JUNO RISING

An ISF-Allion novel

PATTY JANSEN

CHAPTER ONE

"MEDICAL," SAID THE OFFICER with the name tag Private First Class L. Manning. He stopped in the grey and featureless corridor at the door of a room that wafted smells of antiseptic and where, out of the line of vision, someone moved with soft footsteps and rummaged in plastic wrappings.

Fabio's courage sank, then, deep into a place he didn't want to be, a place where he was lying face down on a hard and cold bench and a nurse was shaving his head. Locks of hair tickled over his face on the way down to making black curly snow on the table, leaving an itchy trail on his face. All he could do was blow them away because his hands were strapped to the table; a drip was in one arm, and sensors were stuck to his head, which were attached to beeping machines. A thin tube fed into the drip through which, at the press of a button, the surgeons would administer the anaesthetic to knock him unconscious. The doctors weren't quite doing that yet; they were talking to each other in low voices, a mush of mumbled conversation with medical words like *cranial lobe* and *neuro-reflexes*.

Deep breath.

He was back in the grey and scuffed corridor at the ground

floor of Calico Base, on Io, being shown around by a fresh-faced Private First Class with the name tag that said Manning, who had met him when he came out of the transport tube and who was still talking, ". . . anyway, it's nothing special, just the regular tests. A few months ago, a guy came over from Ganymede and brought chicken pox. The whole base went down with it . . ." He laughed, and the laughter sounded muffled in the woolly space inside Fabio's head. The recent scar at the back of his head itched. He took a breath of the static-dry, sulphur-laced air, and another. The air flowed into his lungs, then, as if he'd forgotten to breathe.

There were no such things as innocent medicals. There was nothing regular about having a blood test. Not for him, ever.

"I have . . ." he started to protest, but he remembered that he'd vowed to keep his mouth shut. And he remembered that he didn't actually remember what he had, or *didn't* have, medically. Worse, he had an audience.

A few troops in dark green Space Corps fatigues sat on plastic chairs outside the entrance of the room, wordlessly staring at him. Two privates, a private first class and a sergeant.

Fabio recognised some of them because they had been with him on the transport, a short-range in-system barge that ferried people from the Galilean sling to various points in the Jupiter system. Hard to miss each other when you're sardined into a tin can for eight hours. Judging by the discussions he had overheard on the transport, they were base relief staff and most seemed to have been sent here as punishment for some sort of transgression.

A private with a shaven head nodded at Fabio and raised an eyebrow at Manning. Curiosity oozed off him. *Look, who's this geezer that he requires a personal minder? What's with the non-standard uniform? Is he crazy or dangerous?*

Manning sat down and Fabio took the chair to the right of him. He stared at the open door to the medical room, where he could only see shelves full of jars and part of a workbench.

He heard voices in the room and wondered what was happening inside. Doctors with vicious needles. Nurses with jars and vials. Those worried him, because those were for collecting things that weren't theirs to collect. He jammed his hands under his legs, but his right leg wanted to jiggle. He clamped his jaws to suppress the jiggling—

"Hey, you're new, too, aren't you?" The voice from his right was young and female.

Fabio whirled around.

The woman jerked back, her expression startled and defensive. She looked quite young, dark-skinned with big brown eyes and glossy black hair in a bun. "Whoa, mate. I didn't want to offend you. I thought . . . I saw you on the transport. I was sitting on the bench against the opposite wall. I thought you were new . . . because you looked like it was your first trip out, with the Sarajevo tag and all that . . ." Her gaze went to the chest of his uniform, where he wore a badge with three tiny embroidered stars. It was a shirt that ISF used for Earth-based recruits. It had been given to him on the transport, and he had no idea whether this meant that he'd been demoted or that they didn't have gear appropriate to his rank.

"Um, yeah." He stared at the opposite wall, grey with scuff marks. "Yeah, I'm new." He was hoping she'd shut up. He did not want to talk and be reminded of the vast areas of blackness inside his head. He did not want to be here. He did not want a medical. He was supposed to work for some Major called K. Doric and he wanted to ask Manning when he was going to meet this person—

"Hey, I'm new, too. Got transferred from Europa. Where did you come from?"

He met the woman's eyes again. Where did he come from? The question twigged nagging unease. Jumbled memories exploded into confusion, closely followed by rage. "Where did I come from? Does it matter where I come from?"

Her eyes widened. "Sorry, I was only asking." She looked away and leaned to the side, away from him.

Fabio took deep breaths and resumed clamping his jaws to

keep from jiggling his leg, but the nerves took over and he jiggled anyway. His knees were shaking with it.

The question repeated in his mind. *Where did you come from? Where did you come from?*

A memory came to him.

He was on his stomach on a bed in the hospital. He could tell he was on a ship because the mattress under him vibrated. There was no one in the room and when he lifted his head, a sharp pain speared through his neck. He wanted to scream, but his throat was too dry. He coughed and that made the pain worse. But he couldn't stop coughing because his throat tickled. He couldn't breathe. The door opened and a nurse ran in.

"Don't move!"

He wanted to scream, *I can't breathe,* but he couldn't.

He wanted to ask, *Where am I?* but he couldn't.

He wanted to know where the ship was going, and what he was doing here, and who had put him here, but he coughed and coughed until blackness encroached on his vision, and someone in the echoing cavern of darkness said, "Keep the sedative up."

That, he remembered. But where he came from? No, that information was lost in the depths of his mind.

A man in Space Corps fatigues came out of the treatment room. The young woman went in next.

Fabio waited, jiggling his leg, clamping his jaws, sitting on his hands. A few Flight Force Ensigns arrived in the corridor, dressed in their black everyday uniforms. One of them asked if this was the place where they had to go for the medical. When the Space Corps troops said that was so, they dumped their duffel bags on the floor and leaned against the wall, talking and laughing. They spoke with drawling accents and used a lot of abbreviations. Fabio recognised some of the abbreviations, but not all of them.

The Space Corps—planet-based—troops fell silent and eyed them with suspicious looks. That he remembered: the continued animosity between Flight and Corps. Flight troops called Corps *dirt crawlers.* Corps troops called Flight personnel *Dreamers* or other less polite words that referred to their aloof stance and lewd speculation about what they did with their time when in between destinations.

The seat next to Fabio remained empty.

His leg wouldn't stop jiggling.

He stared at the opposite wall, ignoring Manning, doing his utmost best to ignore everyone. Where *had* he come from? Getting to Io took months, depending on where you came from. Not from the Jupiter system was all he knew. He didn't remember getting on the interplanetary. The woman said Sarajevo. That was ISF head office. That was—

Admiral Sanchez. A broad-shouldered man with enough gold and glitter on his chest to blind a person. Salt and pepper hair. Penetrating eyes.

His office was a statement of opulence: polished wood, a soft carpet, cool air. Intricate models of big warships—

"Hey," Manning said. "It's your turn."

Fabio's heart jumped. He stared at the door. He rose abruptly, swung his duffel onto his shoulder. It hit the wall with a *thud,* which drew raised eyebrows from the people in the corridor. He went in.

The narrow galley-style room contained an examination table, covered in white disposable liner. The walls were lined with shelves crammed full of jars and sample bags, tubes, pre-wrapped wound dressings. Bottles. Needles. Blood pressure machine. A heart rate monitor. A drip stand. Gloves. A brain activity scan machine with the patches stored in a clear plastic box on top. Fabio knew those things. Each of those items had a story to tell about where it went and what people did with it. All those stories were shouting for attention in Fabio's brain, while he stood there trying to ignore their voices. Somewhere in that racket he found the presence of mind to say, "Oh, hello."

A med officer sat at a workstation tapping at his deskscreen, clad in green hospital outfit, with short-cropped hair.

He said, "Be with you in a mo," without looking up from his work.

Fabio's mouth had gone dry as the ash and sulphur desert outside. "I did all the regulation health checks before I left the Interplanetary Transfer Vessel. They should all be on your system." That, he remembered, too.

The med officer looked up. His eyes were brown. "Your name?"

"Velazquez, Fabio."

The med officer scrolled over a screen, and tapped it with his stylus. "Ah, yes, here you are. Got the details. Lieutenant First Class, Tech Services. Contracted to the Research Division." He frowned at Fabio's uniform. "Did they run out of gear?"

Fabio nodded, hoping this meant that he hadn't been demoted, and that someone soon was going to tell him what had happened or what he was meant to be doing here.

The officer tapped the screen some more and frowned, then shrugged.

"Welcome to Calico Base. Sit down."

Fabio sat, having regained a sliver of hope that none of this prodding, poking and swabbing would, in fact, be necessary.

The med officer—his nametag said Lt. Hansen—swivelled his chair to face Fabio. Manning remained at the door, leaning against the doorframe with his arms crossed over his chest. His arms were thick and freckled, covered in a fuzz of ginger hair.

"First time on Io?" Hansen asked.

Fabio nodded. At least he *thought* it was his first time, but maybe it wasn't. Maybe those black holes in his mind contained previous visits, times when he had done goodness-knew-what, because someone had obviously *made* him forget important things.

"OK, so you are unaware that it's base policy to do our own tests, since we apply quarantine to all new arrivals, regardless of rank." Hansen now took a container off the shelf that held plastic-wrapped syringes and yanked a pair of gloves out of a dispenser.

Shit. "But the officer on the ship said—"

The rubber gloves went on, snap, snap and he took a pre-wrapped syringe from a container. "The ITV med officer would be following regulations from headquarters or Flight Force. They don't meet our requirements. They don't have to deal with the infection risks posed by a high turnover staff population in a closed-system base." He ripped the plastic in a kind of definite way that said, *Headquarters can stick their regulations up their arse.*

That made him uneasy. Did Base Commanders have that level of authority?

"But I . . ." he tried again. Sweat was running down his back under his shirt. His chest suddenly became too constricted to breathe. Only the last week of his trip, as far as he could count, had he been free of medical equipment. He'd only just learned to walk properly in a spinning habitat of the interplanetary. In his experience, any time he went near medical equipment, he became worse off.

The officer gestured for Fabio to put his arm on the desk for a blood sample. Fabio glanced at Manning, still at the door, and considered his options. Refuse, and be treated as difficult from his first day here? Try to run out of the room, and be disciplined? The International Space Force brand of discipline usually involved more medical procedures; he remembered that, too.

He put his arm on the desk. Defeat.

Hansen rolled up his sleeve, applied a strap, and prodded for a vein.

Fabio watched the needle plunge into his arm. Blood spurted into the vial. Blood, the giver of life, the betrayer of secrets.

Something triggered a flash of memory in his mind. He saw lists of results, numbers arranged in tables. Certain figures had been circled with red. He remembered names. "What sort of tests are you doing?"

"Pathogens, a few basic parameters."

"What sort of parameters?"

"HB, blood sugar—"

"Chromosome Normality?" The word *nanometrics* was on the

tip of his tongue, but a vague half-hidden memory stopped him saying it. He sat in a hall amongst lines of Space Corp personnel, a sea of dark green. A high-ranking officer, red-faced, was shouting at him *I don't want any more freaks like you under my command.* He pointed at Fabio and everyone in that hall looked at him.

Hansen laughed. "Chromosome Normality is a long-term health parameter. It's not of interest to us unless you're on a permanent placing. We're only interested in pathogens and your immediate health."

His rubber-gloved hands unclicked a full vial of blood and replaced it with an empty one. Hansen dumped the full vial in a tray where it rolled across the metal bottom before coming to rest against the tray's far side.

He met Fabio's eyes, frowning. "Are you a med officer? I thought you were the contract astronomer."

"I am."

All right, so that was why he was here, apart from meeting this mysterious person K. Doric. He tried to remember what an *astronomer* did, and came up with a big dark space inside him where, clearly, some knowledge was supposed to be. This Major Doric wasn't going to be impressed—

"I've been given orders to rush you through, for understandable reasons. They really want you to start work up there. The tests should be done by tonight. Until then, you'll have to stay confined to your cabin."

Fabio nodded. Confined to cabin was fine by him; he had no desire to talk to anyone except those necessary to do his job. The rushing through made him nervous, though.

The officer withdrew the needle, swabbed away the drop of blood and sprayed a neat round patch of wound adhesive over the site. "Peel off after an hour."

Fabio nodded again; he knew the drill. He pulled down his sleeve, suddenly very, very tired. "Finished?"

"Not yet. Lie down on the bed, please."

Fabio glanced at the bed and noticed the headbands and electrode net on a shelf, and thick braids of leads. There was also a control screen of a scanner with the familiar MediXScan logo. Brain scan.

Panic closed like a vice on his chest.

Any moment now and Hansen would put that thing on his head. Fabio could feel the weight of those leads and the pinch of the net pushing all those electrodes to his skin. Another memory: they usually shaved him when they used that thing. At some point in the past, someone had used that machine on him and produced a three-dimensional image of his brain. He could still see it appearing on the screen. He saw the officer move the stylus to select which parts to scan in detail. He felt the jolt of the current delivered by those electrodes, the pain, the whirlpool of images through his mind—

"No."

Hansen frowned. "We're not going to hurt you, only—"

Only violate my memories. "No."

"It's base regulations, so that we can—"

"No!" Fabio rose, black spots dancing before his eyes. He was sweating all over, feeling sick.

Manning took a couple of steps into the room. "Is there a problem, sir?"

Hansen said, "Not that I know of. I need to complete—"

"Don't touch me!" Fabio backed into the shelf on the other side of the room. Manning blocked his way to the door. Manning and Hansen would gang up on him. They'd tie his hands and force him on the bed. They'd restrain him so he couldn't move and then they'd put the thing on him. They'd *read his mind*. That's what they did with those machines, didn't they?

"Calm down, Velazquez. It's a routine procedure that has never given us any problems. It doesn't hurt, and doesn't tell us anything about your thoughts."

"Then why are you doing it, if it doesn't tell you anything? It's bullshit, I tell you. I don't believe anything you're saying. I retract my permission for this medical." He was shouting and he couldn't stop. There would be trouble, but he wouldn't calm down. His hands trembled so much that his whole body shook with it.

Hansen retreated to his desk and hit a button on the wall and Manning stopped and held up his hands. "Whoa, calm down, calm down. All the doc here wants to check is if you have any implants."

"I don't. That was already tested on board. You have the results already. You have no right to do this."

"Medical examination is a base regulation."

"You can't force me." Then another snippet of knowledge fell into place. "It's in the ISF charter under privacy regulations, section 87a, page 413."

Red spots appeared on Hansen's cheeks. "But we . . ." He swallowed whatever he was going to say. "We have to—"

A woman barged into the room. "Hansen, Manning, what's this?"

She was taller than Manning without being lanky, had a sharp-nosed face and shoulder-length dead straight platinum blond hair, which swung loose over her shoulders. She was in Space Corps uniform with senior officer's stripes. Both Hansen and Manning stiffened and saluted.

"Just a medical test, Ma'am," Hansen said.

"You pressed the emergency," she said, her voice flat. "That's not 'just a medical test'."

"He . . ." Hansen hesitated, glanced at Fabio. "He looked like he was going to fight. I wasn't doing anything except standard procedure, Ma'am. To request backup in case . . ."

"You know this officer's name?"

"Yes, Ma'am. It's Lt. Velazquez."

"Well done. Did you look at your task sheet, Hansen?"

"I did, Ma'am."

"Then what does it say behind Lt. Velazquez's name?"

Hansen looked. Froze. "Oh."

"What does it say, Hansen?"

"Contact Research Command."

"Does it say: submit him to standard entry procedure?"

"No, ma'am."

"Then why didn't you contact Research Command?"

"It was a mistake, ma'am."

"I am getting very tired of your mistakes. The time may come that I will discuss your 'mistakes' with Commander Banparra."

"That's not necessary, ma'am."

She glared at him for a couple of very long seconds. Then she turned to Fabio. "Come."

Fabio scrambled to collect his duffel bag. He was still trembling.

Manning stood at the door, looking uncertain. "Do you want me to come, ma'am?"

She stopped to face him, eye to eye, her nose no more than a hand span higher than his face.

"You'd like that, eh, Private First Class Manning? The more time you spend away from your general duties, the better. Tell me, what need would Lieutenant Velazquez have for your sorry arse if you can't even follow your fucking orders and keep him out of the bureaucracy down here?"

"I didn't get any—"

"Can't you read, Private First Class Manning?"

Silence. Manning went red in the face. "I apologise, ma'am."

"You *apologise,* as if that's an excuse for your dumbassery."

"I didn't know what—"

"Shut up." He shrank visibly with every second of her death stare. "Fucking imbecile. Come with me." The latter to Fabio.

He glanced at Hansen, who waved his hand at the door.

"I'm sorry, but where are we going? I'm supposed to meet—"

She turned her cold grey stare on him. Then she held out her hand. "Major Katarina Doric. Welcome to Calico Base."

JAYKADIA

JAYKADIA LAW, HEIRESS and youngest Executive ever of the Ganymede Mining Company and niece of the Governor of the Council Of Four, sat at her desk in her office. When the door to the office opened, she was busy distilling very long and boring sales reports into a slide show that she could present to the board the next day.

Nobody ever just opened that door, so she called out, "Clarence!"

Because that was the young man in charge of the door who shouldn't have let anyone come in.

She did this without looking up, because she hated to lose where she was with the figures, and it was only after a while that she realised that not only had the person not gone back into the other room, there was more than one person, and they formed a wall of stout-looking men just inside the door.

Then she looked up.

Military uniforms. Four of them.

And, at the same time it dawned on her that this was no ordinary visit, she also realised that Vice Admiral Preston, the dark-skinned man second from the right, would have to have a *very* good reason to come into her office, and that she was being rude to let him stand.

"I'm sorry, Vice Admiral. I was busy. I didn't realise you were here."

She rose from her seat, pulled out a chair from the side of the desk—because she rarely received people in here—and dragged it to the other side of the desk so that it faced her.

Preston sat down, his face prim, eying the stacks of to-scale models tottering on the shelf in the corner.

Great, she clearly had not made a great impression. Did she say that she didn't like receiving people in here?

Running a company as big as this was no job for a twenty-five-year-old, others said.

Jaykadia went back to her own chair and swiped the financial data off the pad and pushed the pad aside.

"It's quite an honour to see you here," she said, heart hammering.

Vice Admiral Preston of the Jovian System division of the ISF was old enough to be her grandfather. She had no doubt that he'd enjoyed a good relationship with her father, established when her father was young and wont to frequent bars where military men came. Jaykadia was not part of that scene and he probably viewed her as some sort of alien.

"I won't take much of your time," he said.

They all said that, right? "Go ahead." And clearly, he wanted to be out of here as soon as possible.

"We need the Ganymede Mining Company's cooperation for a major military exercise. Within the next few months, we will see a dramatic increase in the number of troops stationed in the system. Many of them will bring their own ships, but we need places to house the logistics support crew. We don't have enough space and need large spaces we can rent from the commercial sector."

"You mean?" She hated the blah of words that people of that generation used. Almost as if they were afraid to speak the truth.

"Your equipment maintenance halls."

What? "You want to put people in there? Many of those halls aren't insulated or pressurised."

"I know. We have pressure tents which we can put up inside. We have portable air makers and we'll be bringing all of our own tools."

Jaykadia was still trying to process what he was asking. "But those halls are full of mining equipment. We need to do maintenance there, away from the dust."

"But you're not using all of the space."

"Not all the time, no."

"And the machines can be taken outside?"

"They can, but . . . what is this about? Are the bases on Io really all full?"

"Not yet, but they will be soon. We need accommodation for maintenance crews, who need little secrecy but easy access to maintain and repair fleet craft, and who are not part of the craft's crew. We also have logistics operations that I prefer to be planet-based."

"That must be a pretty big exercise."

"It is." He sounded prim. "And it's of vital importance to the security of the system."

"When . . . would you need these places? For how long?" She was quickly thinking of business operations. It was true that the sheds were not always full, but they were necessary for performing maintenance. She suspected that the engineers would object violently to being told to have to perform maintenance in a hard vacuum. She suspected that some maintenance could not be done in a vacuum.

"A few weeks at the least, and the first troops would be arriving on Sol 154."

That was barely a hundred and fifty days. "But that barely gives me time to organise alternatives. I can't just shift entire maintenance operations to be done outside. Are we meant to be compensated for this in any way?"

In fact, the more she thought about it, the more it bugged her that he dared ask this on such short term. Did he think the commercial mining operations were just hanging around waiting for the military to use their services?

"The compensation will be the safety of the system."

"We're talking about an *exercise*, right? You must have known about your requirements sooner than this."

"Yes, and this is the point of the exercise: to set up logistics in case of an outside attack."

"And who is going to attack us?"

"Any enemy. In this case, a fictitious one. It's of vital importance that we can defend our settlements. We haven't done any large-scale exercises for many years and we're well overdue for one."

And, damn, that was true as well.

Jaykadia remembered those times at school in Ganymede City where a siren would go off at random times and all the kids had to scramble to the emergency room to put on breathing apparatus, or hide in the shelter, depending on the type of alarm. And during those times, the place would crawl with military officers and her father would complain about them at dinnertime.

But that was also the time that tensions were high between ISF and Allion, and now, after Mars, Allion was gone and there was no longer an immediate threat.

There had not been a large-scale exercise for a long time. Hence the massive military operation.

She blew out a breath through her nose. It was annoying, but she would have to cope with it. At least it was only a short-term operation. Despite being civilians and working for commercial operations, most people in the system respected the military and what ISF had done for them: brought the ships and the stations, transported most people and, occasionally, kept the peace.

Not only that, but there would be no business for Ganymede Mining if the military didn't buy most of their products.

She nodded. "All right, I'll look into what we can do."

"There is a level of urgency. We'll begin rolling out the plan soon."

"Have you spoken to my aunt about any assistance from the settlements?"

"Yes, the Governor realises the importance of the operation and I've been assured we'll have her full cooperation."

"So . . . when can I expect these troops to turn up?"

"Some are waiting in orbit."

Crap. The company had contracts to fill and obligations to meet.

Leaving the machines outside all the time added to their maintenance downtime. If she couldn't get the ore to the processing facility at West Plains, then the plant would sit idle and run at a loss. And to say nothing about other companies that relied on Ganymede Mining for their supplies. Those would be livid.

He promised to stay in contact and gave her a direct access code.

"We are going to treat this as if there were a serious threat," he said, while standing at the door, having rejoined his three silent companions who had waited while he was talking. One of them had already opened the door, letting in the moist air from outside. Jaykadia could hear the sprinklers going in the planter boxes outside.

"There may well be some surprise events. My staff has been writing scenarios and we will use a random sequence that none of us knows beforehand to simulate a real scenario. Expect some disruption."

Great. "But at least it will be temporary."

"Yes, it will be."

And then he was gone.

Jaykadia leaned her head in her hands. Just this morning she had made a joke about having sailed through the past few months without major interruptions.

She hadn't actually asked for any interruptions.

And then, because she wasn't the type that moped, she pulled up a map.

If ISF took the sheds and put their troops inside, those resources became lost to her. She bet that they would have guards keeping out anyone and everyone who wanted to visit the area. That meant that not only did she need to move out all the mining equipment housed in the sheds, but all the auxiliary equipment as well. The computers, the testing bays, the stores of spare parts. And most of those things could definitely *not* be stored outside. Keep in mind that when you unpacked a tightly packed suitcase, the contents, when strewn about the room, took up three times the space they did when packed, and you definitely had a problem.

From memory also, ISF sprang large surprises in exercises. This was likely to mean that things would suddenly stop working for no obvious reason or that a huge number of "refugees" would turn up in a ship unfit to be sent anywhere else, and they would have to find space for those as well. At the end, they would be rated on their performance and lengthy reports would be sent to all participating communities.

Yes, the settlements were supposed to have policies that were meant to cope with emergencies like this, for example the failure of a neighbouring dome, but resources were scarce and it was easy to just use an empty hall intended for emergency accommodation for other purposes and forget to check the emergency rations and replace necessary supplies. And yes, they should keep all of this audited, but that whole process was a farce.

Because frankly, no one had seen the need after Allion had been defeated and was gone. Who was going to attack them out here?

Also she loathed the idea of putting a lot of effort into this for an exercise to amuse the military.

So, preferably, any changes that the company made should cater to another purpose after the exercise.

The Law family had not become wealthy by doing nothing and putting up their hands in the air when things got hard. They sought solutions and considered all reasonable options.

She would have to go to see her aunt in Galileo City to coordinate their efforts. Because if it was ISF's aim to show the civilian settlements how unprepared they were, then she was determined not to come last in the rankings.

If the vice admiral wanted the exercise, then let's have the exercise.

But when she turned to her desk screen, those dratted income reports stared back at her. They were not going to go away.

Damn it, she had work to do.

A column with the newsfeed scrolled over the right hand bar of the screen. A delegation of people from the Council Of Four had left for Io.

That was an issue that had been running forever.

The military bases on Io generated a small but very persistent stream of rumours that life inside the bases was hell for those who fell foul of the established majority or the command. Add to that the fact that the troops sent to Io were often on some punitive detention, and the words bullying, deprivation of freedom and even *torture* were never too far away.

Since Io had—finally—agreed to formally take a seat in the Council Of Four—so named after Jupiter's four major inhabited moons—they had to comply with human rights conditions.

And this delegation to Io—one which checked living conditions and interviewed at-risk troops at the base—had been talked about for a long time. Like, years.

The Council demanded it, ISF didn't want it and kept changing the conditions under which they would allow it. But finally they had come to an agreement.

The newsfeed showed a photo of the delegation prior to departure from Galileo City. And there were two people in the picture whom she knew quite well.

One of them was Thalia Hasegawa, a long-standing childhood friend of hers although they hadn't seen each other for a few years. She seemed to have aged little since they had been at university. Her hair was still dark, glossy and very long. She still wore it in a long ponytail that only looked a little bit less messy now that she had an official position. She still looked deceptively elfin-like. Just make sure that you didn't get into her way.

Jaykadia was always melancholy when she thought of that time through secondary school and university when she, Thalia and Kat were inseparable. They'd had so much fun together, until the terrible accident when a truck they were driving had overturned, nearly killing them.

Things had never been the same since, but lately she had run across Thalia a few times and had followed her activities, mainly because she thought that her former friend was doing admirable work.

Life in the higher classes at the Council Of Four meant you were born into a family. Jaykadia had always known that she would need to run the company just like the other friend in the group, Kat, had always known that she would sign up for active duty in the force. Because that was what their respective families did. Thalia had always been a bit different. Because she was the youngest child, her family put no expectations on her future.

Thalia chose to use that freedom to make this part of the solar system a fairer place. And it was not as if that wasn't needed. When the first priority was survival, things like human rights of both civilians and, especially, the military went out the window.

Jaykadia felt a little bit guilty about always considering commercial options and money as priority. Thalia seem to be all about humanitarian causes. And maybe it was time that she considered the effects of the decisions she made, including shifting large populations out of bases and allowing soldiers to occupy commercial space. That was an uncomfortable thought.

The other person in the picture she knew was also related to that group of friends. While she and Thalia had muddled through lists of boyfriends, Paul Armitage had always been with Kat.

When they had all recovered from that terrible accident and were slowly leaving the permanent care of the hospital to the less-permanent situation of many recurring hospital visits, he had asked her to marry him.

Jaykadia had attended the wedding in a wheelchair.

But the accident had changed all of them and as far as she knew Kat had become quite closed. She didn't think she had divorced her husband, but her job in the military had definitely taken her away from him.

So now Paul was part of this delegation that was going to investigate the military record of its treatment of lower-ranked officers. He was an interesting addition to that group. What if he had to investigate his wife—or perhaps ex-wife? Although she had lost contact with Kat, she assumed she was still in the military.

Jaykadia had always thought Paul was strange. He was moody and prone to outbursts of anger. But he also cared deeply for people around him. She remembered joking about how he followed Kat like a doggy. After the accident, though, he had spent as much his time as he could in the hospital sitting next to her bed and later helping her in the gym regain her strength and she had felt stupid for making that comment.

Her own family only visited sporadically and much of her recovery from having the bones in both her legs shattered came through her own efforts.

Being an executive officer of a commercial company was lonely, and she missed her friends.

CHAPTER TWO

MAJOR DORIC CHARGED out the door.

Fabio heaved his duffel onto his shoulder and scurried out after her, drawing curious glances from the troops still waiting outside.

The major set off through the warren of corridors at a pace Fabio had trouble keeping up with. He felt sick and dizzy. His head hurt. The air was so sharp and dry that it stung the inside of his nose. He was on the verge of asking her to slow down, but another memory flashed through his mind.

He was in a classroom with wooden chairs and tables. Children were standing around him. One in particular was a big boy with a round head atop a thick and short neck. He who shouted, *Boys don't do that. You're such a girl.*

Fabio, in the body of his ten-year-old self, got up and punched the boy in the face. There was a moment in which the bully stiffened, looking shocked. Glistening red blood welled in his left nostril and ran down his upper lip. The boy wiped it with the back of his hand, looked at it, and started crying. The teacher ran into the room, because she had been called away. She dragged Fabio into the corridor and yelled at him. He had to stay there, and couldn't come back into the classroom and she kept yelling about how bad he was that it got kind of boring—he remembered the sun coming in through the windows. After the teacher had left him alone in the corridor, he sat down, leaning with his back against the wall and stared at a bird wheeling in the blue sky outside.

A *bird*, in *blue sky*.

He remembered thinking that he wished he were a bird and would fly away as soon as he could, and none of these dreadful people would be able to stop him.

And somehow that memory gave him the strength to quicken his pace, to look at the sterile linoleum floor moving under his feet, to follow the shadow of Katarina Doric.

Doubt still niggled. Where was the school and what was he doing that attracted the ire of the bully? A worrying thought: were the memories even his?

Major Doric led him into the same huge hall where he had arrived off the troop transport bus from the landing pad. The tube where he had first entered the base still showed the *in use* lights, and he presumed the caterpillar bus in which he'd come from the shuttle still sat on the other end. The hall was full of activity from unloading the freight that had come on the same shuttle. A conveyor belt disgorged blue plastic-wrapped parcels out of an access tube. A couple of troops were stacking these onto a trolley. The air was cold here, and being moved around by huge dust-caked fans.

Above him rose the inner ceiling of the dome, with metal struts dripping rusty condensed water from rust-tinged icicles. The concrete below was stained with orange patches.

Two things he knew about Io, from half-remembered pages in a guide. The bases there had never boasted much of a civilian population, because radiation restricted life to the inside of depressing domes, even more than in other places: Ganymede, Europa, *Mars*. That last name kept popping up in his memory.

Secondly, apart from radiation, machines suffered a lot of wear and tear from volcanic dust and the abundance of salt that formed droplets as soon as a vehicle came in contact with air containing traces of water. All this was made worse by sulphur dioxide snow that vehicles and troops carried into the airlock and that sublimated as soon as the temperature rose, and formed sulphuric acid with the humidity in the air and compounded problems with rust. There, he remembered that. Maybe he *had* been here before.

When traversing the hall, he became aware of raised voices. A group of Space Corps troops surrounded a couple of people who had, by the looks of the open access tube behind them, just come in from a transport that was not the ISF shuttle that had brought Fabio here. They were not ISF military either. The three men and one woman wore civilian clothes, quite garishly colourful ones, too, especially the tallest of them, a broad-shouldered man dressed in a bright-blue trench coat and yellow trousers. His head was shaven and his skin possibly the blackest Fabio remembered seeing. Another was a blond-haired man, dressed in reds and whites with a fringed shawl, a vest over a wide-sleeved shirt and patterned trousers.

One of the Space Corps troops had opened a travel bag, spilling clothes and personal items over a table. The dark-haired young man, who Fabio presumed was the bag's owner, was speaking to a Corporal, a defensive expression on his face.

"What's going on there?" Fabio asked the major. "Do you have civilians on this base?"

"Council Of Four representatives," she said, and a tone of distaste coloured her voice.

Council of Four, he remembered, were the civilian populations of the four Jovian moons and their mining operations, commercial concerns owned by a couple of powerful civilian families, the Hasegawas and the Laws and the Mesouaras. Io was a nominal member, lacking a civilian population.

"Why the fracas?"

"The Council Of Four has pushed through regulations that

allow delegations to visit any settlement in any of the signatory members' territories. They made it a condition for use of the Galilean sling. Banparra signed it."

That would be Commander Banparra of Calico Base. He remembered that, too.

He said, "I'm guessing you don't agree?"

She gave him such a vicious look that he quickly added, "Ma'am."

"Calico and Prometheus are both military bases and no one has any say on who comes or goes here except Sarajevo." Headquarters, again. He understood the nervous looks at the Sarajevo tag on his shirt. "So, no, I don't agree. Banparra acted outside his authority when he signed. A lot of people are angry about that."

The young man was still arguing with the soldiers. They had found a small bag in his luggage, and whatever was inside was cause for argument.

Major Doric strode towards another airlock tube and thumbed the panel on the wall. It flashed small yellow lights and a thick metal plate hissed open. When the gap had grown wide enough, Fabio could see into the interior of what looked like another caterpillar truck.

"Where are we going?"

"The Research base is at the Stick Farm."

Whatever that was. He followed her into the tube, a rigid but flexible accessway about ten metres long. Most of it was unlit, save for a single light on the ceiling at the point where it met the open door of the vehicle.

"Across the surface is the easiest access to the base. There's an underground train, but the air quality in the tunnel isn't maintained to standard and is used only for goods." Her voice sounded oddly muffled in the tube.

The truck's cabin had room for a driver and six passengers. The front and surrounding viewscreens were still black and empty, but when Major Doric turned on the power on the door panel, the front viewscreen came alive, showing the outer wall of the dome and a section of the yellow, dusty plain dotted with blinking lights, which Fabio assumed were for landing shuttles. The truck stood in the ink-black shadow of the dome, but the sun was about to come around, and lit a section of the dome, showing its copper-coloured hue.

Major Doric shut both outer and inner doors and waved Fabio into the front passenger seat. Then she slid behind the controls and put on a pair of headphones. While she spoke to the base traffic control, she started the engine.

Fabio looked around. It looked like she had come here just to pick him up. According to his experience, everyone in the settlements was always trying to save resources. She wouldn't have come here just for him if it wasn't important. *He* must be important. He had no idea why. Really, what was he to her, for her to come barging into a medical examination, to put up special instructions about his treatment and come and rescue him when they got it wrong? She was angry about it, too.

Panic closed on him again. Since introducing herself, she hadn't said a single word about who she was and why he was here.

He eyed her while she went through the motions of starting up the truck. There was something familiar about her actions. Check fuel, check air pressure in the tanks, check power, check batteries. He must have done this before, and he tried to think where that would have been. The air tube disconnected with a hiss.

The truck inched forwards, ploughing through yellow dust. She turned the wheel to bring it around. The yellow landscape scrolled sideways over the viewscreen. There was the caterpillar bus that had brought Fabio and the other passengers from the shuttle. A truck waited to be assigned to an airlock, its headlights a brief flash over the screen.

A path made of latticed rubbery-looking mats led away from the dome. Once the wheels of the truck had hit the hard surface, it picked up speed. For a while, the truck rumbled along the path.

The latticed surface made the truck vibrate, which produced a resonating hum that made Fabio's teeth ache. The dome of the base receded behind them and, occasionally, when they crested a ridge, disappeared from view.

"I want you to understand one thing, and one thing only," Major Doric said.

"Ma'am. . . ?"

"As long as you're on this base, I am your commanding officer. You will take your orders from me. Not from Banparra or anyone else on this base. Especially not from those clowns in the med unit, or quarantine officers. Understood?"

"Yes, ma'am."

"Also, understand that it's highly likely that those people I just mentioned don't like you being here. They are likely to force you to submit to useless bureaucratic procedures if they get half the chance. They will try to find a way to get you off the base. I'm sure you can imagine many ways in which they could do that."

"I think so, ma'am." Anyone only needed to test his blood for nanometrics and his position would be history.

"Good. Therefore, you will not leave the research base without my express permission. You will not speak to anyone off-base by any means."

"What about within the base?"

"Within the base, they're all research branch. Our people. However. Your project is on a need-to-know basis only and you are *not* free to discuss the details with anyone else. I guess that concept isn't strange to you either."

"I think you're right, ma'am."

"Now, you're free to speak. Am I right in guessing that you have brought instructions for me?"

"Instructions?"

She frowned at him. "A message?"

"Who from?"

Then her expression became guarded. "Sanchez sent you, right?"

"He did." He thought so, anyway.

"He didn't give you a personal message?"

"Um—no. Not that I know."

"What about something you don't know?"

"Well, in that case I don't know . . . um . . . ma'am."

She gave him an angry stare, and returned her attention to the road, muttering *imbecile* which seemed a word that she loved very much. She breathed out hard through flaring nostrils. A tense silence followed.

"All right, let's try this again. My information says that you're from the rehabilitation program. You were caught embedded in enemy forces when ISF overran the Mars Civilian Army and the freehold revolutionaries, who are known to be a front for Allion. It says no one was sure of your loyalty, so they removed your service implants and wiped you clean. But insiders know that you work for Sanchez directly. Now, where or how would Sanchez have given you a message for me?"

"I don't know, ma'am. He didn't say anything about it."

"The fuck he wouldn't have. In your current state, you're about as trustworthy as a poodle for a watchdog. Someone feeds you and you follow."

"Well, I don't know about a message. I can't make any messages appear where there aren't any."

She snorted. "We'll see about that." And a bit later, she added, "Are you always this coherent?"

"Er . . . tired, I guess." He had learned on the interplanetary that *tired* was always a good excuse for anything. Most people on the ship were tired most of the time. *Tired* got you sent off to the gym, which was a place where people did things, rather than talked about things. Doing suited him fine. It was the talking that got under his skin.

An uneasy silence hung between them. He wanted to say, *I'm unarmed and not dangerous* but that was probably not a good idea. Maybe she had been desperate for news. Maybe this was some-one's way of giving her the finger. *We're sending you someone, but he's not going to be able to tell you anything.* Maybe the information she wanted was buried somewhere inside him in a secret implant that no one had been able to find.

The engine hummed and thumped. The surface was uneven and she drove at a speed that made him sway in his seat. Her hands held the wheel in a white-knuckled grip. The truck's headlights spread their glow, lighting a section of road ahead.

They were plodding through a parched desert of yellows and greens, soft-looking dunes with the occasional rocky outcrop. The road had started climbing up a ridge a while ago. They had left the rubbery latticed surface behind and were now on a path that appeared to have been spray-painted black. Every now and then there was a post at the side of the road with an orange light on top. When the truck faced the right way, the front viewscreen showed this snaking path zigzagging up the side of a huge jagged mountain. As the truck climbed, the plain on the left gave way to a ravine with black rock at the bottom. If he squinted, he thought he could see the glow of orange.

"Is that lava?"

"Yup. We call it the pit of hell."

"And where is the Research base?"

"At the very top. Don't you see the sticks yet?"

Fabio squinted, but didn't know what he was supposed to be looking for. All that messing with his implants had affected his eyesight, but he'd been too afraid to say anything about it. Any undeserved special considerations got you last pick on the shit jobs.

Around a sharp hairpin bend, they came up behind a slow vehicle crawling uphill. It was a huge square thing, and a spray of dust came from underneath.

The truck dropped a few gears as she overtook it.

"What are they doing?"

"It. It's a robot. It's reapplying adhesive. Resurfacing. The surface sediment is mainly volcanic ejecta, a lot of sulphur. It's loose as hell, unstable, bad for trucks and incredible fun to get bogged in, because it gets into everything and fucks up all equipment. So we spray a layer of foam to hold the surface together, to stop it subsiding in the case of earthquakes. You may have noticed the ridges back on the valley floor. They were the earthquake shield rings. With all the volcanic activity, we have to keep cleaning and resurfacing every six months. This place is continuously being turned inside out."

She paused while steering the truck around another sharp hairpin bend.

"Crap falls from the sky all the time. There are bots cleaning the dome all the time, but it still sinks at a rate of a centimetre a year, because the surrounding area is also being covered."

"So, in this hideously, dangerously volcanic place, we're going up the top of a very tall mountain."

"That does sound stupid, but you're going to have to readjust your understanding a bit. Io is ass-backwards. The mountains are uplifted parts of the crust. They're always next to cracks. Lava pits are in the cracks."

"Pele is not like that." He was proud of having remembered the name of the largest active volcano in the solar system.

"No. Pele is a class all of its own."

Whatever had happened to him, whatever they had done to him on the interplanetary ship and whatever rehabilitation program he had attended before that, it hadn't affected his factual knowledge. It had just affected his recent memory. And that made him wonder what was on that implant that had been removed and why he had the nanometrics.

Rehabilitation. He hung onto that word. Picked up with the revolutionaries. Sanchez. Mars.

He remembered he'd gone into the hospital, but remembered nothing except vague flashes just before the operation, something in the back of his head. He'd woken up face down on the bed in a lot of pain, on the interplanetary ship. Everything before that was a blur. He didn't have the scars of being involved in an accident. He didn't know if he'd been sick—

The wheeling bird in the blue sky.

Brown fields of waving grass, soft undulating hills, like the hills of Io outside the truck. Probably less high, and less jagged at the edges. And the sky was blue, not dark grey. The grass was brown, not dirty yellow.

A word came to him. *Pampas.*

Horses. Cattle. Villages with low, spread-out houses. Another word, a name. "Argentina."

"What?" Major Doric said. They had been driving in silence, only broken by the hum of the engine.

"Argentina. That's a country on Earth."

"I know that. What about it?"

"That's where I grew up. My family had a farm." He thought so, at least. It seemed important. Maybe he never had a farm and had never been to Argentina, but someone, somewhere wanted him to remember that he'd lived on a farm. Or something like that. Memories were insubstantial, inconsequential things with no proof whether they were real or had been modified, falsified or misappropriated or were simply outright lies.

She raised an eyebrow.

"Sorry," he said. And then he said nothing for a long time while the truck crawled up the mountainside. He remembered something else.

He sat in a leather chair in an office and someone in uniform sat on the other side of the desk, a dark-haired man with a slab of medals and decorations on his chest and a whole firmament of stars on his epaulettes.

Admiral Sanchez of the International Space Force. His eyebrows were huge and bushy, a mixture of grey and black, and twirled into long points that stood from his head like horns.

"Don't you dare stuff this up, too, Velazquez," he said, putting his elbows on the desk and placing the fingertips of both hands against one another. "I've been involved with your project from the start, but it's getting to the point where your actions have put us in a lot of trouble. I think you can thank your lucky stars that *I* believe that you're speaking the truth, even if no one else does. But I cannot keep you in positions where you are vulnerable to outside influences, not even pretty female eyes, for fuck's sake. I'm going to give you a quiet posting in a place where you can't do any more harm than you already have. Keep your head down, Velazquez, and I might leave it on your shoulders."

The expression in the black eyes was concerned like an uncle's, not like a superior. The memory made him shiver. The memory contained nothing about a message for Doric.

Terrain became rough now that they were higher up the mountain. Major Doric's hands went hand over hand on the steering wheel. The truck bumped and creaked. A panel rattled.

The black, tarry path zigzagged up the mountainside, from orange light to orange light. Fabio stared at the forward viewscreen, as if the grey sky would give him any clues. The huge red sliver of Jupiter, about a third full, hung above, giving off a sickly red-orange glow. Beyond its misty parameter, the sky faded from grey to black. There were stars, the glowing orb of a moon, almost full. Ganymede. He remembered that name. Another bright spot in the sky was Europa.

"Did my . . . my name appear on your Research Division spec sheet? Was that why you came into the med room back there?"

"The transport arrived. I figured you'd be on it. It's not like we get new arrivals every day. What's with all the questions?"

"I just want to know why you . . . needed me badly enough to come all this way."

"Simple. We asked for a mining astronomer, so they sent us one."

"Er—I suppose." Very simple. Except he remembered nothing about doing any kind of job at all. A mining astronomer was someone who scoured the telescope outputs for comets and asteroids and identified their components and calculated what was needed to divert the asteroid's orbit to one convenient for miners, like into the orbit of a planet, or even crashing into a planet—

—Mars.

That name kept coming up in his memories.

He shivered.

"Are you cold?"

"No. It's just . . ." But he didn't know what and he had no idea what to say to someone who obviously thought he was an expert.

THALIA

THE DOORS TO THE TRANSPORT craft had opened.

Thalia pulled her bag out of the locker under her chair. The other members of the delegation, Jun and Paul, had already left the craft, so she went with Sol, who had sat next to her and couldn't get out until she did. They followed the other passengers through a wobbly access tube.

The air was dusty, with a slight metallic tang to it, and ice cold. The tube's walls pulsed with the air pumped into it to keep the pressure up.

A nervous energy raged through her body. She had worked so hard to come here and couldn't believe that she had finally succeeded.

That Base Commander Banparra was such an arse. First he wanted to be part of the Council Of Four, and then he wanted to be exempt from all its regulations.

He had managed to get the military-civilian quota waived—Io was a military settlement after all, and few civilians would seriously consider living here. But he wanted the benefits of being in the Council Of Four, so he would have to be subject to this, the most contentious of rules: obey the human rights laws of the system.

There was some sort of hold-up at the end of the tube, where all the passengers passed a scanner and had to stand still for a few seconds until the screen told them to continue. Thalia could not see what it was about, but the process seemed the same for everyone. The screen told them to stand on a line, and then a blue light would track across the person's body. Then after a second or two, the screen would turn green and the text *continue please* would appear. It did not say what it was scanning, but nobody objected so it was clearly just part of the regular entry process.

When it was Thalia's turn, she stood with her feet slightly apart on the line as directed, and the blue line tracked over her face. It was a very harsh, almost painful light, that went from the top of her head to her feet making a horizontal blue line over her clothes.

She waited.

It seemed to take little bit longer than with previous person.

And then the screen lit up red.

But it said *continue please.*

What was that about?

She looked around, but nobody seemed to be attending this machine, and nobody seemed to care that her scan was different.

She had no idea why it should be different either. She had completed all the tests and had taken all the medication that they had instructed her to take.

Sol, joining her from behind after finishing his scan, flicked his eyebrows.

"Did it do the same thing to you with the red scan?" Thalia asked in a low voice.

"Nope."

Ah well, best not to worry about it. If it was important, she was sure she'd hear about it soon enough.

At the end of the tube, passengers fanned out into a military-grey hall with hard military-style benches, where the only attractive feature was a large viewscreen on the opposite wall.

It showed a landscape outside: a few gold-coloured domes set in a sickly grey-yellow plain. Caterpillar wheel tracks in the dust showed the frequent passage of vehicles. In fact, one was coming in the direction of the camera now.

The sky was dark grey, and behind the base, a mountain range formed a jagged horizon.

"This sure is one hellhole of a place," said Paul, looking up at the screen, a sneer on his face. "Why do people even live here?"

Thalia jammed her hands in her pockets. Even if he just complained about something general, he annoyed her, with his exquisitely quaffed shock of blond hair, with his whiny voice, with his living tattoos that were nothing but a monumental waste of bio-resources that could have been used for medical purpose. Like, to save someone's life. Or something.

Trying to look tough, but having no idea how. He was all air and no substance. Never did as was agreed. The question was not: what are these people doing here, but what was *he* doing here? Never mind that he had married one of her childhood friends, she could think of few people she'd been less keen to have as company on a mission. And the worst thing? He didn't even realise that he acted like a spoilt whining brat.

So now she was going to be stuck here for days with this moron, because that craft that had brought them in was the only way out again, and it wouldn't be back for days.

Thank the heavens for Sol and Jun whose presence would help take the edge off his annoying remarks, or who could serve as alternate pissing posts when she was tired of listening to Paul.

Don't get yourself riled up, Sol would say. *He's just doing it to get a rise out of you.*

Jun, being the youngest member in the team and only there because he'd won the spot through an article he had written, didn't have much to say at all.

They waited in the hall, slightly apart, but brought together by the fact that none of them wore military uniforms.

All the passengers had now come out of the craft. Most

remained standing and milled around near the screen and the entrance to a tube access point on the other side of the hall. There was very little talk amongst the group. Everyone except the four of them were in military uniform of some description, and the group got some strange looks. Civilians didn't come here. Civilians had never come here.

That was why she had been so keen to get involved with the COF human rights movement—because they were said to be able to send a mission to the secretive military bases on Io under the human rights agreements. And under these agreements, she could ask questions, and she could ask to see prisoners without raising any questions. And she would not only report on living conditions to COF, but to others, including a Human Rights committee of which Admiral Sanchez was a member. *He* didn't like the poor name his forces had in the Outer System. *He* didn't want Banparra taking the decisions in his own hand in order to circumvent inspection.

Some noises came from outside: clanging of metal against metal. A light above the access tube door flashed and a moment later the door opened into yet another tube.

This one gave access to the vehicle that had been visible on the screen a moment ago.

Thalia followed Sol and sat down next to him in the bus-like arrangement.

Not too much later, the vehicle bumped across the grey-yellow plain on its way to the base.

Meanwhile, an electronic voice made safety announcements. Arriving passengers were to present their bags for checking for a long list of prohibited items which included weapons and food. Passengers were to report to their units upon arrival and if they had no unit, were to report to the quarantine officer.

"I hope none of this is going to take too long," Sol said. "I'm tired and hungry."

"Me, too," Thalia said. "But sadly, I don't hold much hope that we can just walk in."

She had a letter from Base Commander Banparra that should answer questions, but again, coming here had been one string of frustrations and she had no illusion that the base command wanted them here.

The vehicle stopped and a moment later, the side door opened. Passengers got up and filed out of the door row by row.

Jun and Paul were first and Thalia and Sol followed them, down a ramp, into another tube and finally into the base. A queue formed when the passengers had to wait to clear a checkpoint.

Cold air filtered into the tube from the hall, where several large vehicles were visible through the entrance of the tunnel.

Jun and Paul arrived at the front of the queue. The officer asked them for their ID, and then looked at Thalia. "You're with them?" He had a clean-shaven military face and a hard expression. If she hadn't seen him smile at the previous group, she would never have thought that he could.

"We're part of the same group."

"The human rights activists, is that correct?"

"We're representatives of the Council Of Four." Thalia would not let the word *activists* pass her lips. It was a good thing to fight for the rights of all people. Wherever so-called *activists* turned their backs, there were always people who behaved like animals to each other. Worse than animals, because animals did not maliciously harm their rivals and continue to harm them when they were down and vulnerable. Here was another reason why she hated ISF so much. Shortsighted, entrenched tunnel vision, endemic discrimination against anything and anyone that didn't conform to their vision.

"Put your bags on the table please."

The four of them went where he indicated and placed their bags on the bench. Another officer, wearing gloves, opened the clips and slides so that he could look inside.

Thalia watched while he searched through Jun's bag.

"What's this?" He held up a parcel.

"That's my medicine," Jun said.

The man studied his screen. "The entry log says nothing about medicine on your person. Can I see the active ingredient list?"

"Sure, but the documentation is in my luggage. I can show you as soon as I have it."

"In that case we're going to have to retain this." He put the box aside.

"Hey, I need those," Jun said.

Thalia wasn't aware of his medical condition, but truth was that most people in Council Of Four settlements did have a medical condition that required long-term medication to manage. Moreover, she wasn't aware that they would need to provide proof of the identity of every tablet.

"It's an unidentified substance, and those are prohibited inside any buildings of the base."

"I told you that I have the documentation in my luggage."

"You should have kept that with the substance at all times."

Thalia pushed her way to the front. "Can you give him his luggage so that he can get it out for you?"

The officer turned a withering gaze on her.

A man in the queue behind her said, "Come on, we don't have all day."

The officer glared at her. "Ma'am, please wait for your turn."

"We're travelling together." He knew this, of course, the dick. And also, of course, he was picking on the youngest and most inexperienced-looking member of the group, and deliberately stopping the others stepping in to help.

"It's *his* bag and his medication. Every officer in this base—"

"He's not an officer and you know who we are," said Sol. "It's not like you get hundreds of civilian visitors through here every day."

Paul shifted his weight from one foot to the other and back again, his hands jammed deep inside his pockets. He had already put his bag on the table for searching, as if he wanted to be processed and leave Jun here.

"We have strict protocols to adhere to," the officer said. Not a

skerrick of friendliness crossed his face. "I can't accept this unidentified material in our base—"

"Fuck it, man, just let him get his fucking bag and show it to
you!" Paul burst out.

The officer gave him a wide-eyed look.

"You said—what, sir?"

Thalia bumped his arm. "Paul, keep calm please."

She would rather have belted him over the head. What was
wrong with this idiot? He always did this—hold tirades against
people who could really stuff up their work if they became too
annoyed.

"Let go of me." He pulled his arm out of her grip.

"Paul . . ." The idiot. He was not going to make a scene here?

The quarantine officer waved his hand. "Mister, please step
away while we process your colleague's details."

"He is in my group. And he's right." Paul jerked his head at
Sol. "You know who we are, no need to put on this façade. Give
him his fucking bag so he can show you the documentation."

"Mister, I told you—"

"Paul, keep quiet!" Thalia said. He was going to ruin
everything.

Another officer came to the assistance of the first one. He
pushed himself between the first officer and Paul, who threatened
to jump over the table. He pushed Paul back into the line.

"Keep your hands off me!" Paul called out.

And he *did* ruin everything, because the first officer had
pressed an alarm and a group of armed guards came running from
another part of the hall.

Within moments, the four of them were isolated and their arms
held behind their backs. There were far too many of them to fight,
or even to run if they managed to escape.

But Paul was fighting anyway, with all his pent-up anger. Why
had the Council Of Four agreed to let him come on the mission?
The man was a walking disaster zone.

The four of them were frogmarched to another part of the big hall and pushed into the back of a truck.

In the darkness of the cabin, Thalia glared at Paul, and Sol tried to comfort Jun, who seemed to feel that it was all his fault.

"It's not," Thalia said. "The guidelines said nothing about having to identify medicines on the spot. I think they're looking for a way to keep us talking to the staff."

"We're fucked," Paul said.

It was one of the rare occasions that Thalia agreed with him.

"It's because of me," Jun said.

"No," Sol said. "If they hadn't stopped you, they would have stopped me. I have medicines in my pocket."

And Thalia somehow returned a red body scan.

The message was clear. They had wanted a reason to refuse them access.

A soldier came to shut the back door of the truck and lock it from the outside. The cabin walls were thick and when the door had shut, it became pitch dark inside.

"I wonder where we're going?" Sol asked.

Nobody knew, but it was a long way away, and it was not in the main base.

CHAPTER THREE

WHEN THE TRUCK finally reached the top of the meandering track, they came to a flat area in which the only habitable structure was a low and featureless building made of yellowish concrete. It looked like a field station bunker, and one that had been there for a long time at that.

Beyond, on the flat mountaintop, was an installation consisting of many tall rods, pointing at the sky like a bed of nails. These nails were incredibly tall, reaching almost out of sight and casting long shadows over the surrounding landscape in the weak sunlight. They were arranged in bundles set three by three in frames each about twenty metres across. There was a walkway around each frame at a few metres above ground level. Fabio counted nine such pads.

Just as there wasn't another place like Io in the solar system, there wasn't another place where you could generate electricity off the magnetic field of a planet.

The source of the radiation, Jupiter, hung above, a huge red and cream striped disk, about half lit and waxing visibly.

This then was the Stick Farm. The sight of it brought a memory, but it could have been from pictures. A diagram with lines of magnetic flux. School. He remembered that. Had they spoken about the Stick Farm?

Then another thought: what was the point of trying to do astronomy at this base? Any observations would be severely limited by the radiation generated by Jupiter. Simple communication was hard enough. He glanced at Major Doric. The comment about being free to speak now began to make more sense. *Research* was a euphemism for intelligence. And in this case, the intelligence appeared to be directed at another branch of the force—Banparra, suspected of acting outside his authority, and making agreements with the Council Of Four outside the approval of ISF headquarters. So. ISF Sarajevo plonks a research base next to Banparra's patch to keep an eye on him.

The concrete bunker had two flexible access tubes for vehicles at the back, which made it look like some sort of beached sea creature.

Major Doric drove the truck up one of these tubes and stopped. "Here we are. Welcome to the ISF Research Base at Calico."

"Here?" He frowned at the concrete shelter on the screen. It was barely big enough to house a truck.

"This is the access. The base is underground."

She manoeuvred the tube into position with a remote-controlled gadget from inside the cabin. Something hummed and clanged on the outside of the truck.

"What exactly do you research here?"

"Mostly geology, geothermal research, biochemistry, astro-geology—"

"*Bio*chemistry?"

"We have a team analysing the samples taken from Jupiter's cloud tops."

Something stirred in his memory. "Samples from Jupiter's cloud tops? Did you take them? How?"

"No. Neither Calico nor ISF, for that matter. The samples came off the Allion wellship *Morgana* when we captured her. They're the only samples from Jupiter we've ever been able to lay our hands on."

Fabio glanced at the huge half-orb in the sky, the gravity well that no one had possessed the technology to approach, except the commercial company Allion Aerospace. He remembered seeing that historic footage where the now-defunct communications company Fenosa had paid Allion to paint its logo on the cloud tops of Jupiter. That was something like twenty, thirty standard Earth years ago? Back then, Allion was a strong force to be reckoned with, under the guidance of CEO Eilin Gunnarson. They were unbelievably far ahead of any of the Earth-based militaries, companies or governments. They had been the first to put humans on Mars. Until recently, they had maintained a strong presence there even though most of their population lived on ships and stations—

The *Morgana* had been one of their research ships—

There had been another ship, a huge behemoth called the Forthright—

Which had quite suddenly *vanished* and had never been found.

Yes, that was how events had gone.

He wondered where Allion was now, and if Eilin Gunnarson was still alive.

There had been a war, he seemed to remember.

This place was full of triggers that made him remember stuff. It was good. The interplanetary transport had been boring because there were no triggers and no one had encouraged him to remember. Right now, bits of his life were coming back, even if they were like a bunch of puzzle pieces thrown randomly in a box. Eventually, he'd be able to put it all together in a way that it made sense.

Mars. Sanchez. Allion. Those things were important. Allion and *Morgana* he remembered. Samples from Jupiter's cloud tops.

Meanwhile, the mechanism in the tube communicated with the truck's door. The tube moved over and suckered on. There was a hiss and after a while the airlock opened.

Major Doric got up from her seat.

"Do we suit up?" Fabio asked.

"Not necessary. Just put on a jacket and gloves." The outer door hissed open and let a blast of cold air into the cabin. It smelled of stone with a hint of farts. Sulphur, one of the main components of Io, in all its forms and colours.

Major Doric went down the ladder into the tube, which wobbled with her footsteps. Fabio also climbed down the ladder, still feeling a bit queasy. His feet were unsteady and hands sweaty. It was cold and *dark* in this damn tube.

He had just remembered that back in the days of first settlement, the Stick Farm used to be a *prison camp,* a place where people worked on the stick frame, cleaning and restringing the wires. It was in the time before reliable radiation suits, so they often died from radiation exposure, and sometimes fell off the frame, which was about a kilometre high. Others were electrocuted in the many accidents that happened when the wires arced. He shivered and wondered what the human rights people were going to investigate.

Why did he remember all this stuff and not the important things, such as how to do his job, and what he had done to justify being sent here?

The ground under the tube's flexible material felt hard. Fabio took a step, and the crust cracked under his weight, plunging him half his shoe's height into the ground. He retreated, shocked.

Major Doric laughed. "That's Io. Any volcanic ejecta that are still hot form a crust over the surface. Usually there is soft material underneath. It's the thin ice effect. That's why we have to keep resurfacing the road. Come on, let's get out of this cold thing." Her breath steamed in the glow of the single feeble light that hung from the tube's ceiling. But the steam evaporated quickly in the dry air.

He followed her through the tube, shivering in his inadequate jacket. At the end they came to a concrete door with a pockmarked surface. Major Doric turned the handle and heaved it open. Fabio stepped inside the concrete bunker that was empty, except for a bench in the corner and a line of hooks on the wall next to it, where several environment suits hung. A neat line of boots stood underneath the bench. There was a rust-stained washbasin in the corner. A rectangular opening provided access to a lift foyer. Major Doric preceded Fabio in that direction. She wore hard-soled boots and her footsteps echoed in the emptiness.

Fabio shivered with the feel of dust and grit under his feet. Millions and millions of particles of dust rained from the sky every minute, every hour and every day. It buried any structure that was not regularly cleaned by people.

Dust, tonnes and tonnes of it. Spewed from the volcanoes and slowly raining down on the surface, turning the moon inside out.

The thought of it constricted Fabio's chest. He knew he was being stupid and that people had lived here for many years, perfecting their dance with some of the most hostile conditions in the solar system, but no one ever said that panic attacks had to be rational. He couldn't breathe.

The lift pinged, jolting him from his panic. They went in, and the doors closed in the bare, grey-painted capsule. It was a thing of comfort, this small cubicle that protected him from the outside world, that kept him from being buried under a drift of volcanic crap. And that was a stupid thought, too. He must stop allowing his mind these kinds of thoughts.

He stared at the cubicle's ceiling.

The only indication of movement was a soft rumble in the floor. It was fast, dizzying, and Fabio steadied himself on the smooth metal wall behind him. It reminded him of his cabin in the interplanetary. Cosy, if cramped.

The magic of the moment broke when the lift doors opened and beyond loomed more large open spaces to become lost in.

They came out into a large room where people were working on screens. Some looked up when Major Doric and Fabio came in but continued their work without speaking.

Fabio glanced at the screens, but couldn't see anything that triggered a memory. Couldn't see anything that said these people were prisoners. They wore Space Corps uniforms with the small planet insignia that indicated that they worked for Special Ops. They held ranks. That labour camp *was* some time ago, wasn't it?

People glanced up at him and nodded polite greetings. One or two spoke to each other in a who's-that-guy kind of way.

"What sort of work are you doing here?" he asked of Major Doric's bobbing uniformed back.

She didn't answer the question but led him across the room into the back where there were some smaller rooms, each with a door.

Inside, there was a table, chairs and two wall screens. Major Doric gestured for Fabio to sit down.

Fabio sat, clamping his hands between his knees. His leg was shivering again.

She closed the door and turned on the screen.

This was it. Now she was going to find out that he was a fraud, that he knew nothing and was useless. She'd send him away and he would go into prison or be shipped to another place. Possibly the Saturn system, where he'd had to work in the wet and cold domes of Titan for their terraforming efforts. That would keep him out of circulation for a while.

Major Doric tapped on the screen. Long fingers with short nails, broken or bitten.

Silence hung in the room while she typed. Tap, tap, tap. The people outside in the large room didn't speak, or if they did, he couldn't hear them. Were they ISF recruits or volunteers? Were they recruits from Council Of Four local communities or from Earth or Mars? Were they free to leave if they wanted?

Questions, questions.

Tap, tap, tap. A concentrated look and small frown at the screen. Fabio's heart jumped at that.

His hands felt restless. He wanted to put them in his pockets— but he had no pockets. Then held his hands behind his back, but that felt exposed. He tried crossing his arms so that he could hold his shoulders.

He was too scared to ask her about what he was meant to be doing, but the sooner he came out about his problem, the better. He cleared his throat.

Major Doric looked up.

"Look, I think there has been a misunderstanding about me." His face felt like it was on fire.

She raised a platinum eyebrow.

Another deep breath. Sanchez had said *keep your head down?* The hell! "It may be that you asked for an astronomer, but I don't actually remember anything about my job."

She nodded. "Many people from the rehabilitation program are like that. It will come back soon enough. You'll be fine."

And still they called this *research?*

"But then . . ." Another thought, and one that worried him much more. "Is this an institute? A jail?"

She laughed. "A Research institute, yes. But I guess that's not the type of institute you're talking about?"

He said nothing. She was playing with him; she was a therapist or some such, wanting him to talk about his life or whatever. Therapists asked all these stupid questions: what do you feel about this. What do you feel about that, Blah, blah, blah, nonsense. He didn't *feel* anything. He didn't *want* to feel anything. Any time he felt something, someone abused it. He'd read all the psychology manuals. He knew what they were doing. Winning his trust by getting him to talk. Pretending to feel for him. Making him understand that he was not alone.

Of course he was alone. He'd been alone since they did the thing to his head, or maybe even before that.

"You don't need to be soft with me. I know I'm fucked up. Tell it to me straight. I'm no good for any kind of job, except to be a kitchen hand, as long as you keep me away from the knives."

With a soft—annoyed?—sniff, she turned on one of the wallscreens and navigated through menus until the screen displayed a series of pretty images of objects in space, which she flicked through one after the other. There were about twenty pictures that seemed randomly thrown together—moons, pitted surfaces, sharp-edged segments of a planet with rings: Saturn, he remembered; cryovolcanoes spewing ice dust into space: on Enceladus—he remembered that, too. There were nebulae, multiple-star systems, grainy images of extrasolar planetary systems, suns with huge planets circling in tight orbits. Images in different colours. Blurry scans of spacecraft. She paused a while at these and he felt tempted to ask her if they didn't have any better images of those craft, but somehow the craft seemed important, crap quality as the images were.

She said nothing, but kept flicking the images over the screen, one after the other. Click, click, click.

She said nothing.

He stared at the screen.

Saturn, Enceladus, spaceship, nebula, Hellas Planitia on Mars, another blurry space ship. Click, click, click.

So what? He recognised these places. Did that make him an astronomer? The blackness inside him grew.

Fabio started jiggling his leg again. Sweat trickled down his back. What was she hoping to achieve?

She abandoned the screen and sat on the table. The pants of her military fatigues stretched across broad thighs. She was a large woman, not just tall but with broad shoulders and large hands in the correct proportion to her height. Tall without being gangly. She folded those large hands on her knees. Her fingers were long, her forearms corded with muscle.

"The Research Base on Calico is only four years standard old. Headquarters decided to use the facilities at the Stick Farm that had lain more or less abandoned for fifteen years. Io is too unique an environment not to keep conducting research. In the past few years, we've worked on magnetic fields and radiation. We've worked on predictability of earthquakes, which has had some very useful applications on Earth. I'm both the head of the Research Base and the leader of the very small astronomy division we have here."

"This is no place to do astronomy. Too close to Jupiter."

Something glinted in her eyes. Her mouth twitched. Was that a smile? "That's why the division is small. It's also the most perfect place to study Jupiter." Again that smile.

His heart was thudding hard against his ribs. She wanted something. *Research* was a euphemism for *Intelligence*. She'd squirrelled him away in this secretive part of the base in order to get whatever she could get out of him.

He was half-scared and half wished to flip her the bird and tell her good luck.

She asked, "What did you make out of the pictures?"

"They have no relationship with each other. You're showing me random things." He pointed at the image that was frozen there. "Look here, this says it's from Satscope. You didn't even take it here. And this is an image from a completely different system. You're testing me. You're trying to annoy me into sharing things I don't want to share. I tell you now: there *is* nothing to share because whoever wiped my memories after whatever I'm supposed to have done or found out did a fucking good job. I barely remember who I am."

She looked at him and smiled and that only enraged him more. "We are a genuine research division. Astronomers are hard enough to find, and there is a shortage of skilled ones. We also do rehabilitation. Your name came up. The spec said you were damaged and I said I'd take you on. I'm testing if you can do this job. I think you can. We didn't ask for someone who had political opinions, or someone who wins scientific prizes. We don't want anyone who has opinions on what we were doing here and why. We want someone for the job, and I think you can do it."

"OK then. What is the job?"

"I'll tell you in detail tomorrow, but in short, we need someone who can analyse a wide set of scope data so we can locate some asteroids or cometoids for us to harvest our own water."

"Water?" There was none on Io. It had a dire absence of

hydrogen and not much oxygen either. Didn't they. . . ? More memories came rushing back. . . .

"I thought you imported water from Europa?" That made the most sense. The closest settlement, full of ice. There was an automated barge system that made regular trips to all the moons and space-bases using the Galilean sling. Had been for many years.

Major Doric's face showed no emotion. "We can't use the barges at the moment, I'm afraid. I want you to find an independent source." She flicked through more images. "We need to find asteroids we could divert."

"But that could take quite a while."

"As I said, we can last for about six solars."

Within six solars? One hundred and fifty days? That would mean locating something either in the system or in the asteroid belt. There were millions of smaller ice-covered bodies out there. Yes, he could do that. A memory niggled in the back of his mind that he had done something like this before, but . . . "It will be much more expensive than getting it from Europa."

"I am aware of that." Yes, that angry look. Something was very much out of order here. "I want the work done, and done quickly. I do not want any more dependency on the Council Of Four. We have equipment. We could even shoot a nano-bomb to produce course diversion rockets in situ. We just need someone to calculate the course and amount of thrust needed and the time of arrival."

"I presume you want the ice chunk put into orbit."

"Crashing it on the surface would be unhelpful, not to mention dangerous for us down here."

Another shard of memory: *People are running through a corridor into a shelter. Sirens are going off, and lights are flashing.*

He jammed the palms of his hands into his eyes. If only those flashbacks would stop.

"Are you all right?"

"Yes. Think so. Just tired."

"I'm almost done."

She showed him all the available scans the base had purchased from Satscope—so that was how they got the information. That took care of the "astronomy" department. There must be a small fortune in data here. Someone had been through and flagged all the possible comets of interest.

"You've already done a lot of the work."

"Not me, the previous astronomer. Unfortunately, he left suddenly without having completed the work. We need to go through composition scans and overlay sets of results to make composite and false colour images. It's routine work. I'm sure you can do it."

He nodded, hoping that something would come back to him. Maybe if he just started to look at the data. He hoped.

"Come, I'll take you to your room so you can freshen up. Work starts tomorrow."

She led him into a lift where they descended deep into the mountain, into another part of the base with grey corridors and scuffed linoleum. Every passage looked the same as the next: Black-painted doors with a peephole and a slot for a nametag, lights set at regular intervals. It was claustrophobic. Another memory stirred: the old base at Mars, underground to protect against radiation. There was a room full of pressure suits to his right, where people were getting dressed.

He remembered saying, *But what if we can't find them?* And someone—a pale man—said, *We cannot find those who don't want to be found. It is our task to warn those who want to listen.*

What had he been doing there with this philosophical dude?

Snow. He remembered driving through snow, with the truck's engines labouring through drifts of the stuff. Pink snow.

"Your cabin." Major Doric stopped so suddenly that Fabio nearly crashed into her.

They were still in the same type of featureless corridor and she had stopped at one of the black doors. In white paint, it said 417, like a prison cell.

She took a keycard out of her pocket and slid it through the slot next to the door, which responded by rumbling aside.

A pale fluorescent light flickered on in the room beyond. A bunk bed to the right, with mattresses stripped bare, a cupboard against the back wall, a desk to the left. There was probably just enough room for one person to stand and turn around without hitting his elbows had it not been for Fabio's luggage which sat, tagged *checked*, on the floor. Hello bags, hello medicine. Everything in there had obviously passed scrutiny, and that left him with a fuzzy warm feeling, a little island of familiarity.

"Is . . . anyone else in this room?" Fabio asked, but the musty scent that rolled from the room told him probably not. Or at least there hadn't been for a long time.

"No. We're understaffed. Plenty of room for everyone. Here." Major Doric took the card back out of the slot and gave it to Fabio. "You'll also need this to get into the bathroom and for the mess when you get the medical OK to mingle. Carry it with you at all times."

Fabio took it.

"Also, take some time to study the emergency procedures on the inside of the door in case of volcanic activity. The short run-down: one blast—warning, two blasts—assemble, three blasts—get the hell out. You get five minutes to make your way up to the access lock, where we came in. If you're not there, you'll be left behind."

"Running is useless. In twenty minutes, the earthquake has passed."

"This is not Earth. These earthquakes tend to occur in waves, building up in strength. The Research Base lies outside the earthquake protection zones."

Fabio had seen the rings surrounding the base.

"Even those are only good up to about ten on the Richter scale, which covers about ninety-five percent of earthquakes on Io."

"What about the other five percent?"

"That's what the evacuation procedures are about."

Fabio took a few steps into the room and looked over his shoulder to the inside of the door. There it was in massive letters:

Emergency Procedures in case of volcanic activity and underneath *Claiming unfamiliarity with these procedures is a punishable offence under ISF law.*

There was a long list of dot points with detailed instructions, most of which started with imperative verb forms.

Shit. She wasn't joking.

He met her eyes briefly, and she must have seen the realisation hover in Fabio's eyes, because she nodded. "It's a good old hell hole all right."

Fabio hefted his bag out of the way onto the top bunk. Turned around and looked back at the door, picturing it closed and how much this little room would feel like a prison, with that oppressive set of instructions on the door.

If you can't stand being locked up, don't go into space, one of his instructors had said. Ironic, right—space: endless swathes of nothing, cramped accommodation everywhere you travelled, a contradiction in terms.

Major Doric hesitated at the door. "Will you be fine, then?"

"Yes, I will."

"The showers are down that way." She pointed over her shoulder. "At the T-junction. You'll see the sign on the door. At the moment, there are not many other people in this corridor, so you'll have them mostly to yourself."

"Yeah, OK. Thanks."

"Make it quick, though. The personal water allowance is not good."

"Thanks."

She finally left and Fabio found himself alone, for the first time since setting out, and the silence enfolded him on all sides. There was a faint hiss of air out of the ceiling vents, but not nearly as much as on the sling barge from Callisto. Also, there was no vibration in the floor, all new sensations.

Fabio locked the door, kicked his shoes off and stretched out on the bottom one.

He didn't realise how tired he'd been, and now that his body relaxed his mind was racing. He had lost years of his life, mostly from adolescence and immediately after. He presumed that was when he had signed up for ISF, somewhere in Argentina.

In isolated areas, in space or on land, you couldn't disappear; you just became more visible as someone who didn't belong there. A sitting duck, visible from all over the pond. That was him right now.

And all the while he heard Admiral Sanchez's words in his mind. *You get one more chance, Velazquez. I've gone out of my way to protect your backside, because I trust and value you, but if you fuck this one up, too, I'm going to have to pull the plug. . . .*

Cold shivers that voice gave him, because that old shit Sanchez had a mental hold of him, and if he got Sanchez any angrier than he already was, then . . . then he was dead. If he wasn't dead already.

Head down, Velazquez, don't make any more enemies. Do a quiet, decent job for once.

Decent, that was the word. Food on the table, rent paid on time, money in the bank kind of decent.

If he could just remember what the job was that Sanchez wanted him to do.

He lay there, staring at the bottom of the bunk above him. His arms folded under his head. Aches and pains made his muscles feel tired. His knees were always troublesome, especially his left knee, which had the joint replaced twice and still when he walked too much, he could feel the squishiness in the ball joint. The whole area had been cleared of nerves, but the medical profession just couldn't fix it anymore—

He noticed the control unit near the door, and more memories came flooding back. He realised they'd kept him in a blank room aboard the interplanetary so his memories wouldn't be triggered. There were no such restrictions here.

He rose from the bed and studied the panel. Normal communication equipment. It had a data port. He wondered if he could hook up equipment.

He took his duffel from his bed and rummaged amongst the clothes. A couple of ampoules of clear fluid with a box that contained a syringe. A cable. There was something familiar about the feel in his hands, as if his body remembered what to do, even if he did not.

He inserted one end of the cable into the data port at the hub next to the door. The other end . . .

He ran his hand over the back of his head, fingertips through his hair. And that was where he had the scar. The flesh was still tender under his probing fingers.

They removed the implant.

That was where his memories had gone.

He had always despised the thing. Normal people did not have wires in their brains.

But now he couldn't connect to the data port and he couldn't upload data, and all of a sudden, he wanted to. There would be information in the base's system, no matter how commonly known, on all those things that were currently gaps in his memory. He wanted to see pictures of *Argentina* and *pampas*, and *Sarajevo* and even Admiral Sanchez's face, just to check if he remembered him well enough, or if the much-decorated man on the other side of the desk actually *was* Sanchez. And maybe the information had something to say about *Fabio Velazquez* as well, although he wasn't sure if he would be ready for the results. He didn't think he'd been a very nice person.

He rummaged further in the bag. He was quite certain that at some point there had been an infopad in his possession: a sleek, wafer-thin design that weighed no more than a data stick. He could feel the coolness of it in his hands.

Where was it?

He took all his clothes out of his bag and flung them over the bed and the floor. What the hell did he need thermal underwear for? When had he last worn a charger vest that used the body's heat and movement to generate electricity? There was a plug on that one, too, although the battery unit was missing.

No pad.

Apparently the *checked* label on the bag meant *all technology removed, confiscated in order to be erased.*

What would they have found on it and how could he get the pad back? He opened the door and looked into the corridor. No one, just scuffed white walls and black doors. He held his breath to listen for signs of human habitation, but heard none.

He was sweating all over. He wanted the pad, badly. Now. He wanted it because it would tell him things he'd forgotten. He wanted it because he didn't want to wait until things happened that jogged his mind to remember important facts.

The removal of the implant had turned him into an empty vessel. He wanted to be full again. He wanted to talk to people, even if it was only on the other end of a keyboard. He didn't want to be alone. Bad things happened when people let him wait in a solitary room. He wanted a roommate, and a pad, and news and all the things normal people had.

THE WATCHER

VEGA ANTARES SAT UP in shock, wiping sweat from her face.

Bright light filtered through the window to her right, over the plans, lines of code and mathematical calculations projected around her on the floor.

She must have fallen asleep. The last two days had been so exhausting. She had been working almost constantly.

She unwound her legs and stumbled to her feet, numb from sitting in the same position. Others would laugh that she liked this empty room with projections on the floor. They liked the trappings of furniture, chairs and desks. Vega joked that it made them so much like the bureaucracies they despised. The governments on Earth, the large international organisations, the ISF, the Council Of Four, all instruments of bureaucracy designed to further the aims of the ruling majority from the traditionally rich countries.

She filled her cup from the dispenser next to the cabinet, and drank the cool water.

The large, aquarium-like window looked out over soft clouds, always whirling, as far as she could see. The sky was dark blue, and if she squinted, she could just make out a faint white line that came from the zenith and disappeared in the cloud mass. That was no scratch on the window and no falling star. Those were Jupiter's rings, seen from side on. To the left of those floated a white speck, visibly moving.

Io.

Impenetrable fortress of ISF bases.

In theory she would be able to see Calico Base, located at the subjovian point.

Her intelligence told her that the prisoner had been moved there. It was a definite improvement over his previous locality on Earth, in Sarajevo, the hub of ISF. Over the past few solars, whenever she read her nanometrics memory, he would show up as a distant point coming closer. The computing hub downstairs had constantly worked on trajectories, until it had become clear that he was going to Io. Of course. He'd been reprimanded. Io was where prisoners went.

Not only did the man have secret information that rightfully belonged to Allion, he knew many secrets from within ISF as well.

Secrets that certain parts of Space Corps didn't want Flight Force to know, or information that was only relevant to ISF people from the inner system, and they didn't want the Outer System, and Vice Admiral Preston, to get their hands on it. Oh, the politics were thick with this one. If ISF was still one complete organisation after the dust from this blew over, she'd be surprised.

But Vega did not share the nanometrics with the prisoner. Priya did, but Priya had died on Mars. Vega could not communicate with him, but she desperately needed the information that Priya had given him.

This was why all these diagrams and calculations were around her on the floor. Which approach route they could get the wellship *Thor IV* to fly, and where they could release the moth fighters so that they evaded detection by the dumb ISF radar. Which sectors of Io were safe to send trucks for a pickup by a moth. Which weapons they could carry on top of the weight of the crew and fuel, and allowing for a good margin of error if the pilot passed out because of too many gs.

It was all calculated to the microsecond.

Because when Juno Station had a problem that was what they did: used their minds and knowledge to solve it. Think big, think bold, take risks. It was the Allion way.

A soft hissing noise indicated the door sliding aside.

Vega's second in charge, Taura Shelton, came in.

"Any luck?" she asked.

"They took him to Calico."

"That's a bummer. He'll be hard to reach there, let alone available for rescue. I don't fancy we'll send someone in."

"Oh, we will send someone, but not until everything is ready."

"Into the base? That sounds like a bad idea."

"Probably not the base. I don't like separating our people from their escape vehicles. We'll track him and wait until he's in a place where we can reach him without creating too much fuss. Sian is on standby." As a pilot in the system, she always had access to a suitable craft.

"She may be all the way on the other side of the system. The military will definitely notice when a civilian passenger craft enters their space."

"Don't worry. We'll be fine. The technicians have it all under control."

Taura sniffed. "I'm glad you are so confident. There is no margin for error for this one. We have only six solars."

Vega gestured her second in command closer.

"I know you're a flight technician and nanometrics is not your thing, but just have a look at this."

She flicked her fingers and the projection nozzles in the ceiling filled the floor with a giant image of a pitted and scarred world in shades of yellow, green and red. Jupiter's moon Io.

The image zoomed in, as if they were flying closer at great speed.

Taura went to stand on the edge of the room, leaning against the wall.

Vega laughed. Taura was much more comfortable with traditional technology, workstations, screens and desks.

Vega preferred immersion and as little distraction as possible.

The image on the floor displayed a view of a couple of copper-coloured domes with interlinking tubes. Calico Base. A little rectangular dot moved across the sickly yellow plain. This was a live view from one of the observation butterflies: tiny satellites made mostly of superconducting wire that flew around the system propelled by Jupiter's magnetic field. They needed no energy source—the constant radiation of which could be detected by outsiders—and they transmitted data in short sharp bursts that were too short for tracking equipment to get a fix on the exact location. They didn't maintain location anyway.

Superimposed over the view of the base were three dots of light, and all three were in the same section of the base: the small building on top of the mountain that overlooked that base. Most of that part of the base was underground.

Vega zoomed in again. Corridors and stairwells rushed past, like a veritable warren of passages. "This base used to be much bigger, but not a lot of this room is being used at present. Here." She nodded at the floor.

The projection showed a long corridor. One dot was in a room at the beginning, near the stairs, another was in another room on the other side of a door, and a third was in an adjacent corridor, where the rooms were much bigger.

She nodded at the projection. "That's our prisoner and two of the mindshards."

"If he's not your mindshard, but the other two are, can't we just talk to the other two and tell them to grab him and bust their backsides out of there?"

Vega laughed. That was so like Taura. She was a hardware engineer. Practical, straight-shooting. She shook her head. "The mindshards are a passive technology. We'd need some sort of transmitting capability in order to reach them, and even then it's not sure that we could. It doesn't work that way. The technique was designed to be observant and undetectable. We can plant knowledge and memories in people's minds, but not without their knowledge. We'd need to create hooks and use precise transmissions. As soon as we start transmitting to them, we blow our cover."

"Then we have one chance to blow our cover, so we better use it well."

"I would prefer not to use it on getting the prisoner out. We are not going to blow our cover."

"Then what?"

"The seeds for this escape were sown many years ago."

Taura cast her a disbelieving look. They'd had many discussions about mindshard technology, and if you couldn't send a command to it and it wouldn't fill a screen with data, Taura didn't want to know about it. But Vega knew it was the next generation of technology, way beyond anything ISF was able to replicate or detect.

CHAPTER FOUR

BREATHING HARD, FABIO staggered around his room, forcing his galloping mind to slow down.

Calm down, calm down.

He took deep breaths, staring at himself in the mirror, a technique a nurse had taught him at the transport. He might not feel like himself, but he looked like himself, a normal person, a man, of slight build, with short black hair.

Maybe he should clean up and get changed. That's what normal people did when they arrived in a place. He couldn't remember the last time he washed. Probably on the interplanetary.

The room held a small cupboard that had a space for hanging uniforms and two shelves, one of which contained towels, a bottle of *all-purpose washing gel* which he recognised from the interplanetary, and *dental hygiene paste*, the other a spare blanket and set of sheets. A drawer underneath held the ubiquitous copy of the ISF manifest, as well as an environment suit liner. The vacuum suits would be in the entrance hall.

Fabio picked up his possessions from the floor and arranged them in the cupboard, hanging up his shirts—they looked a bit rumpled—and putting his boots in the bottom drawer and his empty duffel in the very top shelf. He didn't know where to put the medicines, so he left them on his bed, three jars with little pills. Labels said how often the contents needed to be taken, but apart from a code, the label said nothing about the contents. It hadn't worried him earlier, on the shuttle or interplanetary. It worried him now. He'd have to look up the code. He'd have to find out what to do when the pills ran out.

He took a towel and clean underwear and went out to the corridor.

He walked in the direction Major Doric had indicated the bathroom to be. Apart from his footsteps and the sound of air hissing from the vents, there was no sound. No voices behind the doors, no music. The silence pressed on him.

He found the bathroom—couldn't see a men's or women's indication, but that wasn't customary in all settlements. He pushed open the door and peeked in. Well, bathroom was a misnomer for the tiny hole-in-the-wall with two humidi-vac cubicles, which were the same brand and size as the ones on the ITV. Which was: tiny.

Outside the cubicles there was a small change room with white but badly rust-stained tiles. The doors didn't close properly on either of the two cubicles. There was a bench were Fabio took off his uniform. He folded it neatly, but gathered it would probably get wet, seeing as the rubber threshold under cubicle doors showed yellow streaking from where mineral-laden water had squirted through.

Interesting shades of yellow and orange. Did he say anything about the ship's cubicles being dirty?

It was debatable how clean excessively recycled water was anyway. Whenever anything went wrong with a habitat, it happened in the bio plants. If the Ph balance was wrong, the algal baths quite quickly degenerated into a stinking mess. Most closed-system bases operated on a mixed bio and chemical recycling process. The chemical process needed more tech and energy, but at least it was reliable.

Energy this base had plenty of, with the stick farm outside.

A card slot was next to each cubicle. Fabio pushed the door, but it wouldn't open until he had retrieved his card and slid it through the machine. The door creaked, its hinges caked with rust and salt.

Inside the cubicle was barely enough room to turn around. Fabio pressed the release causing jets of heavy steam to hiss out of holes in the wall. It was hot, and steamy. He let the steam massage his skin.

Then he remembered the water rations, and grabbed for the bottle of *all-purpose cleaning gel*. He put it in his hair, but he was halfway through soaping himself when the mist cut out.

What the fuck?

Dripping wet, he went outside. Cold wind blew over his skin from the ceiling vent. He wriggled the card out of his clothes while trying not to get them wet and slid it through the receptacle again, went back inside and pressed the button. No go. Back outside, dripping water all over the floor. The screen on the slot said, *daily shower allowance used.*

What the fuck—seriously?

He shivered, while bone-dry air blasted over him. Already his skin was drying, with the soapy residue starting to itch. Whoever's motherfucking idea of a joke was this? Someone who was watching him on camera, knowing that he was new and wanting to play a practical joke on him?

He opened the bathroom door a crack and looked out. The corridor was empty. There was no sound. He shut the door again, but the display on the machine hadn't changed.

Opened the door again. Still no one. He called, "Hey, can anyone help me with the water?"

Nothing except the hiss of air out of the ceiling vents. Maybe he hadn't been loud enough.

Oh, for fuck's sake! He didn't want to have the whole base out here laughing at him, all those people who had seen him come out of the lift and being taken to Doric's office.

He dried himself in the towel, pulled on his uniform, grabbed his access card, went into the hallway and knocked on the nearest door. No reply. He tried the door handle. It was locked. Where was everyone?

Knocked on another door. "Hey, is there anyone here? There's a problem with the water."

Nothing. He banged on another door with the same result. He went further up the corridor, where his room was. All the doors were closed, and since he'd noticed how the door to his cabin shut hermetically, probably in case of dome failure, no light would be peeping from underneath closed doors either. When walking around with Manning in the other base, he had seen some people. Not many, but this part of the base was deserted.

It was an asylum for crazy people.

In memory, he was in a long, concrete corridor. Smoke was creeping in from under the doors to the left. A cloth over his mouth made him feel claustrophobic.

Hello! he screamed. His voice sounded muffled. A door to his right led into a dormitory. All the beds were neatly made, and empty.

He yelled into the room, *Hello! Anyone here?*

Further down the corridor, he came across a body slumped on the floor. Colourful clothing. His heart skipped a beat. Was that—?

He pushed the woman's shoulder and she rolled over. She was black-skinned, with her fizzed hair cropped close to her head. A trail of blood ran from her nostril. Her eyes were open.

Elsewhere in the building an alarm wailed. He had to get out. He had to find a suit, because he'd left his in the truck. The truck would have gone, taking the refugees to higher ground. It wouldn't be long before the wall of water came and would freeze over the valley floor—

In the corridor in the base at Io, Fabio arrived at a closed door.

There was a panel on the wall next to it. Fabio pressed a couple of buttons.

Nothing. They'd locked him up in here. They only pretended

that he was free to go wherever he wanted. This was a prison after all.

Wait. Think. Deep breaths.

He studied the text on the little display. It said *equalised*. So the panel was not armed—which meant that the other side of the door was pressurised. The display flashed *enter access code*.

Well fuck, he hadn't been given an access code and suddenly entering that door seemed like the most important thing in his life. Making sure that he wasn't locked in. Finding a live person to talk to.

He put both hands on the door and tried to push it sideways. It didn't budge.

He banged on the door with both fists. "Hey, is there anyone in this place?"

Nothing.

Then a thought. Of course he had been given an access code. That was the function of the card. He couldn't see any slot to insert it, so he tapped it against the panel. To his surprise, the door slid open.

Well, duh. Let's not panic for no reason.

On the other side of the door was another corridor, similar to the one that held his room. Grey walls, grey floor, grey ceiling and black doors.

He was about to turn around when he heard the muffled sound of voices. Fabio ran down the corridor, and located the room where the sound was coming from. When he knocked on the door, someone, a male voice, shouted, "Hello? Who's there?"

"Hey, mate, can you help me with the water?"

"I would love to, but we can't get out," the voice replied, in a thick accent that made Fabio sure that this was someone from the civilian settlements, mainly on Europa, Ganymede. "Some dickhead locked the door."

Locked? What the . . . Fabio pulled the door handle, but it wouldn't move. "Why would anyone do that?"

"Some lock malfunction. We tried to go for dinner, but couldn't get out," the man said. "We're hungry."

Dinner. Fabio hadn't even considered that. Doric had said nothing about it.

"Have you tried the comm?"

"They said they're sending someone, but that was an hour ago."

"They'll be coming from the main base." This was another man.

Strange that the research base itself would have no one with a security override. Did he even believe what the man was saying?

In the military, one contacted one's superiors and unless you were on punitive detention, the superior came to help you out. That was the rule.

"Have you called your superior officer?"

"We're visitors. We don't have a superior officer on this base."

That sucked. Should he do something about it?

His subconscious was telling him that he knew how to open doors, but the voice of his rational mind was starting to resemble that of Admiral Sanchez. *Keep your head down, Velazquez. Don't get involved in things you don't understand. You're in enough trouble already.*

That was all very well, but he couldn't leave these people in here all night without dinner, could he? Surely there was no harm in fixing what was no doubt a simple malfunction. It was easy enough to do: forget to change the settings on the door and it wouldn't open until someone gave it the right command. "Wait. I'll go and find someone."

As he went by his room, he saw that someone had put a tray with a covered plate on the floor next to his door. He wasn't hungry, but picked it up and put it on the tiny desk in his room, and then left the room again.

The other end of the corridor led to a staircase, which he had used when Major Doric had brought him here. On the level above was another empty corridor without a living soul in sight.

A second floor up, he met a female private coming out of a lift with armful of mops and brooms and a vacuum cleaner.

She frowned at him.

"Excuse me, have you got security clearance to open doors? There's people down there locked in their room and they need dinner."

She looked at him strangely. "And who are you and where did you spring from?"

"I'm—" he realised that none of his shirts showed his rank and his status as member of the Special Ops division. "Fabio Velazquez. I've just arrived today."

"Ah. You're the mining astronomer."

"Yes. Can you help and open the door? I think their door lock has malfunctioned. They called someone, but no one has arrived yet."

She shook her head. "Sorry. If I had that type of security clearance, I'd get a better position and be out of here in no time. Have you tried the workshop?"

"No, where is it?"

"You can't go there. You need to call them. They're in the main base."

"Oh. I'll try that, then." Although he was reasonably sure that the people inside the room had already done that.

Probably help had already arrived.

Maybe he should go and eat his own dinner and keep his nose out of things that were none of his business.

He returned to his room and lifted the lid off the tray. The plate underneath contained fried protein cubes and mash with a couple of cherry tomatoes and a few leaves of lettuce. He could live with the protein cubes, if they were decent quality, which these ones were, and the mash, which was nothing more than a bland filler, but he forced himself to eat the tomatoes and lettuce first, not because he didn't like them but, man, were there no other vegetables that were easy and quick to grow in closed-base hydroponics?

The tray came with a built-in e-ink display that contained instructions about how to dispose of scraps and where to leave the tray after use. It also described rules of the base's personal allocation of alcohol.

When he pushed the tray aside, the surface of the tiny desk came alive with e-ink. On further inspection, he found that the desktop could be detached from the wall. There was a bracket in the top corner of the room that could hold it, and a controller stuck to the underside. The base entertainment included a lot of local news shows, both from ISF and COF sources. This was going to be useful. Fabio flicked through and came across a news provider calling themselves Law's News. He guessed this had something to do with the Law family which held huge assets in COF territory. This service was based on Ganymede.

One of the first listed news items was *Historic delegation leaves for Io*. It went on to describe that the first delegation ever had been sent to Calico Base as part of a new agreement of openness. They had sent four people: a trade representative, a diplomat, a COF government representative and a security specialist. There was a picture of them before departure, a *historic delegation*. Three men and a woman. He'd seen those people being roughed up in the entrance hall.

The article crowed, *COF governor Anise-Leontine Law said, "We have great hopes for repairing frayed relationships with ISF and defusing tension that exists between civilians and military bases and risk of conflict that might entail. The previous armed conflicts are all too clear in the memories of our older residents. We do not want to go down that road again and we're glad that ISF has seen sense in allowing the delegation to visit."*

Suddenly, he had a thought: what if the people locked in the room were the COF delegation? They were visitors, the man had said. They had no superiors on the base, he had said.

Locking people up in a room was hardly an example of diplomatic finesse. Surely, this had to be an accident that had the potential to cause much damage. He'd better go and check.

That was one thing he remembered: in times of need, you looked after other people.

JAYKADIA

GOVERNOR OF THE COUNCIL Of Four, Anise-Leontine Law, looked up when Jaykadia opened the door to her office, and a smile of recognition spread over her face.

"Jaykadia, what an honour this is, for you to come and see me here."

Jaykadia shut the door behind her, and crossed the room.

"I wish it were a happy occasion that I came see you about," she said.

She sat down in the chair opposite her aunt's desk.

Behind her aunt's chair was a large window which looked out over the many domes and arches and delicate architecture of Galileo City. It disturbed her that all this might be in danger. The settlement was so fragile, protected from the harshness of space only by the dome, transparent and looking so insubstantial.

"I had a visit from Preston," she said.

"I know," her aunt answered. "He's been here as well."

"So you know what it's about?"

"Yes. The situation is quite interesting."

Interesting was not the way Jaykadia would have put it. "Why do you say interesting? I think it's quite serious. He wants me to move all our maintenance outside, he refuses to say for how long, he leaves me with no way to cater to all these people he wants to bring in and, on top of that, it's quite likely that he'll spring some surprises on us."

"Preston plays politics very well," her aunt said. "He's going to tell everybody how important this exercise is and draw a lot of civilians into it, but the only thing that interests him is expanding the force at our expense. You can be sure that when this exercise is over and all the soldiers have vacated your sheds, there will be something left for you to concede. Whether he wants to maintain a permanent unit on site, or wants you to house equipment, or wants you to sign a contract, he will try to encroach on your land and your business. And he will use it to strengthen his position in his face-off with Sanchez."

"I don't have time for his games. If he wants to secede from the inner system division of ISF, let him do that. I don't care."

"But they will care."

"Of course, but why does he need to bother us with it?"

"Because he wants to enlist us as supporters. He wants to make sure that we are so dependent on him that we have no option but to follow wherever they choose to take us."

Jaykadia stared at her aunt.

The Governor of the Council Of Four was not a dumb woman. If Preston played political games, Anise-Leontine Law was right up there with him.

"You can't seriously suggest that Preston is preparing to go to *war* with the inner system section of ISF?"

"Well, he's planning something."

"But why? Why would he care? Why would they care? Space is huge. Let them each control a part of it and be done."

But she knew that her aunt was right, and also that Preston was planning something, and that she should try to keep out of it as much as possible, especially with anything remotely connected to Mars, because that was forever a hotbed of conflict.

"We should keep a very close eye on them," her aunt said.

"Yes, but how can we influence them?"

Her aunt nodded, but did not say anything. She had this infuriating habit of waiting to speak until the other party figured out what she wanted them to see. Throughout the discussion, she would give them little clues to what she thought.

"Come on aunt, I've got lots of stuff to do. I don't have time to play this game today."

"Remember Mars?"

"How could I not remember it?" So many people had died in that disaster, when an asteroid hit the dome where a conference was being held, including most of the delegates.

"Do you remember what the International Space Force said then?"

"Of course I remember," Jaykadia said. "How can that still be relevant?" She still remembered the speech by Sanchez that blamed Allion for the disaster, because they had lax safety procedures. Privately, some people went much further: they accused Allion of deliberately targeting the dome.

There had been lots of military people in her life even then, and they all listened to Sanchez, hands on their hearts. It was a bit scary.

"Things take a long time in space."

"I have no idea where you're going with this. Tell me what you think, please."

"You are so impatient."

"In this matter, yes, I am, and if it's because I'm young, I'm happy to own up to that."

Her aunt folded her hands on the table. "Well, nobody is too sure about this, so please don't take it as a definite. There was a time, many years ago, when space exploration was a lot less conservative than it is today. After Mars, people became much more cautious. Accidents are bad for public opinion. A lot of civilians are in space, and when civilians die, it doesn't look good for anyone. News services spread facts and fiction about the event far and wide. It's impossible for ISF to control the narrative as they do with their own mishaps. It is my feeling that the trend to be less cautious at the beginning stages of a project is not something evil and alien, but something from the time that people set out to conquer space and did lots of experiments. The fact is that we now do less groundbreaking research than people did back then."

"So, what does this have to do with this exercise?"

"Well, he is afraid that someone will come out of nowhere with more advanced technology, having taken more risks, but having succeeded in doing something ISF cannot."

"Like Allion, back in the day."

"Exactly. We're still reaping the profits of their work. For one, you wouldn't be sitting here if it wasn't for Allion technology."

The accident. The hospital, that brilliant doctor to whom Jaykadia owed her life.

"Dr Crawford was not Allion." Sadly, she had retired.

"You are more convinced of that than I am. I think she went to ground when she became stranded when Allion was wiped out. She kept her head down because she had to survive. She won't have been the only one, and Preston is trying to root out dissent. People who might be likely to be informants for other interests."

"Are you seriously suggesting that Allion is still alive in some way?"

"I don't know, but wouldn't be surprised if they were. That's what this exercise is about: increasing the footprint of ISF in the civilian communities to fill the ideological vacuum that has arisen there. They have never liked the fact that commercial companies do things and develop technology that's not in their control. They want to know what we're doing in our sheds, and they want to have control over as much of it as possible."

Damn, that made far more sense than was comfortable.

"Preston asked me to vacate all the mining sheds," Jaykadia said. "What should I do about it?"

"Give him his sheds. But don't take out everything. Make sure you still have some surveillance equipment inside, and make sure that you have some personnel located in nearby locations, and argue the hardest you can that those people be given access to all their facilities."

"You mean we spy on what they're doing?"

"We are great spies," her aunt said. "We would never have gotten as far as we have today if we had blindly obeyed their every command. We're happy to work with them, but when pushed, many of us will come to the defence of freedom and the likes of Allion and Fenosa and all the commercial operations that once co-existed with ISF. We are truly not hostile to the military unless they give us no other option. But if they're smart, they won't go down that path. Preston is a smart man. He won't make that mistake, but we have to keep on our toes. This is why we speak to them and we invite them to join our groups and come to our meetings. We know they're not going to pull their weight in the Council Of Four, but just having them in there gives us the authority to send delegations to Io."

"Have you heard from the delegation yet?"

"No, but we don't have direct access, and I expect there to be something soon."

She smiled, and Jaykadia was starting to like this. It was true, life these days was boring, even in the hostile environment of space.

Playing the political game would be a good thing to do.

CHAPTER FIVE

FABIO LEFT HIS ROOM again, and went back to the door where he had heard the voices. It was shut.

He knocked. "Are you still there?"

Footsteps. A male voice. "Finally. Are you from Base Ops?"

"Um—no. I'm the guy who was here before. Has anyone come to open the door yet?"

"We've heard nothing. We've complained several times. They say someone is coming to fix the problem, but no one comes."

This was very odd. "I asked upstairs, but there seems to be hardly anyone here. I'll see if I can open the door myself. Wait a moment." He glanced around the corridor for something to bash the door down, but the corridor was entirely empty, and besides, an airtight door would be hard to bash in, never mind that a damaged door would get him into all kinds of trouble that a malfunction didn't justify. He ran to his room, opened his cupboard and stared at the contents, trying to remember what would be useful. His hand went unbidden to the back of his head. If he still had his implant, he would know what to do.

He glanced at the comm hub next to the door. Security clearance.

There was something niggling at him. His scar itched. He did have an external data patch in his bag, which he'd found in his room on the interplanetary, stuck to the bottom of the top shelf of the cupboard. It had been live, and no doubt used by security to spy on him, but he had disabled it by sending worms from the room's hub, little bits of code that day by day stripped away layers of security that hid the patch from the system, until he could access its data and erase it. He had taken pride in this work, proof that he was not mad and that he could do things, if only he remembered what those things were. He had taken the patch as a trophy, an empty patch with layers of top-level-approved security that he could use to his advantage.

It would probably open the door.

He took his duffel from the top shelf, and picked apart the lining in the corner where he had hidden it. The device was no bigger than a pill, but much flatter, with one side made of adhese-latex. He stuck it to his collarbone, under his uniform. A patch of warmth spread across his chest. That was his nanometrics jumping into action, a particular type of dendromers dumping their coating and releasing the naked nanobots into his bloodstream. He watched the screen of the PCD on his wrist until it registered the heightened activity, and it started to flash *corrupt software detected.* Yeah, duh, that was all the stuff he'd planted on the patch. If someone was going to take a blood sample tomorrow, he'd be seriously screwed.

He went back to the door and knocked. "Are you still there?"

"We're not going anywhere," the man said.

"I'm going to try something. I may need your help."

He knelt on the ground so that he was face to face with the door's lock. He took off the PCD and pressed it against the metal surface of the lock, where it stuck like it had on his skin.

Now. This kind of activity felt very familiar.

A memory: he saw a brief flash of a dark and derelict concrete corridor, felt a brief chill of freezing air against his skin. It stung like boiling water.

His heart thumped. Only a vacuum was that cold. Where the hell had that been?

He pressed a button on the PCD. The screen flickered briefly, and then came up with the Calico Base logo and security prompt. *Entry code.*

Well, fuck that, he had no entry code.

Sometimes, doors released automatically in case of a general power failure. He could simulate a power failure. While being bored on the interplanetary, he'd found many worms in the ship's systems that did just that and had stored them all on his secret datapatch. Really, command had no idea how corrupted their supposedly secure systems were.

He subvocalized *List DIR COMMAND BREAKER.*

The PCD's screen showed a list of about twenty-five worms. The one called Death of Night would do nicely.

Seriously, he wondered about the sanity of people who wrote these things, although rumours went that some of the worms were self-perpetuating and hundreds of years old.

He tapped on his PCD. The worm transferred.

The little light on the door started flashing.

"Can you try the door?" he said. Because in an emergency, doors could only be opened from the inside.

There was a thump against the door. And then, "Nope."

Fuck.

The light was still flashing.

Another memory. He was in a dark room, and a display on the wall flashed in blue letters 15 . . . 14 . . . 13 . . . 12 . . . He pressed himself against the wall, holding the gun with both hands, listening out for footsteps.

Someone shouted outside, *If I get my fucking hands on you, I'll wring your neck, you little slime.*

Fabio breathed fast, still seeing those letters. Then he knew what he had to do. High-level security codes did not release the lock in the event of a power failure. You could not have criminals running around your closed-environment facility each time there was a power failure. Rather, these locks required a human response that it was, in fact, OK to release them, because you could also not afford the families of convicted criminals sue you for negligence of care. If there was a real emergency, *everyone* should be given a chance to escape, not just the "good" people.

"Are you listening? I want you to do something for me." The light was still flashing. They probably had another thirty seconds before it was reset and the system would detect the worm.

"Yeah, OK."

"I want you to go the comm hub and find the menu."

Footsteps. A short silence, and then, "Got it."

"Go into something that says, *Enter manual code.*"

"Got that, and then?"

"Enter S1."

"Done."

"Can you open the door?"

The door rattled. "Nope."

"OK, try pressing reset and receive at the same time."

A small silence. "Nope."

Fuck. Well, the implant memories would come in handy here. Meanwhile, the seconds were ticking away. Surely Major Doric wouldn't be impressed if she found out he'd been messing with the security system. *Keep your head down, Velazquez.* The hell. Trouble had a way of finding him. And what was wrong with helping people, anyway? "Are you still in the manual mode?"

"Yes—oh—hang on. Now I am. What was that again?"

"Reset and receive at the same time." One of the most-commonly used lock overrides.

There was a brief burst of power that made the PCD's screen flash. Fabio felt it going through his veins. His skin prickled, and a feeling of heat spread through from his arm into his shoulder. The nanobots in his body aligned; he could feel it.

The light stopped flashing. The lock clicked.

The door opened.

A waft of stale and sweaty air drifted from the room. The man on the other side was the tall and dark-skinned delegate he had seen earlier that day in the arrival hall. He had startlingly grey eyes.

Fabio clambered to his feet, rubbing his arms and taking the man's outstretched hand. He was at least a head taller than Fabio, and his hand was huge, but long-fingered and delicate.

"Thank you for opening the door. I thought they were going to abandon us for the night," the black man said. His voice was very deep.

He stood in a narrow hallway to what seemed to be a small apartment. There were four doors in the hall, one open. In this room—a bedroom with two bunks—sat the three other members of the delegation. The young man sat on the top bunk, the woman on the bottom, and a blond-haired man of indeterminate age stood by the door. He was also very gangly and tall, and much of his skin was covered in green-hued bio-tattoos that moved. Not cheap, those.

For a moment, they stared at each other. Fabio realised how odd he looked with the spiked-up hair and caked shampoo. "Well, I had a shower malfunction." He was still shivering from the burst of power that had gone through him. "Um . . . you're free to go to dinner now." He held out his hand. "Fabio Velazquez."

"Do you normally work here?"

"No, I just arrived on a temporary contract."

The dark-haired woman wormed herself off the bunk and rose in a fluid motion. "And he's the only one in this place who's shown any kind of help to us." She was shorter than Fabio, with a thin frame and long black hair. Her eyes were black. A smattering of freckles covered her nose and cheeks, which reminded him of someone.

He asked, "Er . . . have we met before?"

"If you've been to Europa, maybe. Before the embargo."

"Um . . ." He didn't know if he'd been to Europa. What embargo? What sanctions?

"I'm Thalia Hasegawa," she said. "Communication officer for COF."

"Paul Armitage," said the tattooed man and gave an absurd little bow.

"Sol Whitaker," said the black man.

"Jun Hasegawa." That was the youngest member in the group, and Fabio was surprised just how young his voice sounded.

He did remember that the Hasegawas were a major mining family in these parts. The immigrant Yoshi Hasegawa had nine children, who each had lots of children, and as a result, there were many Hasegawas everywhere.

"I'm afraid I can't help you with anything at all," Fabio said. "I don't know what embargo you're talking about." Probably something that Major Doric wouldn't want him to learn about.

Paul scoffed. "What planet have you been on? Do they keep force deliberately innocent now?"

"Paul. . . ," Thalia warned.

There was a brief and tense silence.

Thalia said, in a measured voice, "He wouldn't know about politics of the system if he came from elsewhere. In short, the Council Of Four is an independent body of civilian and mainly commercial interests that represents the four Galilean moons. The Council Of Four raised money for the sling to be built and it belongs to the Council's cooperative. The Council has agreed that in return for the use of the sling, individuals, organisations or commercial ventures need to declare what they're using it for, and outline the projects they're working on. This is to increase stability in the system and avoid situations such as on Mars. Banparra has been a most accommodating Base Commander. He sees the value in working together with local systems, rather than relying on his orders to come from Sarajevo. We value him a lot, because without him, we would never be here as inspectors of the Council Of Four. Frankly, I don't see how Sarajevo can have any idea of the issues we're facing out here."

Hmm, that was a lot more enlightening than anything he'd

heard so far. And he was probably also not supposed to learn of it in this manner. Was he supposed to support Banparra or Sarajevo? The latter, he thought, although instructions on what he was supposed to do had gone MIA.

"So now Vice Admiral Preston has 'innocently' announced the largest military exercise the system has seen, in which Calico Base will be the epicentre. But in order to get enough resources delivered to Calico, they need to use the Galilean sling, and the commercial operators of the sling have put a limit on how many transfers they will process. Part of it is simple logistics: they don't have that much spare capacity, but some of it is definitely political."

Hang on—Preston. That definitely rang a bell. But she was wrong about him: Preston was not a supporter of Sarajevo. Preston was Sanchez's rival.

That man has been trying to undermine me. If you find any reason to bring him down, don't hesitate.

"Is this . . . exercise and embargo why you're here?"

"No. We're here to inspect working conditions and talk to the base crew, especially the ones in lower rankings and those who have been sent here as punishment. We'll spend a few weeks in various places of the base. For the time being, the first mission seems to be to find something to eat. Does anyone know where to find the kitchens?"

Fabio checked his PCD, only to find that the bypass of the base security had dumped a lot of information on it. "I think I can find out."

So he set out with this odd group, Thalia walking next to him, Sol following with Jun, who had not said a single word except his name, and Paul trailing the group, a scowl on his face.

The PCD showed the canteen as being two floors above the room.

Again, there was no one on the stairs and even the canteen was empty, but there was a light still on behind the serving counter, although all trays and serving counters had already been cleaned. Where were the people who had eaten here?

As the group proceeded into the room, a man came out of the doorway of the kitchen. He stopped and frowned in consternation.

"These people would like to get some dinner," Fabio said.

The man stared. "Yes, sure. D-corridor, right? I was coming to that. Sorry I'm late, but we've been very busy."

It looked like they had, too. A huge pile of plates stood on the counter. There were at least two hundred chairs in the room, and the floor was still dusty and covered in footsteps and the occasional spill.

"Your dinner is being made right now. I'll go and check if they're ready. Wait here. Sit down."

They sat one of the long tables.

Jun sat next to Thalia, Sol at the head of the table and Paul next to Fabio.

Noises of rattling of plates and cutlery drifted from the kitchen.

"Too busy to attend us, my arse," Paul said.

Thalia said, "Oh, stop it. You know they don't want us here, so why are you surprised?"

"I hadn't expected them to be quite so blatant about it," Paul said.

"They're military. Subtlety is not their thing."

Thalia leaned her elbows on the table and her head in her hands. Jun stared into the distance. Fabio wondered how old he was.

Thalia asked Fabio what his task was at the base, and he told her that it was to find icy celestial bodies that could be diverted to use as drinking water.

Sol said, "What? Isn't that the job of the Galilean sling?"

"It's just a job."

"But it isn't really, is it?" Sol said. "It's not that simple."

Fabio shrugged, which was a very good gesture in a situation where he had no idea what to say for best effect. He felt like he was in a crowd where everybody knew where to go next, except he didn't.

"It's not going to make anyone happy," Thalia said. "The Council Of Four will be very pissed off if Io is found to bypass their services."

Fabio met her eyes, dark and sharp, but said nothing about nano-bombs.

"I agree," Paul said. "It would be easier if the Io bases just cooperated and signed that agreement so we could resume the supply of ice from Europa, but they're too stubborn. The COF laws require openness. For the safety of all citizens, but especially against the growing threat of another war breaking out, we demand that all bases declare what they're doing and where. But Io refuses, citing military security. And that is rubbish, since we're all people, space colonists, and we can't afford to start fighting each other. So Io has become isolated and now not even their military friends on Earth want to help them."

Jun said, "Starting to look like a North Korea kind of situation, isn't it?" It was the first time he'd said more than a few words.

Paul looked at him in an irritated way. "For once, speak in terms that don't show off how smart you are. Give a body a chance to understand what you're talking about."

"North Korea, a small country on Earth that two centuries ago stubbornly held onto its ideology, only to starve its people. Only when the borders finally came down did the first foreign soldiers find the extent of suffering by both soldiers and civilians. In space, such a situation would be much worse. Without outside resources, these bases will die."

This was followed by a silence.

But damn, the youngster was right, and Fabio wasn't sure if ISF cared. In fact, something about his jumbled-up memories about Mars told him that they probably didn't, and they might be ready to cut their losses and Banparra knew this so he cosied up to the locals.

Paul said, "I think the real risk is that the base command at Io will jump sideways. If ISF headquarters keeps tightening the screws on Banparra and keeps isolating him from the COF, then he may associate with other elements, and heaven knows we've already faced this situation once in relation to Calico Base, when they were infested with spies. Banparra was welcomed by COF as a hardliner to clean things up, but I'm not sure if all the troops here are under his full control. In fact, going by our experience, I'm pretty sure they are not."

"Yeah," Sol said, his voice dark.

A brief silence. Fabio thought of the jostling between Research and the rest of the base. Disagreements between the base and Doric. Different orders, different security systems.

A kitchen hand had come into the dining hall with a steam mop on his back, and started to clean the floor.

Jun said, "We may as well name the beast. You think Banparra is in with Allion?"

Paul nodded. "That scum never goes away."

Thalia whirled at him. "I don't get why you keep circulating those stories. Allion is gone from the system. They have no interest in playing petty local politics. They were into big projects and long-term goals. Why would they hang around here if everyone is infighting and there is all of space to be explored?"

"I suggest that you don't underestimate their vindictiveness," Paul said.

"Oh, come on, give me proof." She spread her hands. "Why are we even talking about this? Why are you Ganymedeans so damn suspicious? When they were here, Allion was a commercial partner. We bought their stuff. They bought ours. They are not mysterious evil forces or mythical ghosts. They are gone."

"Can I say something?" The soldier with the steam mop had stopped at the table on his way to the serving area.

Everyone looked at him, and he blushed.

"Well, I just overheard what you were saying about Allion, but I don't think you know all of it. There are definitely ghost ships in the area. We've had quite a few reports recently."

Sol raised one eyebrow over the rim of his drink. "I thought those were well and truly relegated to the realm of imagination."

"With due respect, sir, I've seen the data and believe there is some merit in them."

"You think so? How?" Thalia's voice sounded disbelieving.

The kitchen hand blushed again. His young face looked very inexperienced. Guess Doric hadn't subjected him to her *need to know* speech.

"I've seen the scans. They clearly show something moving in the system. There's a very faint signature of an engine. It's about the right size for a ship. Some infrared scans match up with the visible ones, that's always a good sign. Don't you agree they are likely to be Allion ships? No other commercial company I know is still in operation in this area, or at least not independently, in space. Fenosa has fully retreated to on-surface contracts. They work mostly for the families. Some of the families have ships, but they're mining barges, often robotic boats whose behaviour can be fully predicted. These ships—"

Paul said, "If they are ships. Sorry, but I've seen the blobs of light that you call ships. You can watch them all over the fear-mongering networks."

"I think they are." The man sounded more confident. "Anyway, these ships move independently. They're not in orbit. They're not in radio contact. The only entity we have no control over in the system is Allion, in their base, floating down there in the clouds. And they haven't been up for years, not that I've heard at least."

"Oh, there we have the mythical cloud bases again." Thalia rolled her eyes. "I really don't understand why these rumours keep persisting. A ship of the size you suggest would leave a signature. It would be a flashing beacon of electromagnetic radiation. Everything on board a ship uses electronics. Same with a base in the cloud tops of Jupiter. That at some point Allion had ships which could dive down to that level doesn't mean that they're down there still. Ships of that calibre, like the *Thor* series or the *Morgana* leave a whole furrow of signatures we can pick up. Their

engines, for starters, would be a flashing beacon in some frequen-
cies, depending on the energy source. If—as rumours have it—
they used antimatter engines, they would spit out visible light.
Seriously. Has anyone seen any new stars in the firmament lately?"
She breathed in through flaring nostrils.

"They'd have shielding."

"Oh yeah, and now we're in the realm of magic." She snorted.
"No ship that we know can move without leaving some signature.
No base exists without emitting a crapload of radiation that we can
detect. This is becoming the busiest section of space after the Earth-
Moon route. You cannot hide in space. Everything you do sends a
big, flashing signal that screams *here I am.*"

There was a brief angry silence, in which the kitchen hand
shrugged and went back to mopping. The cook returned with a
trolley that contained a couple of trays, which he proceeded to set
out in front of everyone in the group, including Fabio.

Paul lifted the cover off and pulled a face. Base food was obviously not up to his standards.

Fabio agreed with what Thalia had said. If you wanted to hide
somewhere, the best place was somewhere amongst lots of other
people that generated lots of noise. Open space was a very bad
place to hide.

For a while, everyone ate. The mash was bland, but filling. The
water was cold, and even in this dryness, a bit of humidity
condensed onto the outside of the glass. Fabio wasn't hungry, but
he drank with deep gulps.

"Anyway," Paul rose from the table, his plate still half full.
"We're digressing, and it's been a long day. I'm going to bed."

Sol and Jun rose as well, but Thalia said, "I'll come later."

KATARINA

IN A ROOM IN THE RESIDENTIAL part of the Research base, Major Katarina Doric sat at her desk writing the old-fashioned way: with a pen on a sheet of plasti-paper. It was very old-fashioned indeed. It had been years since she had written anything by hand, since most communication was electronic and much of it went through scans, voice recognition and thought sensors. Her handwriting was clumsy and reminded her of having to learn to write at school. Not in a good way.

But she needed to send this message.

This morning in the arrival hall with that oaf of a new guy, she'd done her best to hide her surprise: her husband was here.

What he was doing here and how he had managed to get into the delegation from the Council Of Four was a mystery. As far as she knew, he wasn't interested in politics and he wasn't the easiest person to get on with, prone to mercurial outbursts, during which he would shout at her and she would shout at him and the neighbours would come to check if anyone had been killed.

And then they'd make up and cry and say they didn't mean it like that. Kat had thought of leaving the shambles of a marriage many times, but the fact was that he was the only one who had ever cared for her in times of need.

Having been "promoted" to Io marked a time of dire need for her. He hadn't been able to speak to her for years, and he still hadn't abandoned her.

He was a migrant because all his family lived on Earth. He could just as easily have gone back to his family after declaring the rocky marriage over.

No one would ever have explained to him what had happened to her when he'd come home from his work as engineer, finding her gone, no matter how much he'd bugged ISF for information about her whereabouts—and he would have.

They would have stonewalled him all the way.

Classified information.

She will contact you when she can.

But he was still faithful to her, even if he might have thought that she was dead.

He was as faithful to her as he'd been back when she'd been in an accident and had spent time in the hospital with a broken pelvis, learning to walk again.

He'd helped her walk along the railings, crying in pain all the way. He'd helped her walk her first steps unaided, and when she came out, he'd asked her to marry him, knowing that she would spend long times away from home.

This morning, he'd looked old and tired and cranky, and his hair showed patches of grey that hadn't been there before.

He hadn't seen her, and that was just as well, because it looked like there was some sort of problem with one of the delegation's papers, and now she heard that the delegation was confined to their rooms and she had to be oh so careful that nobody found out that she knew that he was here. Or that they realised that he was her husband.

Therefore she resorted to this clumsy way of communicating: handwriting. It was untraceable, and once you destroyed a letter, it was truly gone.

How was she going to get it to him?

She needed to write only a few sentences: where to find the information about who had sent the asteroid into the Mars dome, and who had ordered the senseless killing of many civilians afterwards—all in the name of security. She needed Paul to send that proof to Sarajevo, or failing that, to Ganymede City, or failing that, just to give it to the rest of the delegation, who would take it to Ganymede City, and there it would be brought to the Council Of Four, and ISF—or at least the Outer System Division with Preston at its head—would come out looking very bad indeed.

And hopefully that could happen before she got shot, and before Banparra had flooded the place with troops, and before any war broke out—real or simulated—between the two divisions of ISF or between ISF and the Council Of Four, because something was afoot that was not covered by the excuse *exercise.*

And before any of that happened, her only and final wish would be to spend one more night in her husband's arms.

She had been through so many military exercises.

They were always planned—not so much at a low level, but at a higher level. There would always be performance sheets circulated prior to the event. Aims, strategies and outcomes would be discussed at her level. She would be informed and would have to report on her part of the exercise, which was usually to track fleet movements and keeping fleet captains up to date with the latest in intersecting objects—bits of rock and ice that could seriously disrupt fleet operations.

She would have to give her guarantee that vital information be kept secret from the troops so as not to spoil certain surprise elements of the exercise.

This time, there was nothing.

When Mars happened, her father had a high military position, and he had later told her how no one knew that ISF was about to go into a major operation that later turned out to have been meticulously planned. They had merely been warned that there might be trouble, but the warning didn't extend beyond the normal levels of caution applied to large gatherings of different groups of people, as the one at Johnson Base, near the north pole of Mars, where a historic meeting between ISF and "commercial interests", but mainly Allion, was about to take place.

Her father said that all of the ISF's planned hostile activities were hidden from him. And he was not in a position where he should have been kept out of this information.

The parallels between her current situation and his remarks were very strong right now. She was not being told things. She had been told to come here, to this secluded base where—frankly—doing any kind of astronomy was a joke.

All right, Banparra didn't trust her, but he was not the one authorising who passed which information to whom. And he clearly trusted her enough to give her a team of computer monkeys—because he needed her and work had to be done—but she had nothing to do with the arriving troops or had even been told about them.

Ostensibly, they were here for the *exercise,* but, as had happened to her father all those years ago on Mars, she didn't think that was the whole story. What, for example, was the purpose of the installation they were building on the other side of the main base?

Because of her rank, she should have been informed, even if she fell within a different division from Banparra.

She couldn't trust anyone, not even the lame spy Sanchez may or may not have sent—seriously, what a useless piece of shit.

Sanchez had let her know that there would be instructions about information that she needed to collect, and when she heard of this person coming all the way from Earth, she had thought this was it. But the guy was an idiot. She didn't even think that he remembered his own name, and the only way that he'd entered the base was in the same way that she had: by having been sent as a form of punitive action. What he had done was an utter mystery.

And so she wondered how genuine Sanchez had been when sending her here.

"That Preston is up to something," he had said to her when

meeting her in his office. "He has been taking matters into his own hands far too much. I need some people on the ground in the Jupiter system."

Katarina had done some intelligence work before. Most importantly, she had worked as ISF contract astronomer in the asteroid belt, doing exactly the same thing she was doing now—flinging small celestial bodies into different orbits so that they reached those who had had plans for them. She had seen the asteroid veer off-course and had assumed that it would be corrected. The day that it had crashed into Mars remained forever etched into her memory, as did the day when her calculation of the asteroid's trajectory had been complete. She knew the asteroid had been sent from the belt. She knew this wasn't an accident. She knew the then-commander of the asteroid belt Preston was directly responsible, and when Sarajevo had gotten wind of her data, they had asked her to become an informant.

They needed to keep Preston in line, Sanchez said, because there were persistent rumours that the Outer System Division of the ISF was going to break off.

So he had asked her to fill a position on Io. He called it a promotion, but she knew it was a way to keep her silent and out of the way of agitators who might go to the various news sources with her discoveries.

Just then, she hadn't wanted to think about her mercurial husband and his outbursts and his increasingly political stance. He was right about most things and wrong about how he dealt with them. She didn't want him to cause a conflict in her job.

Maybe some time away on Io was just what she needed.

But staring at the wall in her room when her shift had ended only made her think and worry more. She worried that Base Command would search through her data and find the calculations she had made that proved that the wayward asteroid had been sent from their facility. She worried that they would find out that she was aligned with Sanchez and wanted to rid the force of people who thought they were a law unto themselves, like Preston, like Banparra, men who thought that "the need to survive" justified the continued need to keep the population under a warlike martial law that brushed over atrocities like Mars.

So she had erased the document with her discoveries from her military account and put it in a private account outside the military that only she could access.

She wiped her PCD of all info that would be used against her.

Command was always warning troops not to use encryption on private documents, because they'd assume that encrypted information concerned something troops shouldn't have.

The important points in her handwritten letter were how to find this information, the hints about the passcodes—which only Paul would understand—and the information that the situation was urgent.

It was all starting to sound familiar.

Use an excuse to put a lot of people in a dome, then send an asteroid into it.

Mars.

She was disgusted that ISF had tried to blame the incident on a commercial company. What they had done with Allion was nothing short of genocide.

But nothing was keeping them from doing it again.

And if she didn't speak up, then who would? Paul, obviously, but his voice would be stronger if she added hers.

She wanted to, very badly. More importantly, she missed him.

CHAPTER SIX

THE MEN LEFT, AND FABIO and Thalia remained at the table, silent.

She was looking at her hands.

Then she looked up, her eyes meeting his. "So, what is your story?"

"My story?"

"Yeah, you didn't say anything about yourself during that discussion."

"What is there to say? I arrived here today. I don't know much about the base. Never worked here before."

"Why did you get involved in this mining water business?"

"Orders."

"You work for these people?"

"Yes."

"You're not a prisoner?"

A prisoner? Was he a prisoner? Could be, because he didn't think it was his own choice to come here. Also because Sanchez had said—

"If I was a prisoner, then where is the prison?" He spread his hands. "Is this your prison, too?"

Was that a slight uncomfortable look over her face? "Well, like a prisoner in rehabilitation." She sounded annoyed.

"What am I supposed to have done?" Fabio's heart was thudding. He wanted to know this. Was he being punished or what else was going on? He might have called himself a victim, or a fallen spy in need of protection. Someone who needed to spend some quiet time away from attention. Not a prisoner.

She frowned. "Where did you come from before you were here?"

"I was on the interplanetary."

"All your life?"

"For a long time."

"Where did it come from?"

"Earth." At least, that's where Sanchez was and he assumed that he had seen Sanchez there.

Her frown deepened. "The Mars treaty prevents ships going out directly from Earth to the Outer System."

"Look, I don't know where it came from. What do you want from me? I'm new here, and I have no personal involvement in whatever disagreement you have going on between the military and civilians, about water or about other things. I'm just doing my job. I don't care. I can't give you any information that you want."

"Do you know anything at all about what you're doing here?"

Fabio half-rose from the table. "Look, miss, I said I'm not getting involved. If you want to discuss the particulars of this water plan, you should discuss it with Doric."

"No need to get defensive."

"Yes, there is a need. You have no right to ask anything from me. I'm an ISF officer. You're a civilian. I am not obliged to give you anything."

"Oh yes, you are. Article 275g of the act says that the military forces shall retain no information and undertake no action that conflict with the safety or wellbeing of the civilians."

He stared at her.

"In short: the force is here to protect us, and not to be a law unto itself."

Was the force ever a law unto itself? ISF had been his entire life. He didn't remember a life where it had not dominated his life. Maybe with the exception of this *Argentina* and the school with the bird in the sky.

"Do you even know anything?"

"Of course I do."

"Would you want to get out of here?"

Fabio stared at her. What sort of question was that? Get out of here and then what? Where would he go by himself? "I am not a prisoner." But then again, what was he?

"You can help us. The Council Of Four is concerned about the treatment of low-ranked people on the base and those who have been sent here for punishment. After years of negotiation, we finally have in Banparra a base commander at Io who is willing to listen to civilian concerns about the reputation of the military. He may not care about punishment, but he cares a lot about the relationship between the bases and civilians. Banparra is a local, went through Ganymede University before signing up with the force, and although he's known to be a strict disciplinarian, he's also aware that the non-military sectors of the system look at Io with suspicion and he is working to improve relationships. But it's too slow. There are many people like yourself, prisoners—"

"I'm not a—"

"—who have been treated with forbidden substances and treatments to wipe their memories so that they become like meek sheep—"

"Hey, watch who you're calling—"

"You will understand that this concerns us, the civilians in this system, and we want to do something about that. All you need to do is to agree to speak to me—"

"I'm already speaking to you—"

"On the record. I want to do an interview, so we can put pressure on Banparra to release you and to open up the detention files to see who else they're holding, because people have gone missing—"

"What part of 'I'm not involved with your local politics' do you not understand?" He now fully rose from the seat. "I helped you open the door. I made sure you got dinner. As far as I'm concerned we are now finished!"

She stared at him, her expression intense.

He stared back, feeling the anger seep out of him and the fatigue come in. His head throbbed.

"Sorry," he said, sat back down and buried his face in his hands. "I'm not well. Very confused."

"They wiped you, didn't they?"

"I don't know what they did or who did what."

She let a silence lapse. "I have heard about you from before whatever they did to you to put you in this state. I believe you have your heart in the right place."

Fabio said into his hands, "Well, thanks. Not sure I deserve it."

"You do. Take it from me, you do."

Fabio didn't intend to become involved, but just these last few days, he had begun to believe that he was a bad person, a selfish traitor with double standards, who had, at some point in the past, done something so vile that all of humankind would hate him. It was good to hear from someone that this was not necessarily the case.

"I'm so tired. I want people to stop bothering me." No, he wanted . . . to know where his home was.

"Then tell me when we can meet you for the interview." Her dark eyes met his.

"I have to clear it with my superior."

"No. You can't tell anyone. Tell me when you're free. Same time tomorrow?"

What was the time, and when was tomorrow?

And then he looked into Sanchez's dark eyes. He said, *Keep your head down, Velasquez, and I may just leave it on your shoulders.*

"I don't know if I can—"

Doing interviews was not keeping his head down. Sanchez would disapprove. Heck, Banparra would certainly disapprove, because whatever his feeling towards locals, he clearly didn't like these snooping civilians on his base. Whatever Fabio had done right by this woman, he certainly had a reputation for being a turncoat, even if he had no idea what caused this or what he had done.

Mars.

If ever he could dredge up the memories from the woolly depths of his mind, but increasingly he feared that those things were gone, never to be retrieved. And that in itself gave him nightmares. All these people knew something about him that he didn't, and he couldn't very well ask without looking like a fool, which he probably already did.

"Please," she said. "We have come here just for cases like you, because it's scandalous how they're ruining your life."

But that set Fabio more on edge. Who, exactly, was ruining his life? And why did they think that ISF were doing so? If nothing else, he was only here because of them. "What are you going to ask me in this interview that you can't ask me now?"

"Nothing, except it will be a formal interview with witnesses and a video feed."

"No. I'm not doing that."

"But you just agreed—"

"I'm not doing that. You can use what I've told you, but I suspect you already know more about me than I do." And he didn't know why she glommed onto him. All of a sudden the feeling that she wanted something scared him. There were too many people everywhere who liked to take advantage of others when they were down. He was in no state to tell all the local scams from a real situation.

"Please calm down, it's just for the record, because when we report to the Council Of Four about a situation, we have to be able to justify our sources. That's standard practice."

"No, no." He didn't want anything to do with the Council Of Four. That was moving into the dangerous territory of politics.

"Excuse me." There was a sound at the door. A soldier Fabio hadn't seen before stood there. He wore Space Ops fatigues with the Sarajevo tag and his badge declared him to be Private C. Allen. "Base regulations say that you're not supposed to be out here outside allocated times."

Thalia whirled around.

"Base regulations also required us to be locked in our room? We had no food and all our calls for help were ignored."

Private Allen briefly met Fabio's eyes, registered Fabio's higher rank and nodded politely. "Sir?"

"Um. That's how I found them. Locked in their room. I don't understand what happened either, but I think they were entitled dinner at the very least."

"I'm sorry about that, sir. We're very busy."

"Why was their door locked?"

"Probably a mistake, sir. I guess the kitchens had no idea that they were staying here. Normally visitors would stay at the main base and we only cater for research staff who live in a different section of the base."

Thalia said, "I'm afraid my colleague will lodge a complaint."

"I fully understand, ma'am, and I'm sorry. My superior tells me that no one should roam about the base on their off-shift times, so I have to urge you to return to your rooms."

Fabio said, "No one is roaming the base. We came up here from their apartment and will be going straight back."

"I'm sorry. Someone must have forgotten to change the security settings on your door. It won't happen again, I can assure you. It's about to get very busy in that corridor. Anyway, we're entering the night shift now. Everyone should be in their cabins, because the heating in this part of the base doesn't run at night."

The private escorted Fabio and Thalia down the stairs, and then to Fabio's room.

In the corridors, there were a few more signs of life now, as if a large number of people had been away previously and had now returned to their rooms for the night. Fabio didn't see any of these people, but he could hear them talk behind the closed doors.

Fabio went into his cabin where he was alone with the disturbances of his empty mind. Something inside worried him deeply. Keeping his head down meant not getting caught up in politics, but some part in him seemed to *like* politics and seemed to have a knack for getting people to talk. Not only that, but talking politics had a comforting familiarity that fitted him like a well-worn coat.

Who was he and what had he done in the past? Something that Thalia thought was good and everyone on the base thought was despicable.

He opened the door to the empty cupboard and stared at his reflection. The face that looked back at him was almost a stranger. He was pale-skinned, thin. His body was hairless, his beard no more than a stray fuzz on his chin. His hair was a bit messy for a military officer, his face fine-featured. From the front, he couldn't see the scar where the implant had been removed, but he could feel it, running his hand over the back of his head. One spot, in his upper arm, had been itching consistently today. He held it up to the mirror and when he ran the tips of his fingers over it, he could feel something hard under the skin.

What was that? He pushed and squeezed the skin.

It felt like a tube-like thing, about a millimetre across and four or five millimetres long. *Big enough to be a tracking device.* Or a capsule releasing a steady dose of numbing chemicals.

For a long time, he stood before the mirror fingering the lump until the skin was red. He didn't think it had been there before. Was this part of his nanometrics? He couldn't imagine that all the checks they'd done on the interplanetary would have missed this. Or maybe they had inserted this thing in his arm.

He kept seeing the incoherent flashes of his memories. He had once known how to break into things, how to open doors. He'd once had a weapon. He'd driven through a snowstorm in a truck. In a *pressurised truck*, he realised. It didn't snow anywhere in the solar system apart from on Earth and on Titan. There would have been no need for a pressurised truck on Earth. He didn't think he'd ever been to Titan. Another mystery. He'd done something on Mars. Something to do with warning people against the wishes of others. Saving people. Pink snow. What the hell.

You get one more chance, Velazquez.

Shards of memories chased each other through his mind.

He was so messed up.

THALIA

WELL, CRAP, THAT INTERRUPTION came at an inopportune moment, although Thalia doubted that she would have been able to talk Lt. Velasquez into an interview. He seemed a really odd sort. Nervous, flighty, knew nothing. To wipe someone's mindbase wasn't usually that successful, she thought. Or maybe that was because there had been almost nothing there.

Thalia expected to come back to the room and find all three men in different corners, sunk in their own world. Jun moping, Paul being angry about something and muttering under his breath. Sol would be the only one actually doing anything useful, like writing a report, although he'd get Jun to help him, and Jun might actually do it, because he was a good kid, even if far too young.

But when she entered the room, she found all three men standing at the little desk on the far side of the room.

They had their back to her, and turned around when she came in.

"What's going on?" she asked.

"Have a look at this," Jun said. He moved aside so that Thalia could see the screen on the wall.

It showed a section of the sickly yellow plain with a lot of activity in the form of trucks and containers.

"Where is that coming from?"

"It's one of the base's outside camera feeds. They only gave us access to the general communication and news hub; but, although it may be hard to get into this base, once you're in it, the security is pretty lousy."

"Meaning: you hacked into it?"

Sol snorted. "Don't act like you're surprised. That's why he's with us."

Actually, there were other reasons why Jun was with them, mostly to do with his well-to-do family, but admittedly his skills in electronic systems were useful.

On the screen, a huge crate was loaded onto a very long flatbed truck.

"What are they doing?"

"Well, while you were away, another one of these trucks left this field and went in that direction." Sol pointed at a grey mass of jagged peaks at the horizon.

"Is this camera facing to the base?"

"Away from it. They're taking this stuff to the next valley."

"What are they doing with it there?"

"Your guess is as good as mine."

They watched the screen for a bit, but loading a truck with something bulky was slow business, and Sol grew bored and made everyone some tea.

"Did you learn anything from that guy?" he asked Thalia. Jun had joined them at the tiny table, but Paul was still watching the screen.

Thalia sighed, blowing steam off her cup. "He doesn't want to cooperate. He said I could use whatever he told us—"

"Which isn't much."

"No, I agree. He's an odd one. But as soon as I mentioned that I wanted to do an official interview he refused to cooperate."

"He's weird," Jun said. "Creepy. Something's wrong with him. I don't know what."

"He's had his mind wiped," Thalia said.

Sol's eyes widened. "That's highly illegal."

"That's why we're here. Because ISF still sanctions these practices."

"How are you so sure?" Paul asked, without turning around from the screen.

"Because he told me."

"How could he tell you they wiped his mind if he doesn't remember that he has lost memories?"

"Because he has no memories left. It's also in how he behaves. He's numb with fear. He doesn't want to speak out in case he says something dumb or asks a question about something he should have known. He's trying to bluff others into thinking that there is nothing wrong with him."

"I'm glad you're the psychoanalyst," Paul said.

Thalia put her cup down with a thunk. "Will you just stop it?"

"Stop what?" He had the temerity to look surprised, which made her even angrier.

"Stop acting like you don't want to be here and complaining about everything."

"This place is not exactly great, is it?"

"Then why are you with us, why did you did you volunteer?"

"I didn't volunteer, in case you missed that. I never volunteered for any of this stuff. I'm a fucking engineer. I would have been so much happier if I'd been left alone doing my job, but no—look, why the hell do I need to explain this?"

"How about: because you've been an arse ever since we left and being cooped up in this little apartment is not going to improve the situation?"

"I also don't want trouble."

"Then you could have stayed at home and stuck to being an engineer."

In fact, she didn't even understand why the Human Rights

division had picked him to accompany her. Jun might have bought his way in, but at least he was competent in computer systems. Sol was a lawyer. Thalia had worked in media. But Paul? He was an engineer, and a blunt and grumpy one at that.

Governor Law had called these people *the best we can send*.

"You would want to know, huh? You'd like to think that each of these *prisoners* are interesting cases for you to study or prove that you're right, that oh, the ISF is such a big baddie because they lock up innocent prisoners. Let's write a report and get all the credit."

"If it isn't to expose the injustice, then why are you here?"

"Because we're not talking about prisoners like they're numbers. They're fucking people. That guy we spoke to, Fabio whatever, you can see the pain and anguish on his face. He is a person, and he's been ruined by the military. And as you may have noticed, he is still a serving officer. We are not talking about *prisoners*, we're talking about their own personnel, people who have done something they didn't like, or even made an objection to something said, and they're being sent here to cool off or to make sure they shut up and don't spoil ISF's reputation with inconvenient facts. Like, that it was actually ISF who sent the asteroid into the dome at Mars, because they needed an excuse to destroy Allion."

What? "Oh, come on, that conspiracy theory was put to bed long ago."

"It's true. I did the calculations."

"But—"

"I'm a fucking engineer. I did the calculations."

"But a simple malfunction could have—"

Paul shook his head. "No. I've seen the commands that were sent to ignite the rockets. There was no malfunction."

"I never heard about that."

"You wouldn't have, because the officer who found these commands was reprimanded and sent on several useless *secret* missions and may be dead."

"Who is this officer?"

"She is my wife."

"Kat? She left. She wanted nothing more to do with us."

"Did she ever tell you?"

"Why would she—"

He said, louder, "Did she ever tell you?"

"No, but—"

"There you go. She never told you, so you made up stories that fit with all the bullshit narrative you're being sold about this whole fucking place. That it's a secret base, and that's OK because they're military. And that it's a punitive settlement, for prisoners. It's not about the fucking prisoners. It's about what the prisoners knew that caused them to be prisoners."

"Whoa, man, keep your hair on," Sol said. "A prisoner is a prisoner."

"No, man, there is a real distinction. Prisoners are criminals. These people here, at least those who are smarter than your average dumbass walking around the corridors, they're fucking political prisoners who know something that the bosses, you know, upper-fucking-command, vice-fucking-admiral Preston, doesn't like. That's what. And if Kat is alive, this is where she will be. Because she saw the meteorite's trajectory, she knew who'd given the order, she raised objections, she found herself on the wrong side of Preston, she contacted Sanchez, because he wants to get rid of this rot, and then she got promoted. So she's here, filling a commanding officer role."

That was actually a pretty impressive piece of knowledge. "How did you find that out?"

"I took years to piece it together. I spent all my free time scouring the news, and delving into boring reports and corners of reports where no one goes. Because I refuse to believe that Kat would just abandon me."

Thalia would have believed it in a heartbeat. She could never see what her childhood friend saw in a piece of grump like Paul.

"I've seen what is publicly available of the reports she sent from the asteroid belt. I have files of cases with precedents of what

Preston does with dissenters. The only thing I have not been able to find is a personnel list of Calico Base. Probably it doesn't exist, so they don't have to justify if people disappear."

"Well . . ." He managed to make her feel guilty about disliking him, about breaking the friendship between the three of them. She didn't *like* being made to feel guilty. She believed she did good work and there was nothing she should feel guilty about. And if he would prefer that people liked him, he could just stop being such an arsehole.

But she *did* feel guilty, and jealous. Let's face it, no man had ever cared for her in this way. Her parents hadn't even cared in that way.

Of course she *shouldn't* feel jealous, but should was different from reality. Damn, she wanted a knight in shining armour who would spend years combing files in obscure depositories in order to find and rescue her. Even if he was also an arsehole.

"Well," she said again. "We can make it about rescuing Kat."

CHAPTER SEVEN

BACK IN HIS ROOM, Fabio turned on his communication hub, detached the screen and put it in the bracket on the wall. Then he stretched out on his bed, his feet up against the opposite wall.

He wanted to sleep. He wanted to forget whatever was left of his memories. He'd start as a fresh officer without prior history. He'd obey all orders without question. He'd be a good little soldier, and he'd never again—

Free people from rooms where they had been locked in by some "mistake".

Or save people's lives, even if they were supposed to be enemies.

Or, for that matter, his own life.

Fabio flicked through the channels, of which there were many. He cared not for sport, or drama, or reruns of old shows.

The ISF military news channel made him feel uneasy. It was too obviously cheery and staged. A female, pale-skinned newsreader churned through items of news of all ISF worlds. Head office in Sarajevo had employed some new high-ranking staff and the channel went through all their awards and achievements.

There was increased surveillance of the surface of Mars where, according to the news reader, things had been calm recently. But the red planet looked nothing like Fabio remembered. It had become a white-and-pink planet.

The newscast didn't say what had happened there, so people must consider that common knowledge.

Fabio remembered driving through snow. He sat at the wheel of a large terrain vehicle and had to divide his attention between looking where he was going and looking at the air gauge on the cabin environment. The truck contained many more people than it was designed to carry and the air was depleting fast. It was fifty kilometres to Jackson, and the plain *should* be easy to traverse if it weren't for the raging blizzard. The truck's windscreen wipers were designed to shift dust, not snow.

The memory made him shiver. He flicked to the next channel.

The information channel was well-stocked, but base-controlled, and there was no search function for past news to fill him in on the vast chunks of time that had been wiped from his brain. He didn't even know what he was looking for.

He typed *Mars* and came up with a lot of information about military activity there. About the bases, their command structure and who filled what position. Also cheerful touristy stuff.

Boring.

While flicking through the other channels, he came across a security login screen. Well, that was careless of them to leave it there. Rather old-fashioned.

He put his finger to the screen—where they really should have installed a more secure entry method, even if it was just a fingerprint or iris scan—and the nano pad under the tip of his middle finger took less than five seconds to find a valid password.

Not that the stuff he found on the other side was terribly interesting. Oh, ouch the black and grey design was so old-fashioned it hurt his eyes.

What was *Vantage*?

He selected that option, which took him to a screen with many thumbnail images.

Hmmm, live camera feeds from outside the base.

One offered a view of the landscape from a camera at the top of the concrete bunker. The horizon was jagged and curved notice-ably. The golden dome of Calico Base sat in the valley on the other side of the lava lake. The sky was grey, the massive disk of Jupiter now almost full and giving off a wan glare. It meant it was almost midnight, but the only time it became really dark on Io was during the daily eclipse when Io went through Jupiter's shadow for two hours at local noon. Natural daylength at Io was forty-two hours and forty-five minutes, but like most other bases, Calico kept Sara-jevo time.

While the view was pretty and very unusual, it was also rather boring, so he flicked to a few other live cameras. One was a close-up of the seething lava lake at the bottom of the cliff. He found that he could manipulate this camera and spent some time scanning the perimeter of the lake and the patterns of cracks in the lava and the bubbling rock. But then he got bored with that and switched to a camera further up the mountain. It showed him details of the surrounding areas, including the track that led from the base to the cliff top. And by chance there was a truck halfway down the slope, winding its way down to the main base. Fabio wasn't entirely sure, but he thought it was the same truck that had taken him to the base. Maybe there only was one truck.

He moved the camera around a bit more and focused on the copper dome of the base which glinted in the sunlight.

He had to zoom the camera in as much as it would go to make out details. Another shuttle must have arrived, because there were lights and a lot of activity on the landing field.

Fabio peered at the screen. At this magnification, the camera's resolution reduced all objects to blurs. Mostly white, like passenger vehicles and shuttles, some grey, like trucks carrying cargo.

The white vehicles lined up to connect to the access tubes to the arrivals hall.

Cranes unloaded crates and other objects from another vehicle.

One truck carried two very large tubes. Rocket launchers?

Lights flashed at the top and sides of the vehicle and a couple of smaller trucks accompanied it at a very slow speed. Instead of going to the base, the convoy disappeared into the craggy terrain on the other side of the field. The last Fabio saw of it was a piece of the machinery on the back of the truck sinking over the ridge of the hill.

Hmmm. Interesting.

He flicked back to the main menu.

Safety Instructions.

He didn't want to read those, because his mind reeled from bad memories of stuff that happened when things went wrong. He saw exploding glass, people collapsed on the ground, and snow everywhere.

But he had to look anyway, just to make sure that the base had proper safety instructions. Imagine just how much could go wrong in a place like this. It was highly likely that all personnel coming to the base voluntarily signed an agreement that they understood the danger and that they would not hold ISF responsible for dangers that were known.

Like exploding volcanoes.

Like earthquakes which might rupture the dome.

Apparently every room was meant to have an air tank and a set of four masks. There were supposed to be hazard stations that held a store of pressure suits and nozzles to refill the tanks. The medicine box was meant to contain various types of anti-radiation medication, and also items to help with major trauma.

From experience, though, he knew that people trying to save their own lives were too busy to attend to someone else. When something happened, it was bad, and there were two options: get out and leave or stay and die.

He'd been on a trip, and he happened to be near an air tank and a pressure suit. He remembered shouts and people pointing at the sky. He remembered peering through the haze of the dust scratches on the outside of the dome's clear cover. A streak of light went through the sky and hit the ground over the hill. It looked like the next valley, although he knew it had to be further away. He remembered the ground shaking. He remembered feeling the shockwave. He remembered the *foomp* of emergency locks closing. He remembered that despite being locked from the main base, debris flew. He remembered the crack appearing in the dome and the sound of air sucking out. The dome just flew open like a flower, and snow fell in the soundless pink dusk.

He remembered the mad scramble of people through a hallway that was still pressurised. Someone was screaming at the front and no one listened. It was everyone for himself.

In order to save themselves, people had to clamber over the bodies of those who had died. In a single moment, the civilised base had turned into a bear pit.

He remembered all those things and knew that none of these silly safety precautions meant anything, especially not on Io where you couldn't even stick any part of you outside without shielding or die of radiation poisoning within an hour.

This was space. If something went wrong, you died.

In case of damage to the dome structure, retreat to your rooms. The base command will be working to restore services as soon as possible.

No, they would be dead.

In case of an earthquake, make your way to the nearest shelter. If that is not possible, sit on your bottom bunk with your feet off the ground.

Just in case lava came into the room. Great, everyone would be dead if a volcano decided to erupt underneath the base.

Seriously what a load of rubbish. Who wrote this?

All you needed to know in a dome breach was: how to get out. Find a vehicle, any kind of vehicle and get out.

Hey what was that? A map of the layout of the buildings in this location.

There was the spaceport, and the main base. It consisted of a large dome and several smaller ones, all interlinked. A winding road led from the base up the hillside to the research station. But what was that dotted grey line from the base to the station and through to the spaceport? He enlarged that area until he could read the small letters. *Goods train.*

Well, that was interesting, Doric had mentioned this briefly, but the other map had definitely not said anything about a train. There was an access point right next to the main lift, too. He knew where that was. That was a handy thing to know. He would have to investigate how big the entrance hatch was, and whether the tunnel would be pressurised. He guessed it would, but that the air quality wouldn't be good.

Fabio tried to sleep, but he was alternately hot or cold. The ceiling vent made odd sounds and the walls in the base groaned and creaked each time there was an earth tremble. There were many small quakes, and each time the ground rumbled, Fabio eyed the door panel to see if any warnings came through. Once, the system mentioned the strength of a quake as 5.2. He thought that was quite a lot, but he listened out for people in the corridors and no one seemed to share his concern.

Either there was no one in this part of the corridor or they would leave him here to be buried under tonnes of volcanic crap.

Don't be ridiculous.

Then he would start all over again: notice the silence, notice the air hissing from the vents, almost falling asleep—another earthquake. Staring at the door panel—nothing. Listening for footsteps—nothing.

Eventually, he grew too tired to worry about the quakes and he must have dozed off, because next thing, someone banged on his door loud enough to make the walls shake.

What the fuck. . . ?

Fabio dragged himself out of bed. The crisp air was cold on his bare feet. It was dusty, too, as if the floor had seen a vacuum a long time ago.

When he opened the door, there was a young private in kitchen garb outside.

"Breakfast, sir." His voice was much too cheery.

Fabio took the tray from him with some sort of mumbled thanks.

Back in the room he put the tray on the desk and let himself drop in the sheet, dragging his hand over his face.

Waking up suddenly was never kind on him. That hadn't changed when they messed with his head.

The tray contained a bowl, a closed cup with a lid and a sealed bag containing a spoon and a fork, all made from extruder plastic of the type made by recyclers.

When he removed the cover from the bowl, a sickly sweet smell met him. What was that white stuff? Some sad excuse for porridge?

There was also a small plate that contained two sausages and two pieces of puffed corn toast.

He put the tray on the floor, detached the deskscreen, flipped the plastic protective surface back, reinstated the tray and started eating while flipping through the latest news.

The COF delegation to Io had not reported in, said the Ganymedean news services. There had been some talk about this in the council, where some councillors asked if this was a matter of concern, to which councillor Anise-Leontine Law had said that she would be contacting ISF to see if there was a problem with communication. *Calico Base often goes into radio silence,* she said.

That was an excuse for a human-enforced silence, because if Jupiter was between Io and Ganymede, they could just use a different satellite relay path. It was slower and less reliable maybe, but got there in the end.

But he'd made the resolution that he was not going to get involved in politics, so he stopped reading and speculating, because he seemed to be a magnet for controversial stuff, and could do very well without controversy right now.

He flicked to the next page and found that it—damn it—continued about the visit.

Base Commander Banparra, the news service said, had not commented on the situation and had also not made a joint statement with the delegation after their arrival at Calico Base. This caused several minor councillors to raise suspicions about Calico's and the ISF's intentions.

He wondered why the military-controlled news service let this through.

While he ate, the comm unit chimed and Major Doric's voice told him that his call for the tray to be picked up would double as notification that he was ready, and that someone would come to take him to her. With the map he had obtained, he could easily find his own way, but that was probably best left unsaid.

His excursion to the mess last night was probably also best not mentioned.

So he got dressed when he had eaten as much of the white goo as he could stomach. He rummaged through the medicines in his bag, but had no idea what they were. He didn't think he'd taken any yesterday and he was still alive. He was going to take a chance and not take them today either.

There was no time for another go at the shower, so he combed the last residue of dried shampoo out of his hair in a shower of white powder. It felt disgusting.

He still hadn't been given a base uniform, so he wore the unmarked, unranked Sarajevo fatigues given to him on the transport. Their greyness would blend in with the bland corridors of the base perfectly well.

A female private came when he pressed the button. She made no move to take the tray, and when he asked her about it, she said to leave the door open and kitchen staff would come to take it later. He didn't like that. They would go through his things. There were probably clues in his luggage about who he was and what he was doing here. Maybe they worried about him breaking into the COF delegates' rooms. Maybe they wanted to know what all his medicines were for.

But he could do nothing except follow her, because he had no doubt that anything he did or said would be reported. She took him to the big room with the workstations where he had been yesterday. There, Major Doric waited in the office.

She gave him a terminal, and set him to work on huge datasets and comparing images and collating them. Plotting orbits. Calculating composition. There were many datasets and the work became automatic, the skills needed still his. Yes, he had worked on mining and exploration before.

There was a name that kept bugging him: Dayol Mining. His workstation had access to the registered ships' database. He searched by company name and found that they were a medium-sized mining venture in the asteroid belt. Head offices on Ceres. The company's CEO was someone by the name of Dorian Salazas.

Another piece of the puzzle that was his life, but he had no idea where it fitted, or if it was important. The name meant nothing to him.

But this data fit in with his previous experience. Once he found a suitable chunk of ice, a company like Dayol Mining would be called in to go out and divert the comet or asteroid. If Fabio could determine a handy asteroid from which to mine the water, which could be diverted to Io in less than six solars, which seemed ridiculously short. Normal mining contracts ran for years or more, like the case of that asteroid with a high content of ammonia ice that a company had smashed—

—into the northern ice cap of Mars—

—by order of the Martian Board, which was the Martian civilian division of the International Space Force under the command of a man named Preston—

And another chunk of memories fell into place.

Fabio had started with Dayol Mining after the asteroid had already been diverted. He had read, in horror, that no civilians had been informed of the impending impact on their doorstep. His superior said that it was a matter for the local authorities.

But they, when he investigated, didn't seem to care. One official said that the only people who lived there were nomadic project workers who lived in trucks and moved in teams. They would be able to get out, he said.

"But can't they at least be told?" Fabio remembered asking.

His only response was a blank stare.

Throughout the parts that he remembered about his life, Fabio had cared about the underdog, and he cared that a big asteroid was coming down on these people's doorstep, and especially because domed communities were nearby and he learned that a conference was even planned at the time of the impact and that nobody knew anything about it. The meeting was of a political nature.

The nomadic settlements in the area belonged to the company Allion. They owned a lot of these very nimble mining units that crawled over Mars' ice cap like harvester ants, scraping ice and turning it into pure water, hydrogen and oxygen for industry and fuel, and who did this while their community and families lived in blow-up tents with entire farms on the back of a flatbed truck.

He had tried to contact those people personally, but it had been very hard.

He remembered talking to a man on a crackling connection, barely hearing the words. Who had this person been?

He remembered being called into the superior officer's room.

"You are forbidden to interfere with the local population," he had said. "This is not in our mission statement."

"But there are lives in danger."

Something bothered him about those memories. Why was he working with a commercial company and answering to someone from the International Space Force? That man had worn Major's stripes.

So Fabio had done what he did best: he had made himself scarce and gone to Mars.

JAYKADIA

"YOU WANT TO—WHAT?"

Governor of the Council Of Four, Anise-Leontine Law had a loud voice that often made Jaykadia cringe no matter what she said.

Jaykadia always turned the volume down on the speakers when she spoke to her aunt, but even so, the words came through like a blast that made Jaykadia cower like a naughty child.

"I think it's only fair," she said, but it was already more than clear that her aunt did *not* like her idea. Which was strange, because hadn't her aunt highlighted that ISF might be talking up the military exercise for political purposes?

"My dear niece, these are high-ranking, highly trained soldiers we're talking about. You don't play games with them."

"They play games with us."

"Yes, but that is different. For all that they play politics, they keep the peace in this area, and you young ones undervalue that."

"I can't see who is going to disrupt the peace that they need to protect us from. It's an exercise, against a hypothetical enemy! Just so they can show off their skills and intimidate us. We've never had any interest in fighting wars, and I think ISF can get a little carried away with how much protection we need from an invisible enemy that is yet to materialise. You've said this yourself. I don't understand—"

"You can't withhold access to the maintenance buildings that they have requested."

"Why not? No one has moved in yet. It's just a way to let us talk to the delegation. They want their sheds? Let us talk to the delegation. They can solve that in two seconds flat."

"No."

"But do we need to let them walk all over us?"

"Don't worry, they will talk."

"Do I then have to wait patiently like a good girl until they deign to allow Thalia to contact us?"

"At this point, yes. The four of them are deep into ISF territory, a place none of us have visited before. The force will be nervous. They may not want certain information to come out. They're a military base."

"And the military is just playing stupid with us. If they were serious about cooperation, they'd allow us to talk to the delegation and get on with it. It's not as if they won't talk about their visit when they come back, so unless they've witnessed something they shouldn't have, I can't see the point of not allowing them to talk to us."

"There are many points. For one, they haven't actually refused contact."

"No, but they sure have stonewalled our attempts to contact them."

"They may do this for the protection of the base. ISF itself is in turmoil, and most of us expect the section from the Outer System to break away from Earth. There are many security reasons that would sway their decision."

"And now you're taking their side!"

"I am not, I assure you. But ISF is an organisation that you do not want to anger. Despite my agreement with some of your points."

"They were your points to start off with."

"I have enough experience with these military types to know that they don't compromise, they never apologise, and they never go back on their word. If they have it in their mind to have these armies in your warehouse, they will have them whether you give permission or not. They have also promised to guarantee the safety of our delegation. That promise is not taken lightly."

"But why then did Preston make a show of coming to me and asking for permission?"

"Because this whole cooperation with the Council Of Four is only show. It is really the council of three and the fourth one is a little off to the side and doesn't quite belong there. They don't like when other people meddle in their affairs. They are a dangerous organisation pretending to be friendly. It's never been any different."

"But then what am I supposed to do? I have to bend over backwards for them, while they hold my friend hostage?"

"We can only wait. Believe me, it's the best option. And meanwhile, attempt not to use hostile language, like *hostage*, because no one is being kept hostage until it is clear that they are. There may be many reasons why we haven't heard from the delegation. There are none for you to go back on your word that they could use the sheds."

Jaykadia signed off.

She slammed both hands on the table so loudly that Clarence came in to enquire if there was something she needed.

She was tempted to say, *Yes, a drink.* Or better still, *Yes, a space ship so I can check on my friend.*

What did this arrogant oaf of a Banparra think he was doing, withholding communication from a group of people who had come into the base under the banner of increased openness?

Thalia was a friend. What was the point of having friends if they didn't come to your aid?

A little voice inside her said, *You haven't spoken for years.*

True, but she had no other friends.

Being a company executive in a company full of older people, mostly men, was *lonely* and *boring*.

She had never had so much fun as she had with Kat and Thalia during her university years. Company people were grey-faced, mouse-like accountants. Prim and proper office workers, miners with big hands and oafy smiles who tapped their dirty hands to their helmets and said *ma'am* when she passed them in the hall-ways. Workers' unions who invited her to come to their lunch breaks to ask them about things that frustrated them, and who then told her, very politely, about the computer system that had too much downtime and the room where the air was always too stuffy to work. Engineers who showed her plans and then went on to explain as if she were a toddler, forgetting that she was also an engineer.

She glanced up at the portrait of her father on the wall. His death had come as a shock.

People said his poor health had been made worse by the fact that she had nearly died in the accident and spent so long in hospital, forcing him to continue to work longer than he had planned.

But the truth was, she had a very different character than he did. When he walked into the room, people noticed. When she walked into a room, people had to be told to stand at attention.

She didn't want that sort of relationship.

She wanted to walk into the worker's suiting room and laugh with them. She wanted them to feel comfortable enough to tell her what they really thought, swear words and all. And now she was going to have to ask them to move all mining equipment outside and do their maintenance while wearing pressure suits.

She had already heard rumblings about it, but nobody dared protest, including herself.

It was ridiculous.

She had not become the youngest executive of a mining company ever to sit there and do exactly what the older people said. It could well be that her aunt was right, and it could be that she was wrong, but things had always been done in the way aunt said.

And maybe this was why there was such an uneasy situation, because nobody had ever been willing to stand up to the bully that was ISF, nobody had ever questioned the news releases that they gave, even though half the time they did not produce much evidence for anything they said. ISF had the equipment; they controlled what they saw and how it was interpreted.

And dammit, Thalia was her friend. She wasn't going to sit here and wait while her friend was kept hostage.

Not only that, but ISF had also taken the freedom of another friend, Kat a few years ago.

She had not spoken to either of them for years, but that didn't mean that they were not important to her.

She crossed the room to the door.

"I'm going out," she said to Clarence, who gave her a surprised look. From the cupboard next to the door, she took a suit liner and pulled it over her clothes.

Several people gave her strange looks while she made her way from the office complex to the big hall where the residential section of the settlement met the industrial section.

The hall functioned as gateway between the offices, living areas and the mine. Workers could drop off their laundry, and grab fast food for breakfast or lunch.

Because Jaykadia had drawn the hood of the liner over her head, most people didn't pay her any attention.

Via a set of double doors, she let herself into the worker's suit-up area. One shift had just ended and the next shift was getting ready to go out, while the mining trucks were undergoing refuelling.

The sound of talk and laughter filled the room. The air smelled of oil, sweat and that special stuffy smell that often dominated poorly ventilated closed environments.

A man said, "Hey, there's the boss!"

People looked, and moved aside for her, and more people looked, and a silence spread across the hall.

Jaykadia had to speak, because that's what they expected, so she climbed onto one of the benches. "A few days ago, some of you received some communication that ISF has requested the use of our maintenance halls for a military exercise."

A man in the audience said, "What?" and others hushed him.

"That was my reaction," Jaykadia said. "But Vice Admiral Preston is a respected figure, and I assumed that he would not betray our trust."

It had gone very quiet in the hall. Hundreds of pairs of eyes were on her.

"You may also be aware that the Council Of Four, led by my aunt, sent a delegation to Io. Their task was to investigate whether there is any truth to stories of the poor treatment of troops at Io, especially those who have been sent there as punitive measure. It seems that our delegation, currently at Calico Base on Io, is being prevented from communicating with us. So, on the one hand, the vice admiral expects us to comply and vacate the sheds, and on the other, he expects us to simply accept poor treatment of our delegation—"

Someone yelled, "He shouldn't have the halls either!"

Jaykadia smiled. "I don't know if I want to go that far, but it may be necessary. Meanwhile, I wanted all of you to know that the request to vacate the halls may be delayed while we sort this out, and that you shouldn't be surprised if you do the work and then nothing happens for a while."

CHAPTER EIGHT

OVER THE NEXT FEW DAYS, Fabio didn't see Thalia and the delegation again. At first, he didn't worry. Then silence on the news services about the delegation got to him. There had been reports on the first day. Why had they stopped?

He wondered if the lack of reports about the visiting delegation meant anything or if he was getting paranoid. On second thoughts, he was probably already paranoid, so worrying about whether he was paranoid or not was likely a lost cause.

Meanwhile, more and more troops arrived in the section of the base where he was staying. They kept to themselves and didn't speak to him other than giving him a polite greeting when meeting him in the corridor. He wondered what they were all doing here and tried to search for clues.

The arrival of new troops in this section of the base necessitated increased supplies, and one day when coming into the lift foyer, the sliding door on the other side was open, giving him a view of the train: a single cylinder-shaped carriage with doors that slid open. The space inside was big enough to stack two of the blue crates that were often used for shipping. Two people were unloading these crates.

A control panel to the side flashed, *Departure in 14 minutes.*

Interesting.

Fabio didn't ask any questions.

He looked on the news every day, but there was nothing about the influx of troops either. He wanted to ask Doric about them, but he was sure it wouldn't fit under his *keep your head down* order. For one, whenever extra troops were mentioned, she made it clear that she violently disagreed with their presence on the base, and she would disagree even more that overcrowding in the main base necessitated that they stayed at Research. Although she may well have volunteered one of the Research base's empty corridors, because those corridors were easy to isolate and there would be no wayward soldiers talking to any of the regular base troops. Unless, of course, those troops were called Fabio Velasquez, who didn't have a clue where he stood in this debate, but he cared about the COF delegates, because . . . because he did, damn it, and because lying to people and locking them up was something he could never stand.

Never mind it was the story of his life.

And he just happened to be good at opening doors.

And because Thalia had said that the delegation would be here for a few weeks and he'd heard nothing since the first day, he thought that maybe he should check out how they were doing. The notion was rather strange to him. He'd not needed to care or look after anyone else since waking up from his surgery. Caring about someone was a human thing, and surely a sign that he was returning to normal, right?

So at night before his dinner had been brought, he left his cabin carrying a towel with the excuse to have a shower. He'd found that water allocations didn't reset each day, so unless you wanted to shower for a few seconds every day, it was better to shower once every second day, because you had decent time to wash and shampoo your hair. And even rinse it out.

This wasn't his shower day, but no one needed to know that. He was armed with his card and a small pocket tool that included the tiniest of screwdrivers, a tiny paint knife with a blunt tip and a bunch of worms on a datastick.

But as he walked through the corridor with the towel over his shoulder, the door at the far end opened and a large group of people came in. Mostly men, all of them wearing grey base overalls. Dirty overalls, with smudges of dust and stains of goodness-knows what. A couple carried environment suit liners over their arms.

They talked and laughed and took little notice of Fabio until they had reached the spot where he stood.

"Hey, new guy. Hurry up in the shower. All of us want to go in."

"Yes, I'm on it." Fabio walked quickly into the shower while all those people went into their rooms. The room next to his, the rooms opposite his, and a number of other rooms in the corridor. They left a smell of engine oil and sulphur in their wake.

What were these people doing during the time they were not in their rooms? His only guess was that they'd been in the field, possibly at the secret construction ISF was building on the other side of the base where he had seen the truck disappear behind the mountain ridge.

Or maybe he was seeing things.

But his plan to try to see the delegation wasn't going to work out today. With all these people here, he couldn't pretend to walk in the wrong direction in order to see the delegation, not even while he was carrying a towel. He wasn't sure what he wanted to say to Thalia anyway. Just checking they were all right, he guessed. Checking out that they hadn't been locked in their room for all that time. On the other hand, the COF delegation definitely didn't fit in the *keep your head down* section.

So he stood in the shower cubicle without turning the water on, rubbed his hair with the towel—which acquired a few smudges of grey dust—and left again. By now, there was a queue outside the door. People were talking and joking and laughing, but none of them spoke to Fabio, so he went to his room until a kitchen hand wearing an apron came to bring him dinner.

While the door was open, a group of people in clean base uniforms walked past, giving him strange who's-that-geezer-that-he-requires-personal-service looks.

"When can I go up to the mess hall?" he asked the kitchen hand, not really sure if that was what he wanted. Meeting people seemed to draw him into situations that his superiors found undesirable.

The man said, "Not my decision. You'll have to check with Doric."

"I'll do that, then."

He took the tray inside and sat eating his dinner while watching some sort of stupid show, not really taking anything in, but mulling over the shards of his shattered memories and wondering where all the pieces went.

In the end, he couldn't stand not knowing, so he rummaged in his desk drawer and found a few sheets of plasti-paper. He butchered a sheet into little pieces using the knife from the dinner tray—which was extremely blunt—and wrote events that he could remember on each piece.

A bird in the sky.

Lying on a treatment table in the hospital, likely on the interplanetary.

Driving through pink snow.

Working for Dayol mining and deciding to go to Mars to warn people.

Walking out of a corridor into a courtyard, wearing a pressure suit, while people without suits lay dead on the ground.

Talking to Sanchez.

He spread the pieces on the ground. The bird didn't fit with the other pieces and he moved it aside. The rest seemed to be connected.

Sanchez was last. That had to be just before he went on the interplanetary, but he had no recollection of how or when he'd boarded.

That left the other three pieces.

Working for Dayol Mining seemed to be the start of the trouble, because that's when he'd decided to go to Mars.

The snow—was that before or after the dead bodies? It could have been caused by the impact of an icy object with the planet, so likely the snow was *after* the dead bodies.

But why had he been out in the field driving around—

—With families and children in the back of the truck?—

—Who spoke a language he didn't recognise—

—And who were mostly dark-skinned—

—And didn't wear uniforms?

Those must have been the nomads he rescued.

He remembered arriving in a big hall and being locked out of a large section of Johnson Base because there was an event going on with many people in attendance.

On the other hand—he'd had little trouble getting the truck so that must have been when he went to visit the nomads. . . .

This was giving him a headache.

One major question remained: why did all of this make him a spy? And if so, what was he spying for?

Over the next few days, Fabio went over all of Major Doric's datasets. He worked hard, and even remembered which programs to use and how to use them and how to interpret the results. Apparently the wipe job had been less blunt than he'd assumed.

After three days, he'd identified a few possible chunks of ice. He went to see Major Doric with his conclusions. She sat quietly, nodding while he pointed out the possible comet candidates for capture and diversion. He hadn't done costings yet, but she didn't seem too concerned about it. One unnamed comet was fairly close, but not moving very fast. Another was further out. Yet another would need a huge correction to bring it into the right orbit but it would move quite fast.

"I think it is time to start discussing this with possible mining corporations. I presume you will not be using any located in the Jovian system."

She nodded. "We have people on standby."

"From Ceres?" He wondered if Dayol Mining had regular contracts for the Space Force bases.

She shook her head. "These are people from the Saturnian system."

"You'll probably only need a contractor for one comet. That should keep you happy for a while."

"I want you to calculate arrival times, costings and yield of all elements for all three."

"So that you can make a choice?"

"No. All three."

Fabio frowned. "You don't need that much water. Your population is small and the bases are closed systems. It would be a waste of time and money to—"

"I want you to do costings and yields for all three." There was an edge to her voice.

"Understood, ma'am."

Fabio went back to work. It seemed Thalia had been right about her suspicions and there was indeed something else going on at the base.

Those trucks he'd seen vanish over the horizon might contain machinery that might need cooling, or turbines that used steam power, or they might be for hydrogen fuel production. Or something else that couldn't see the light of day, and they had placed this installation at the only point where satellites couldn't easily see: directly at the subjovian point, where Jupiter's radiation glare interfered too much with equipment. Where satellites didn't orbit for that reason.

Fabio continued to work, hunched over his screen. He was developing a headache and his lips were raw from the incredibly dry air. He also had this feeling that he was losing hair because every time the screen went black he could see hair stuck on it by static electricity, never mind that he wiped it clean every time. He rubbed his hand through his hair, and studied his palm, but all those hairs seemed firmly attached. Then he rubbed his face, but he'd shaved this morning, and his beard was not really worth mentioning anyway. Then his arms, and he dislodged a couple of the longer hairs from the back of his forearms.

What the. . . ?

He pulled at the hairs. A small bundle of them came loose. Well, that was really strange—

"I take it that you're Lt. Velazquez?"

Fabio jumped. He hadn't heard the man come up behind him. Worse, the man was not alone. He'd come with two companions, and while the man, whose badge said Zanetti, looked like an officer in a senior position, the other two looked like thugs.

"It's about your medical."

Crap. The small cocoon of safety he had built around him in the last few days broke apart. The big black hole in his mind opened up, sucking him into a vortex of panic that constricted his chest. "What about it?"

"Hansen needs to see you."

"I'm very busy here," he managed to say. His mouth was dry. "I thought you were from different divisions."

"I've spoken to Hansen, and he has asked that you see him. You are going and that is an order."

THALIA

TIME WAS ENDLESS if you couldn't see daylight and if you were cooped up in a small apartment with three people you didn't particularly like.

Three days went past, in which the delegation didn't leave the apartment and had no contact with anyone in a senior position.

By the end of those three days, Thalia was just as livid as Paul.

The command sent a message and gave as excuse that the group was *in quarantine*, and it needed to be established that they did not bring diseases into the base.

"When that guy came and let us out, we should have run," Sol said, his voice dark.

Thalia agreed, although she had no idea where they could have run to.

Prometheus was a long way away, and it was also a military base. None of them were pilots, so they couldn't "borrow" any of the shuttles. And they had no contact off-planet, so they couldn't warn anyone from outside.

"But why do they treat us like this?" Sol asked. "Why allow us to come all this way and then not allow us to do what we've come to do?"

"It's still about that medicine, isn't it?" Jun said.

"It's about my wife," Paul said.

Sol shook his head. "I think it's more political. Something has happened in the council and we don't even know what it is. We probably won't know until we get home."

Thalia said, "We might as well go home. Why haven't they put us on a ship already? If they don't want us here, why keep us here?"

But ultimately, no one had an answer, much as Jun thought it was because of his medicines and Paul thought it was about his wife, Kat, who had been one of Thalia's friends when they all hung out together.

Thalia replied to the base command's message asking that, since they were not welcome at the base and *all meetings have been cancelled* they should be sent home.

There was nothing to do while waiting for the reply.

It now made sense that the door had been locked. It remained locked except when the private came to deliver food.

Paul and Jun got into devising plans to overwhelm the man and run out.

"But we don't have access to the main base, we need a truck, and access to the shuttles is only via the main base. We couldn't get in there without being noticed."

They were only jokes, but Thalia couldn't help but consider these plans more seriously.

Moreover, she couldn't imagine that the Council Of Four would keep quiet about this incident. Governor Law was not someone who would take no for an answer and she would demand, not impolitely but insistently, that she'd be told about the issues that kept the delegation here. Even if the group themselves never got to hear this. She would also not stand for the continued detention.

But there was nothing to do except wait. There was no reply from Base Command about being allowed to leave. What was more, a lot of the information channels were cut off. Jun could no longer access the outside cameras. The news also cut off halfway through the day, and there was nothing left to do except sleep and annoy each other.

And damn it, Paul had changed so much. He'd gotten old and cranky and complained about everything. She told him, minus the old and cranky part.

"No, it's you who have changed. All three of you, since you had that accident. You were constantly in each other's pockets. After you came out of the hospital, there was none of that. It was all about making your own career."

"Well, nearly dying in an accident gives you a perspective on life."

But in a way he was right. That trip in the truck outside Ganymede City had been the pinnacle of their friendship and things had never been the same since. Jaykadia had felt responsible because she had been driving the truck. Kat got all funny about her military career. Of course she was in the military before —that's what her family did—but she had been talking about finding a job elsewhere because she was unhappy with the way people were treated and with some of the opinions of senior officers. And all of a sudden she just turned around and re-signed for a long-term contract. After she got married.

Thalia had got into political life, because she felt compelled to do so. All the ideas they'd talked about as friends had gone out the window as both Kat and Jaykadia did exactly what their families wanted them to do.

Someone made a sound at the door to the apartment.

Everyone looked at the door. It was not time for dinner yet.

The light on the panel flashed and a moment later the door opened, letting in an officer who Thalia had never seen before.

He turned to her. "Come with me please."

Were they finally being released from this prison?

"Do we need to bring our bags?" Thalia asked. Oh, the hope of being let out of this prison was so high.

"No. Just you."

"What about—"

"I can't answer any questions. I have my orders to bring you. Leave your stuff here."

"What for? We're all part of the delegation."

"I can't answer that."

Thalia had no choice. She didn't like this one bit, but she was sure that if she made a fuss, there would be even more trouble. She told herself that most likely the officer hadn't been told why she needed to come, because that was not his job.

She got her jacket—because it was cold in some of the rooms— and followed the man out the door.

The last person in the delegation she saw was Sol, and his eyes met hers before the door slid shut again. He gave a tiny nod.

The officer took her to the end of the corridor, up the lift to the access point of this part of the base. Via an access tube they went into a truck.

Thalia asked questions, but the officer did not respond with more than no or yes.

Yes, they were going to the main base.

No, the officer did not know exactly what it was about.

No, it had nothing to do with the Council Of Four.

Yes, there was some sort of problem with the information that they had entered on their entry forms.

Yes, that concerned only her, and not the rest of the team.

She wondered why they had made such a fuss over Jun's medicines. That issue still hadn't been resolved.

The officer did not know whether, when she answered all the questions, they would be allowed to leave. "That is not for me to say. The base command will make a decision about that."

"But you do realise that all of this looks really bad in the eyes of all the people, especially those of the Council Of Four, who are watching every step of our visit here?"

"I am just following my orders."

And so it went on for most of the journey. By the time they got to the yellow plain, she had become sick of it.

They sat in uneasy silence while he drove the truck, getting closer and closer to the copper domes of the base.

Once they were inside, a couple of different officers were waiting just inside the airlock. They took over from her minder.

They took her down a low-ceilinged corridor into another part of the base.

It seemed to be part of the hospital. From what she understood, newly arriving troops had to come here to have blood samples taken, and have themselves cleared of disease.

The four of them had undertaken this procedure while still at Ganymede. Maybe there was a problem with communication?

But she also remembered the red flashing screen when she came in. What did that mean?

Thalia was told to sit on a row of hard plastic chairs inside a room that was full of bandages and shelves full of equipment. There was a treatment table in the room, and a few monitors and other things that looked far too familiar stood at the end of the table.

Not long after she had sat down, a man in medical scrubs arrived. The tag on the shirt said Hansen.

"Get on the table, please," he said. He did not look at her or take any kind of other interest in her.

"Can I ask why I'm here?"

"We need to do some tests."

Well, duh. "I had all those tests done before I left. Was there anything wrong with them?"

There was that niggle in her mind.

After the accident, she had spent far too much time in hospital and knew far too much of the things they did there. This sort of uneasy silence by medical officers was never a good sign.

There was nothing wrong with her, was there? On the other hand why would the military care about her health? They certainly wouldn't test her for any of the diseases that came with having been knocked out and having had to take vast quantities of radiation medicine. She had already been tested for infectious diseases. What else was there to test?

But Hansen seemed impatient, so she could do nothing else except the thing he asked her. The four of them had no power here, even less now that they were separated, and it was stupid to let herself be separated, but again she could do nothing about it. The Council Of Four had no jurisdiction in the military bases; civilian laws did not apply.

Once she had taken off her shoes and climbed onto the treatment table, Hansen rolled a piece of scanning equipment next to the table. He slotted a couple of bendable strips into the rails on the side of the table so that she lay in a tunnel.

Memories came back to her.

In the hospital there had been an elderly female doctor called Dr Crawford. She had white elfin hair that she wore in a bun at the back of her head. She was tall, slightly stooped and very thin. Her hands, like spiders, would deftly poke and prod and insert needles and drips.

It had been through her that Thalia had survived the accident at all, but every time she saw the doctor, a deep fear crept over her, because every time the doctor spoke to her, she mentioned some other part of Thalia's body that had been damaged, or another painful treatment that would be necessary.

It was only because of Dr Crawford that she was still alive and not needing to use a wheelchair. It was only because of Dr Crawford that she had any kind of career at all. Without the doctor, she would have lived as a vegetable in one of the homes where, sadly, so many of the mineworkers ended up as result of terrible accidents.

Hansen used the scanner that rolled over the arches over her body.

An image appeared on the screen next to her. It showed all the parts of the body, and a network of bright white lines expanded continuously.

"What are those?" she asked.

"These are your blood vessels."

Thalia didn't understand. Why should they show up like that? Normally you would have to drink some sort of fluid in order for organs show up like that on a scan.

She wanted to ask, but before she did, another man in scrubs came in. He stopped at the door, looking at the screen.

"So, that's what it looks like."

"Yes," Hansen said. "This is a pretty clear case."

A clear case of what?

And then a man and a woman came in, also in scrubs, also staring at the screen.

"Can someone just tell me what is going on?" Thalia said.

Hansen came to the table, and yanked out the struts. "You thought you could get away with this? You thought we were stupid?"

"Get away with what? I have no idea what you're talking about."

Hansen gestured at the screen, where by now a full picture of almost all her blood vessels had appeared. "You don't know? Do you think everybody's veins light up like this? You are still going to pretend that you don't know that you have nanometrics and that you are a spy? I will say it to your face. You are trying to deceive us. This whole humanitarian mission by the Council Of Four is nothing but an effort to spy on us."

While he spoke, anger had made Thalia's cheeks glow. "I have absolutely no idea what you're talking about."

CHAPTER NINE

ORDERS WERE NOT to be disobeyed.

Fabio went with the three men in the lift to the top of the mountain where a truck waited at the access tube. This was definitely a different vehicle, smaller than the six-seater that had brought him here. It was also much faster, and the men seemed to think that getting back to the main base was some sort of off-road rally. They didn't seem inclined to talk much, and that suited Fabio just fine. He'd prefer if the hoon at the controls kept his attention on the road, anyway.

He also wished this whole episode were over and done with. Let them discover the nanometrics and draw their conclusions. It was not as if they could be extracted from his body anyway. The worst they could do was dishonourably discharge him. And that suited him fine, too. They would have to provide him with transport to the nearest civilian settlement, presumably Europa, where someone would find a use for him, even if it was cutting blocks of ice. Somehow, a boring job like cutting ice would also suit him fine. No thinking, no politics involved. No superiors breathing down his neck. Sanchez . . . Sanchez should really go and fuck himself. Fabio was done with crawling on his knees for people. He was sick of hiding. He was sick of not knowing what he was supposed to have done and making apologies for it, because from all the shards of memories that had come back to him, he'd done good things.

But the shred of determination that had built up evaporated as soon as Fabio left the vehicle and entered the arrival hall.

Goddamned Hansen was waiting for him, wearing his full med-hazard suit. He nodded at Zanetti. "Thanks, I'll take it from here."

Zanetti left but the two thugs remained.

Hansen handed him a med-hazard poncho and when Fabio had pulled it over his head, he said, "Let's go."

Hansen's voice sounded kind of muffled through the suit's hood.

Fabio followed him through the maze of corridors to that horrid med room where he had first come when he arrived at the base. His vision was restricted to the narrow field of view of the visor and its crappy Perspex that made all the walls wobble and warp when he moved his head.

"Sit down." Hansen sat at his desk.

Fabio sat. He asked, "Can I take this off?" He pointed at the mask.

Hansen ignored the question. He pulled a menu up on his deskscreen and flicked through a few pages. "Ah." He faced Fabio. "What do you know about yourself?"

"Me?" That was an odd question.

"According to the information I've received, you were treated on board the ITV. What do you remember from before, about yourself?"

"Not much. I grew up in Argentina. I think. I don't remember signing up. I don't remember any job I did before. Except I think I worked for Dayol Mining, but I have no idea how I came to work there and what it has to do with the military. Is there anything wrong with me?" His heart was now thudding so loud that it was hard to hear anything through the roaring of blood in his ears. That was why no one had said anything to him before: he had a terminal illness and he was going to die soon. That was why his hair was falling out and why he had that implant under his skin in his upper arm.

"Not *wrong* as such, but you're a very interesting case. As far as I've been able to trace, you're the last surviving chameleon."

That was clearly meant to be significant, because he gave Fabio an intense stare.

"Chameleon," Fabio repeated, now sweating inside the hood. "That's a type of lizard, right?"

"Yes, it's a lizard that can change its colour depending on the place where it sits. If it's on the ground, it becomes brown. If it's in the trees, it turns green."

"Oh." He pushed aside his sleeve, clearly noticing the part where he had pulled out the longer hairs. "I'm not turning blue to match the seat of this chair."

"Chameleons were part of a secret ISF program that was run, as you remember rightly, on an isolated farm in Argentina. There were only twenty of these people, specially bred to be spies. They were called chameleons because they could change their appearance."

Fabio frowned at him. "Anyone can do that. Cut your hair, dye it, wear a wig, grow a beard—"

"From male to female and back."

What?

"You are a hermaphrodite. You have two X chromosomes and one Y chromosome. You need to take hormones to keep yourself male—"

Fabio took in a breath. The medicines in his duffel. The ones that he *hadn't* been taking. The ones that would have kept his hair from falling out.

"And you need to take hormones to keep yourself female."

"But females usually have . . ." He cupped his hands in front of his chest on top of the bright yellow poncho. Seriously, why couldn't he take this fucking thing off?

"Yes. Every time you start taking the female hormones, you go through a few months of puberty and grow small breasts. When you decide to be male, you change hormone supplements, the breasts shrivel and excess tissue is removed surgically. The point of having people like this is that they can change appearance and move in different circles."

"You said there were only twenty."

"Yes. Sadly, you are the only one left."

The black hole opened in him again. Next, Hansen would say that they'd all died of the horrible infectious disease he had just caught. But he had to ask. "What about the other chameleons?"

Hansen folded his hands on the table. The rubber-gloved finger-tips touched each other. "The reason that the chameleon program was discontinued was that people discovered that you cannot breed for luck and you cannot breed for character. There will be a next generation, fully artificial human, but the chameleon program is dead. One problem with the chameleons was that they had a character trait that made them unsuited to serving as intelligence officers in an army."

"They were dumb?"

"No, Velazquez. They were actually selected for intelligence, although you have done your utmost best to disprove that."

"Sorry to disappoint you, then."

"That!" Hansen pointed at Fabio's mask. "That is why you're unsuitable. You give lip. In fact, you give so much lip that superior officers beg the training posts to take back these supposedly superior weirdo poofters that end up turning discipline into a mess. You have no discipline. You have no respect. You have no loyalty. The other chameleons are all dead because ten of them were executed for treason. Six got 'accidentally' killed while serving, and three were killed by our own troops for the sake of safety. No one even went to court for any of those killings."

Fabio let those statements hang in the angry silence. Then he said, "But what does that have to do with this?" He pointed at the facemask, which was starting to fog up.

"I was getting to that."

"I would like to take it off."

"You're not going to be able to. Your blood contains so many infectious nanometrics that it's a wonder that you haven't yet started a rebellion over there at Research. They're the worst kind: mood-altering drugs. You do something and people follow you and they don't even notice that they're doing something stupid. The ITV said nothing about your condition. We are going to complain to Sarajevo about this. You are a plant and a spy."

He took in a deep breath and continued in a calmer voice. "You are to wear a face mask and protective clothing at all times when you're working with people. We're going to have to increase your protection and give you a personal minder. You are not to leave your room without this person."

"You mean I'm under personal arrest?"

"I don't care what you call it, but if you want, yes."

"What about Major Doric?"

"You can't keep working for her. She will be sent a replacement worker."

"What is going to happen to me?"

"That is not for me to decide."

"Can I contact someone?" Not that he had any idea who to contact. Sanchez, maybe, but he had a feeling that even Sanchez might not care very much, and would probably be glad to be rid of him. Maybe Sanchez had even sent him to this base to cause trouble and get killed in the process.

"No, you can't. Sorry."

Hansen called in the two privates who had waited outside, and they frogmarched Fabio to a small room in the med section behind Hansen's office.

It had a bare examination table, bolted to the wall, and a cupboard with a security lock on it. In the corner stood the familiar round, stool-like contraption which, according to the sign, was for the *collection of human wastes*.

They pushed Fabio inside the room and went through all his

pockets. They took his PCD. Fabio protested. "I need that thing."
Everything he remembered was on it.

"You'll get it back once we've checked it."

They left, telling him to wait.

Once the door was closed, the first thing Fabio did was take off
that mask and poncho. He flung them onto the bench next to
the bed.

The walls seemed to close in on him. He studied the door, but
without the worms on his PCD he could do nothing. It was solid.
They activated the vacuum lock even though the space on both
sides was pressurised. And would remain so. He hoped.

The opening of the ceiling vent might just be wide enough to
crawl through, but when he climbed onto the bed, he found that
the grate was bolted on tight, making it impossible for him to
remove it without tools.

So he paced. The room was two steps wide and three steps long
and he walked that strip of polished linoleum many times. There
was a black scuff mark to one side of the table leg. There were no
manholes in the floor, or loose panels in the walls.

He rattled the doors to the cupboard a few times, but it was
shut securely.

There were no news screens, no outside information.

What would they do to him? Nanometrics were illegal, highly
experimental molecules engineered to deliver specialist—psychotic
—medication to precise locations. They did things like vastly
increase a person's memory, or increase knowledge or change
someone's personality. After some highly publicised botched
experiments, they had been banned.

Getting rid of the nanometrics already deployed, however, was
a lot less easy.

They were a type of dendromers, molecules that grew outward
like a patch of fungus, coating themselves with water-soluble
branches. They self-replicated. If you destroyed the original molecules, the outer edges kept growing. Once in the body, they could
not be eradicated.

Nanometric actions were normally controlled by an implant, so if that had been the implant at the back of his head, removing it would have set the nanometrics free in his body. Without the implant, the things were likely to be feral.

Interrogators were likely to use electrical shocks. They would reprogram the nanometrics. Or, realising he had this technology, they might send targeted signals that made him tell them whatever they wanted to hear. All recorded and under oath, of course.

On the other hand, if he still had the implant, if it was the thing under the skin of his arm . . . He rubbed the spot. It was sore from having been fingered so often already in the last few days.

If that thing was the implant, then . . . what could they do to him? Was it even big enough for a proper implant? It was definitely something hard and cylindrical under the skin. It moved a bit when he pushed it, and if he dug his fingers under it, the other end pushed up the skin like a tent pole.

That little thing could mean the difference between life and death. If they could reprogram it, they might be able to get information out of him that he didn't know he had. They might be able to turn him into a traitor. They might completely wipe his personality and turn him into someone new. Someone who blindly obeyed orders and never questioned anything. And somehow that scared him more than anything else. If they changed his personality, then would the old him be trapped inside his head or something? Would they force him to take medicines and turn him into a woman?

Then another thought: how often had they done this already?

He paced through the room, up, down, up, down, up, down—

The door opened.

Hansen came in, while talking to another man. Both wore face-masks, gloves and clear plastic ponchos. The second man was someone whose stiff ISF-grey jacket had so many decorations that one needed sunglasses to look at him. This had to be Base Commander Banparra. He had the stocky build of someone who had grown up in space with the excess of physical training advocated by some bases.

His skin was black as the sky outside, his head bald and shiny, and the shiny skin formed a couple of deep folds at the back of his neck.

Like a hippopotamus.

He leaned against the room's closed door, arms crossed over his chest. A muscle twitched in his temple.

"Take off your uniform," Hansen said, while going to the cabinet against the back wall. He pressed a combination of numbers on the security panel. When he slid the door open, it revealed leads and cables, and bandages.

Fabio felt sick. "Do I get any say in what happens to me?"

"No. Take off your uniform and lie down on your stomach. I'm not in the mood for tricks."

Fabio did as he was ordered, glancing at Banparra, who returned an empty, emotionless stare. He was shivering. He felt small and thin and weak. He needed to pee.

Fabio climbed up on the table and clumsily turned around. Nerves were getting the better of him.

"Hurry up." Hansen pushed him down on the table, while Banparra fiddled with his PCD which he had taken out of his pocket.

Hansen pulled the straps *snap, snap.*

The he slid the headband over Fabio's head, and paused his gloved fingers in Fabio's hair over the scar. He pushed the hair aside. "He's had an implant removed, Sir."

"Yeah, well, that doesn't surprise me." Banparra's voice was rich and deep. "Is there anything about Velazquez that's as it seems?"

"He's not a chameleon for nothing, sir." He pushed Fabio's shoulder up and stared at that part of his pale chest he could see, while the straps cut into Fabio's wrist. "Hmmm, must have had a decent plastic surgeon to take those boobs off. He's been taking supplements to suppress female hormones and to make his beard grow, rather poorly, I might add."

Banparra snorted. "You're sorry a piece of shit, Velazquez, built to change gender at any time, pumped full of nanometrics to control you. A product of people farms. The fools. Nanometrics never worked that way, and they won't work that way, ever. And then Sarajevo sends you to spy on me?" He laughed. "To sow discord in my base?"

Hansen shoved Fabio back onto the table. He pulled the headband snug, and attached leads to a monitor in the wall at the back of the security cupboard. "I'm ready, sir."

Banparra pushed himself off the door. Up until now, Fabio had not realised how tall he was. He bent over the table and regarded Fabio with a look of one observing an unusual animal. With the headband on his head, and strapped face down on the table, Fabio could only see him from the corner of his eye.

"Tell me, Velazquez, where did you work before you were sent here?"

"I don't remember. I was on the interplanetary. I think I had surgery either on board or just before departure. I don't remember anything further back than that."

"Do you remember who sent you?"

"No." He sure as hell wasn't going to mention Sanchez.

"But you do remember your work well enough to be listed as a mining astronomer."

"I didn't list myself, someone else did; but I do remember most of it. Enough to do all the basic stuff."

"And your appointment here was coincidence, right?"

"As far as I'm aware, sir."

"Where did you come from before you came here?"

"You know that. I don't."

He snorted. "Don't try any funny talk on me, piece of shit. You're a piece of shit, did I tell you that?"

"You did, sir."

"And what do you have to say about that?"

"I don't know, sir."

Banparra hit the side of his head with his flat hand. The slap made Fabio see stars. "I'm getting sick of that answer. It there anything else you can say?"

"I don't—um—yes, sir."

"Good. Did you perhaps come from Mars?"

"Could be, sir. I don't remember any of that. Why do people keep talking about it?"

"Because you single-handedly caused the biggest military fuck-up in the history of mankind. That's why."

He—what? Fabio searched his mind, but there was just a big black hole.

"That happened on Mars," Banparra said. His eyes were startlingly grey. "In case you've forgotten. You lying, cheating creep. They should have put a bullet in your brain the moment they caught you, but someone obviously sees some value in you, because they marked you as needing to stay alive by order of the fucking Admiral. No one says anything about why. So they send you to my base, and that Doric bitch claimed you straight away, another Sarajevo plant. Don't you see anything wrong with that? With what they're trying to do to my base? Send a fucking research division to keep an eye on me, and now send me the last fucking chameleon alive to keep an eye on me, to report back to Sarajevo, because the fuck they want to tell me how to run my base and how to interact with my neighbours. You may record that."

"I don't record anything. I am not a traitor, sir. I don't know what I did, but I would not betray my comrades." Of that, he was certain. He saw a couple of men sitting on a bench opposite him. They were in the cabin on a truck which bounced over rough terrain. He had to hold onto loops hanging from the ceiling. The other men—were they colleagues?—looked familiar but he couldn't remember their names. Or what they were doing there. Or where they were. But they had been friends. Fabio did not hurt friends.

"So you did not fail to listen to your commander's orders when he told you to stay away from the plains settlements north of Johnson on Mars?"

"I don't know if I did, sir." He did remember the man in uniform, before he absconded from Dayol Mining. Had he been a military spy working at Dayol?

"You did not visit the ISF's base at Johnson under a fabricated reason? You did not tell lies about your plans for the next day even though it was base policy to always fill in a book of intended movements?" His eyes were penetrating.

"I don't remember, sir."

"You did not drive off in the middle of a snowstorm, and disconnect the beacon of your truck so that the base could no longer track you?"

The snowstorm. He remembered that. And with it came another memory: the inflatable dome of a settlement tent loomed ahead, the plastic cover being whipped and groaning under the snow. It wouldn't be long before the thing collapsed and was dragged away by the wind. Several trucks had already detached from the structure. People in overalls were trying to undo the coupling to the access tube. A couple of faces showed behind the truck's fogged window. *Children's faces.*

"Get out," he screamed even though they could never hear him yelling inside his suit. "Get out, before the tent blows away!" Even if they could, they probably couldn't understand him. In all these settlements people spoke in an ancient dialect.

He said to Banparra, "There were children's lives at risk."

"So you do remember."

"Bits of it." But as he said that, other things came back: ISF had wanted to free up water resources on Mars. There were huge frozen reservoirs underground. Mars was low on nitrogen. They had directed a nitrogen-rich comet at the ice caps of Mars' north pole.

But the ice on Mars was always mixed with carbon dioxide. The geologists called it clathrate. A more apt term was soda water. When it melted suddenly, it would blow and snow out; they knew that. They did not warn the nearby settlements.

The reservoir's spout turned into a massive snowstorm, and he had gone out to rescue the settlers. Against orders. Yes, they were Allion supporters, but they were civilians and had nothing to do with the conflict that was going on between ISF and Allion.

He met Banparra's eyes and said slowly, "The only thing I did was try to save civilians who were in the way of the water when it would come out."

"You had *orders*."

"They were civilians, who had prospected the desert for at least two generations." He saw the wizened faces, the people towering over him. He must have gotten some of them to safety.

"Those people were dangerous rebels, hiding themselves amongst civilians like the cowards they are. Most of your so-called civilians were aggregates anyway. Not people."

He remembered aggregates, those people who had bones of steel and hardened polymers, whose skin doubled as pressure suit. Yes, those people who'd been fixing the trucks didn't wear suits. On Mars.

"You went into their hideouts. They could have read your implants. These were Allion people. What the *fuck* were you thinking, Velazquez?"

"I don't remember."

"There's not much point in asking him, sir." Hansen said. "They've taken out his implant and fried him. He won't recover those memories—ever."

"Who has them?"

"Headquarters, I presume."

Banparra snorted. "And what else have they put inside his head so that he can pull the same trick with us?"

"That's what we're going to find out."

Hansen pressed a button on the control screen in the back of the cupboard.

Fabio sensed the current going through a split second before everything in his vision turned white. A sharp jolt of pain went through his head.

He might have screamed, his body may have turned rigid or

may have convulsed—he didn't know. He was carried on a maelstrom of pain. The room vanished before him, and he was . . . nowhere.

"Careful, he's no use to us dead."

Hansen slid the dial back and the feeling eased a bit. Fabio managed a moan.

Lines danced over the monitor's screen and an image of a human head appeared.

Banparra said something but Fabio didn't understand any of it.

For what seemed like an eternity, he lay stiff and motionless on the examination table. Then Hansen flicked the machine off and the stiffness disappeared as quickly as it had come.

Hansen yanked the sticky pads off his back. The plaster pulled at his skin hard enough to leave a mark, but it was nothing compared to the pain of the electric current.

"Get dressed," Hansen said.

Fabio clambered stiffly off the examination table. His legs were still shaky and he wasn't certain that they would support him enough to let go of the edge of the table. He put on his shirt with trembling hands, half-leaning against the table.

Banparra and Hansen were looking at the monitor. Rows of text scrolled over the screen. Mindbase files. Fabio had seen them often enough.

Where, though?

And another piece of the puzzle fell into his mind.

He'd been in a room with a lot of workstations. He'd been sitting in a wheelchair and there was something heavy and itchy on his head, like he was wearing an inside-out pincushion on his head.

Two technicians were pointing at the screen and talking in low voices about things to remove and add, occasionally casting a glance in his direction. As if they were talking about a computer they were programming rather than a human being.

Where did that piece go in the scheme of things? After he'd seen Sanchez?

"Doesn't look like there is anything unnatural here," Hansen said.

"They wiped me," Fabio said more to himself than anyone else.

"We'll be the judge of that." His voice carried a shut-up tone.

"What are we going to do with you?" Banparra said, stroking his chin. "I don't want you on my base. They may say that you've been treated, but I don't believe anything Headquarters says, especially not when it's part of something they send to my base without my asking—"

The door to the room opened, and a woman's voice said, "What the hell are you doing with my employee?"

Katarina Doric.

THE WATCHER

"YOU SEE, TAURA, ISF doesn't know how to use nanometrics," Vega said.

She was standing in front of the window overlooking the white cloud tops. Jupiter's distinctive patterns were only visible from a great distance. When you were as close as the orbiting base, all the clouds were white, misty and fluffy.

"They try mechanical things. Sure, you can charge them and they will hold information. Oh, the wonder! Turn a person into a data storage device. But the long-term retention rate is rubbish because the particles move in the bloodstream, even if they don't always move much. But as soon as they move, they interfere with each other and mess up the memories. You can make nanometrics release chemicals. Oh, the wonder! You can change their mood, their nature, their eye colour, even their gender. You have created the perfect spy. Except the molecules move, and they interact, and the spy is loyal only to one thing: survival of the human species. People with nanometrics make for really bad spies but very good ethical workers. They will always stand up for the oppressed."

"That doesn't help us get the guy."

"No, I understand that you want to use engineering and brute force."

"Well, we only have one chance, and time is short. We need those codes."

"Sure, but once we give away our position, we need to be ready to abandon the base."

It was still astonishing that years after Mars, Juno Station remained undiscovered. Nobody knew that it was even possible to live on the tops of the clouds of Jupiter. Only Allion's wellships, the *Thor* series and the *Morgana*, which had sadly been lost to ISF, could ever go down to the outer layers of the planet—to harvest Helium—and Juno had been a small unknown harvesting station before becoming the refuge of the Allion people who could reach it and who had survived the great purging. Sheltered by Jupiter's immense radiation and the fact that no one thought to look for the base, it sat in low orbit and scooted over the cloud tops at a crazy speed. But they were also located right next to the most militarised zone of the system, and once someone knew it was there, the bases on Io would have no issue or problem taking them down.

They had one chance, and by that time, the population of Juno, numbering fifteen thousand, had to be elsewhere.

Taura understood that, for sure, but it did not dampen her impatience. "So, is this nano-stuff getting to any kind of point soon?"

"Yes, because with nanotech is how we're going to get our target. I know you're keen to fly missions and use weapons, but I think we'll get plenty of opportunity for that later."

"We're just sitting here and doing nothing!" She spread her hands and turned away from the window. "I can't stand this airy-fairy stuff anymore. I want proof that something is happening."

"It is. ISF have captured the delegation because of some technicality. They're getting angry because they get no responses to their questions. Our man is going to feel some kind of kinship with them. He spoke to them before, and even if one of the mindshards put him in a difficult spot, he will feel responsible for getting them out of their confinement."

"I'm glad you're so sure."

"I am, because that is what he does, and has done, repeatedly. He's a chameleon. In ISF's eyes, he's broken, but they don't understand that in a situation where he hears about something unfair, he will always choose the underdog. That's how he first got into contact with Priya and presumably why she trusted him enough to carry the information. He had no personal need to come to the ice fields north of Johnson to warn our communities that ISF was about to drop an asteroid into their home. And it's that ability we'll use."

"Seems like a very risky way of doing it, seeing that all we need is the implant that's about this big." Taura held her thumb and index finger a finger's width apart. "So, what, he's going to bust his own backside out of there, because he feels compelled to free these people he doesn't even know—"

"—Two of whom are my mindshards."

"That may be, but you can't communicate with them. How do you know they will be happy to go along with this crazy character? They're not our people at all."

"Trust me. They're Laura Crawford's. She knew what she was doing. All of them already exhibit clear signs that they're not happy and that they know vile and unsavoury things were done and continue to be done in the name of eradicating us."

"That doesn't make them allies."

"No, but it makes them good spokespeople. They will get themselves to a position where we can pick them up unobtrusively, without having to use weapons or give away our position. We will get our prisoner and release the mindshards back into their community. They will help further our cause and they won't even realise they're doing it."

"I hope you're right. That implant is worth more than all our lives put together." Taura went to the door and left.

Vega let her gaze slide over the room and the sections of the outside of the station visible through the window. She thought she was right. She *hoped* she was right. To consider the alternative—that ISF had suddenly developed far superior technology—was unthinkable.

The whole operation was dicey enough. Things could go wrong so very, very quickly.

Back in the time of the Johnson disaster, Allion had been a major force in the solar system's space settlement. They, after all, had been the first to put a person on Mars. They had been the first to use space stations extensively.

But ISF had been unhappy about the situation, and they had been catching up, because they could not let a company—and an egalitarian company at that—comprised of mostly women from developing countries run the show in space exploration.

The conference at Johnson on Mars had been about sharing precious resources. ISF argued that space was a resource that belonged to all people and could not be commercially settled.

Allion argued that they put the effort into developing the technology and therefore they should reap the greatest benefits.

But in reality they needed each other. The environment was hostile. Doubling up on technology served no one.

At least that was the core premise for the meeting.

ISF had not come to talk.

They might be represented by all countries—all rich western countries at that—but they were a military organisation.

They simply wanted control over the bases, so that the governments of the countries on earth could exert their usual control over the populations of the poor who made up most of Allion's workforce.

Of course no one ever put the events on Mars in those terms. There were as many interpretations of what had happened as there were people.

Surprisingly few things were commonly accepted knowledge:

There had been a meeting at which Allion and ISF delegations were present.

There was disagreement about the purpose of this meeting. Some said it had been merely a meeting of scientific minds for the exchange of information, some said Allion was desperate and asked for help because they had trouble with their settlements. Others said that it was the other way around. Others still said it was to lay a framework for what would be acceptable experimentation with humans. ISF objected to Allion's aggregates—people with partially mechanical bodies—even if they had since started a similar program.

Everyone agreed that there was tension at the meeting between the two factions. It was the first time either had met in official capacity—the ISF had always acted as if a lean and agile company consisting of mostly women from developing countries could not do serious science, especially not those who bought fifty-year old space junk after the decommissioning of old—and often failed —projects.

But it had been Allion who had not been afraid or hamstrung by governments and regulations to turn this old junk into something amazing, like a ship that took the first person—a woman named Chandra Lee—to the surface of Mars.

Allion's scientists, trained by venerable universities but from poor countries, had nothing to lose. Cutbacks to immigration meant that they couldn't keep working in the countries that had trained them, and their home countries were too poor to support research that they had trained to perform.

They had nothing to lose.

Too western to work in their home countries, or as refugees without families, or women unable to work in oppressive regimes, they'd been happy for the chance to go into space. They'd given their lives to the cause.

Of course they moved much faster than the behemoth of government-funded space exploration.

But ISF didn't like it.

Under the guise of holding a conference on the future of joint bases of Mars, they had visited and infiltrated the Allion communities. People had been too forgiving and naive. And there was the curiosity. The only men that a lot of these women knew were the aggregates, and they weren't really men in the usual sense of the word.

What had happened during this historic gathering?

The only thing that people agreed on was that there had been a catastrophic breach of the dome, resulting in the deaths of thousands.

Also that the small asteroid that hit near Johnson had not impacted the dome, even if some reports said it had. Despite large numbers of survivors, no one knew why the dome had failed. It could have been through earth movement caused by the asteroid impact, or because the dome was not designed to be covered in the weight of snow, or because of more sinister reasons.

In any case, having blamed Allion for the failure, ISF searched out and destroyed all Allion bases and killed all Allion members that they could find until Allion was officially dead.

Except for Juno Station, the one that no one knew about.

Nobody knew that Allion had survived. They had one chance to make a big impact, but they absolutely needed to save that chance for later.

CHAPTER TEN

BANPARRA'S FACE WENT DARK. In one step he was at the door and shouted in her face, "What are you doing in my base?"

She didn't flinch. "What are you doing with *my* employee?" Her voice was soft and menacing.

Banparra's nostrils flared. "That amounts to disobedience of a superior officer. I'm reporting this to Preston's office."

Doric glared at him. "Good luck with that. You need me."

That was amazing. Disobedience of orders from a superior was no laughing matter. And he outranked her in every way. Even if he hadn't, the fact that he was Base Commander would have made it so. She was acting in a way that was utterly stupid, and even Fabio could see that. What was wrong with her?

Hansen said, "Why are you not wearing safety gear?"

They faced each other wordlessly for a few moments. Doric's nostrils flared. Hansen tossed her a facemask, which she dangled on her index finger.

"Base regulations," Hansen reminded her.

Doric strapped the mask over her head in a look-I'm-wearing-your-fucking-mask kind of way. While she was doing all this, she didn't once look at Fabio, and he wondered what earned him the privilege of her protection and, to be honest, self-destruction.

"He's my employee, and I need him," Doric went on. "You want your chunk of ice delivered to your doorstep? I need him to do the work with me."

"He's a spy," Banparra said.

"He's working to keep all of us alive." Doric's eyes glared over the top of the mask. "Before you try to have me arrested, know this: he comes with personal protection of Admiral Sanchez."

Did he? Personal protection? Fabio thought he'd only annoyed Sanchez. He didn't even think he'd seen Sanchez more often than just for that fabulous dressing-down he'd received. *Keep your head down.* To hell.

"Sanchez's man, with a fancy Sarajevo shirt and fancy Sarajevo implants. That's exactly what I thought. He's a fucking spy from fucking Sarajevo. I'm going to undress him completely, until he's a crying heap of sorry arse on the floor. I do not want spies from Sarajevo on my base."

"This is exactly why people like him are here: because you treat dissenters like animals. What happened to the military code of honour?"

"Fuck all of you. I'm trying to keep everyone alive. There is no room for human rights pansies. I was even taken in by them. Doing the right thing by one's neighbours and all that, but they're all spies, the lot of them."

"So now are you officially declaring secession?"

"No. It's Preston's call anyway. He will not make it unless Sarajevo meddles any more in my running of this base than they currently do. And, frankly, it's getting to that point."

"As long as you don't forget who pays you."

Banparra laughed a big roaring belly laugh. "That's how screwed up your thinking is with the Sarajevo mob. What use do we have here for money? What use do we have for orders that are made for us months' worth of travel away from us? What point do we have in being a political football?"

"That's disobedience of the Admiral's orders. I will have to report that. Just like I will report on the gross negligence of the rights of your troops across the system, like this man here, like Ceres, like Mars."

"Don't talk about Mars! What do you know about it, anyway?"

"More than you can imagine. I know what ISF did on Mars, and it will come out. I have a report ready to be sent, with evidence. Don't go looking for it, because you won't find it anywhere in the base systems. I will send it when I'm ready."

"You won't or you'll be sorry."

"You know what the penalty is for threatening a fellow officer?"

"You know who has the higher rank?"

"I don't care, because I'm not part of your command structure."

"That's it, I'm writing a formal complaint to Sanchez."

"About what? You don't even care about Sanchez. That's the whole point of what you're doing: secession."

They glared at each other.

Fabio's heart was hammering. Where did he fit in this? A spy.

Then Banparra snorted. The rank thing was a problem for him, Fabio guessed. Yes, she could be reprimanded for speaking up, but Research was in a completely different division so the chain of command was muddled at its best. Banparra knew that he couldn't take this any further unless he went to Doric's superior and that was always a risky thing to do. Doric might be of lesser rank—besides being in Research and not in his line of command—but he would be stupid not to realise that anything he said to her would go straight back to head office. He snorted again. Probably figured he'd already said too much.

"That does not change that this man is a spy."

"Why are you so certain about that?"

"Because he failed all his medical tests, tests that you were trying to prevent him from being subjected to. He failed his blood test and he failed his mind scan. He is full of nanometrics."

"That's rubbish. You're just making that up."

"Show her, Hansen."

Medical officer Hanson brought the image to the screen that he had just produced before Doric came in. It showed an image of a human head with all the blood vessels clearly marked white. Both Banparra and Doric glared at it.

"Jesus," Banparra said, shaking his head.

"Explain to me what this actually means," Doric said.

"It proves that he is full of nanometrics," Hansen said. "Because when you run a current through the patient, the nanometrics take on a charge. That's what you're seeing here."

"And what is the proof that anything untoward has been done in his case? Nanometrics can be used for other things, or can just be latent in the system. You have prodded him, you tried to read him, you've wiped him and you have found no evidence that he is in anyway compromised or that his mind or body contains any information that is harmful or secret. It is not about nanometrics, it is about how they are used."

"Yes," Banparra said, and he laughed. "I remember there being a debate about whether or not guns kill people or people kill people. In the end people came to the conclusion that it was a whole heap of a lot easier for people to kill people with guns than without them. Where there's smoke, there's fire. He has nanometrics and therefore I don't trust him."

"I still need him for my work, unless you can provide another astronomer."

"This man stays here. I do not trust him anywhere on the base in any place that has any sensitive information, which is most of the base and especially the research division, and if you need some help you will have to find another officer. Certainly plugging numbers into a computer is not that hard."

"That's what you say. I'd like to see you try to do it."

"You can argue all you want but my decision is final. This man will be locked up and he will stay here."

Fabio looked from one to the other, listening to this discussion fought out completely over his head. He couldn't move, even though he very much wanted to. He struggled against the bonds that kept him onto the table. He didn't want any medical tests. It seemed that all that they'd ever know about him they already knew. He had no idea about nanometrics and where they came from. Maybe he was born with them, maybe it had something to do with Sanchez.

All he knew was that he needed to get out, because this room was too small for all these people here, and if people were going to decide about his fate, he might as well run out the airlock.

Doric said, "Let him sit up. He's not a prisoner."

"Who are you? You would think this whole human rights rubbish has rubbed off on you."

"I saw things that were indescribable. If ever the people on earth hear about this they will never place any faith in ISF ever again."

"Isn't it a good thing then, that we don't really care about people on Earth. We are in space and living in space is hard. You either obey or you leave. Put up or shut up. In case you hadn't noticed, the environment out there is trying very hard to kill us. We have no time for soft politics."

"You keep trying to distract me. Hansen, let the man sit up."

Hansen looked from one to the other, confused.

"Come on, let him sit. You've already read enough of his data."

Then, when nothing happened, Doric crossed the room from the door, and yanked loose the straps that held Fabio on the table. Then she wheeled the machine aside and took the sensors off his head.

Hansen protested. "Hey, keep your hands off my equipment."

"Then let him go."

But Banparra, whom Fabio had fully expected to butt in, was staring at the screen. His face turned red. "So that is how it sticks together."

They all turned to where he was looking.

When Doric moved the machine, it had still been on. The scan on the screen showed part of a human head—Fabio's—and also part of an arm—Doric's. While the veins were clearly visible in the head, they also lit up bright white in the arm.

"You're a traitor."

Doric's face had gone pale.

"What is this?" she asked.

"You tell me," Hansen said.

"This is nonsense. You're just making this up about nanometrics in the man's body. That scan you showed earlier is a fake."

"Either that or you're spiked, too."

"That's ridiculous. How do you even dare to suggest that? I came up from the ranks of Dorics that always served in the force."

"Well, obviously you had had a change of mind," Banparra said.

"This is nonsense, and I will prove it to you. Start a new scan."

They got Fabio off the table, shivering in his thin gown, and put Doric on. Hansen only started scanning equipment when she was convinced that it had been set up properly and the screen wiped. The first scan showed exactly the same thing as it had shown for Fabio: all the veins in her body brightly lit in white.

There was only one conclusion: if he had nanometrics in his blood, then she did, too.

"I think you'll have some questions to answer," Banparra said. "I always suspected that you were a plant from Sarajevo. This is my proof. Your game is up."

The two thugs came in from outside and grabbed her by the arms. As Katarina was dragged out of the room, her bewildered eyes met Fabio's. *Please help.*

JAYKADIA

JAYKADIA STARED AT the middle-aged man who had just entered her office. Haigh Denman was one of her executives, an experienced man who did not often look as upset as he did now.

"They have—what?"

"Taken possession of the maintenance buildings. A whole bunch of soldiers barged in and told everyone to get out. They've started moving equipment outside. All the workers are going home, including the new shift that was just about to go out."

"What about the people who are in the mines waiting for the new shift to turn up? Have they been warned and taken care of?"

"They have. I told them to shut down everything, take their keys and controls and come here."

"Thank you."

Jaykadia pushed herself to her feet.

"I'm going to have a look what's going on. Come."

She grabbed her overalls from the cupboard next to the door, pulled them on, and grabbed her mask and suit liner and went out.

Haigh followed her to the waiting buggy.

"I'm sorry about this," he continued while the buggy took them through the settlement. "I insisted that they speak to you first, but they didn't want to listen."

"Really, thank you. I don't know that you could have done anything to change the outcome." Heck, she didn't even think she could have made a difference herself.

In the big hall, a lot of the workers stood talking to each other. The sound of confusion hung in the air.

"Hey, boss!" someone called, and people turned around.

"What's going on? I thought you said that they wouldn't need the shed for a while?"

"I'm going to have a look at what's going on," Jaykadia said.

"Show 'em, boss!"

"Yeah, she'll get 'em under control."

A number of people cheered.

While it was not strictly necessary to suit up in order to get to the maintenance shed through the long access tube, Jaykadia did so anyway, because the suits that fitted her were all here—the maintenance hall only had ones several sizes too big—and because it would make her look more serious and ready to talk to any intruder, no matter who or where they were.

The suit did make walking more awkward but, on the upside, she acquired a nice swagger.

All along the walk down the tube—which seemed so much longer than it really was—Haigh was talking and Jaykadia played over various scenarios in her mind. If the ISF people had come with a maintenance crew, she'd turn off their power and demand to speak to their commanding officer. If they were soldiers moving out mining trucks, she'd tell them to stop or be accused of theft. Preston would have sent a few small units of people in order to prepare. She'd demand to speak to them and ask them what they thought they were doing, that this land was the property of the Ganymede Mining company, and—

They arrived in the hall.

It was full of people in white jumpsuits and orange overalls. There were hundreds of them, and they had brought a large array of vehicles that stood parked around the walls of the hall. They were all ISF trucks. All the mining equipment had already gone. The troops in white were putting together pressure tents, presumably to be dragged to the unpressurised hall of the maintenance area.

"Holy crap," she said in a low voice.

"I told you they had invaded the hall," Haigh said.

Yes, but she had not quite expected an invasion of this scale.

A female voice came from behind, "Please, we can't allow civilians in this hall."

Jaykadia whirled around.

The woman who had spoken was quite a bit older than her, black-skinned with greying frizzy hair closely cropped. Her eyes were dark and the look in them sharp.

"Excuse me, but I am the owner of this company," Jaykadia said. "I was not informed of this impending . . . invasion."

"Did the vice admiral not talk to you?"

"He did, but. . . ."

Preston had said nothing about when or how the troops were going to arrive, or even that the deal was sealed. She had, perhaps foolishly, assumed that she'd be asked to remove the mining machines and be asked for permission to enter the hall.

"Is Vice Admiral Preston here?"

She gave Jaykadia a *who do you think you are?* look. "No, he is not."

Obviously, the vice admiral had better things to do than talk to the biggest mining company on Ganymede, whose orbital sling he had used to get here, whose industry he was using in the form of the vehicles on the floor.

"I would like to speak with the officer in charge."

"He is very busy."

"I am busy, too. I don't have that much time to deal with an invasion of my company's space keeping my workers from returning to their jobs. I don't have the time to deal with trying to extract stranded workers from the mines, shutting down machines that never shut down, and making sure the operators get back to the surface safely. I didn't ask for any of this."

"Come along, ma'am, but I ask you to please keep it brief."

Jaykadia and Haigh followed the woman across the hall. Once they got past the line of trucks, the full scale of the operation became evident. Had she thought there were hundreds of people here? It looked more like over a thousand.

That changed her perspective on things.

There were no small teams of scouts that she could send away and shout at into halting their work while they contacted their supervisor. More people were here than worked in this entire section of the mine. There was no way they would listen to her.

In the far corner of the hall, an entire command centre had sprung up, with a number of people at workstations facing a couple of large screens. Everything—from the screens and control panels, to the desks and chairs—had been brought in.

This was not some simple maintenance centre. This was a huge operation.

One of the screens displayed a telescope image, showing a starfield with, in the middle, a bright white spot. Scrolling numbers down the side displayed various parameters which Jaykadia didn't recognise, but it also showed the abbreviation ETA: estimated time of arrival.

What was that?

The screen's operator, a woman in a spiffy white uniform and her hair in an immaculate bun, looked over her shoulder and then hit a button that replaced the starfield image with a screen full of data.

Jaykadia turned around to Haigh. He flicked up his eyebrows. What was that about?

They continued past the workstations to a small partitioned-off area, where the officer announced herself by knocking on the fold-up screen.

"Sir?"

A man inside answered.

"There are two people here to see you."

She gestured Jaykadia and Haigh into the makeshift office.

The man who had spoken looked quite young, stout, with reddish hair and freckled skin.

"Operations Commander Donnell," he said.

"I'm Jaykadia Law."

"Wait, are you the company owner?" He sounded incredulous. It was a reaction Jaykadia often got, because of her young age.

"I would like to know what is going on."

"Didn't Vice Admiral Preston inform you of our operations?" He sounded guarded. Jaykadia had often noticed this with people from ISF when they had to speak to civilians.

"He visited me, but he told me that he would contact us when operations were about to start. I've heard nothing, especially not about any operations of this size."

"I think you misunderstood our intention. Our use of this facility is not optional. There were rumours that the company was debating blocking access."

Jaykadia's face grew hot. She had spoken to the workers about blocking access until they could speak to the human rights delegation with the suspicion that the information would be leaked, but it was another thing to hear that it had actually happened.

"Rumours," she said, making an attempt to sound as miffed as possible. She didn't think she was doing a very good job. "Did I ever mention anything to Vice Admiral Preston?"

"You didn't."

An uneasy silence passed.

"My employees are not happy," Jaykadia said.

"I'm sorry. Unfortunately, there is little I can do about it."

"I would like to be kept better up-to-date with your plans. Preston never even mentioned how long you would need to stay here for."

"I can't answer that either."

"Can't you? This is an exercise, right? Exercises go on for a

limited time. I only want to know when I can have my maintenance halls back."

"I'm afraid you will have to ask Preston."

Jaykadia was not going to get any answers from him.

On their way back through the access tube, she asked, "Did
you see how that woman hit the screen when she knew that we
were looking."

"I did," Haigh said.

"What were they looking at?"

"Some sort of approaching ship, my guess."

A cold feeling went over her. "This is an *exercise*, right?"

But he couldn't answer that.

CHAPTER ELEVEN

ONCE DORIC WAS GONE, Hansen tossed Fabio his clothes.

Banparra said, "Take him and his sorry arse back to his dungeon and lock the door. I don't want to see his creepy face here anymore."

Hansen jerked his head at the door. Fabio awkwardly jammed his feet into his shoes and half-stumbled after him into the corridor. As he passed Banparra, the man grabbed him by the front of his shirt.

"Keep your nose out of base politics." From close up, his skin was uneven and pockmarked with acne scars. "I don't like you, Velazquez. I don't like the sneaky look of you and I don't like your file, or the girly, poofy look on your face. You're a dishonest, creepy guy and the sooner I have you off the base, the better."

He released his grip suddenly, making Fabio stumble. Hansen steadied him with a hand whose fingernails bit into the soft skin on the underside of his arm.

He dragged Fabio along the corridor, muttering, "Arsehole."

Fabio was feeling weak all of a sudden. He badly needed to pee.

Hansen's fingertips trailed over Fabio's upper arm, where a

bruised spot marked the place of the implant under his skin. "What do you have here?"

"Don't know," Fabio said, but his voice came out as a croak.

He pinched the skin. "Too small to be a transmitter. In the wrong place to be a memory implant. It could be a tracking device. Who put it there?"

"I don't know. I honestly don't know." He was exhausted and felt closer to tears than he dared admit.

"There is far too much that you conveniently don't know. Don't think you're off the hook now. We're going to subject you to a full investigation. Wait, we'll go back. I'll cut this thing out." He pulled Fabio back to the treatment room.

"I don't know anything. They wiped me."

A deep fear took hold of him. In the last few days, he had started to remember more and more things, and, to be honest, they did not look good for ISF. Failing to warn civilians of a major impact, failing to care for the lives of nomadic communities, sweeping under the carpet that they had—

He was back in the collapsed dome inside Johnson base on Mars. A couple of armed men burst out of a door on the opposite side of the hall, wearing masks and full pressure suits, *shooting* at civilians, shooting at the transparent cover of the dome. Cracks grew across the sky.

Well, damn. Had he actually seen that?

Soldiers had killed those people and caused dome failure?

"Can we stop here for a moment?" He motioned his head at the bathroom they had just passed.

"What—oh. Better be quick." Hansen released his arm.

Fabio pushed the door open and stumbled into the cubicle, but once he was there he found that needing to pee was not the same as actually being able to do it. Not in the stiffened state his muscles were in.

He ran his hand over his upper arm, where the tiny implant still itched under the skin. What was in it? How would it give him away? If it was a tracker, would it have told Banparra where he had been on his first night here?

It was important, he knew.

He had no idea how it had evaded his earlier scan.

He pinched the skin at the spot where the implant sat. There was only one option: he would have to get rid of it. He scratched at the skin, feeling the bump, which was fairly shallow, just underneath the skin. If he had a knife or something, he could cut it out. But he had no knife.

The bathroom was sterile and held only wet wipes in a dispenser—which had no parts that could be removed—and the usual toilet things. Not even a cleaning brush.

His pockets were empty. Hansen had removed his belt, and his shoes had no buckles. He pulled out the small washbasin, but there was nothing that came off or unscrewed. In between looking for something, he squeezed the bump like a massive pimple. If he squeezed hard enough, the lump showed up as a bit of white. It *moved* under the skin. If he could just cut it, the thing would come out by itself.

Damn, he didn't have anything sharp.

He could just reach it . . . with his teeth. He bent down and clamped the fold of skin between his front teeth. It hurt like hell but left only red teeth-shaped marks on the skin.

There was no way he could do this. Those stories of people cutting their arms and doctors operating on themselves were all bullshit. No one could do that.

There was a knock on the door. "Are you all right in there?" Hansen.

He leaned against the wall, staring at the ceiling. Sweat collected on his upper lip.

He had to do this.

Damn.

He bent his head and clamped the skin between his teeth. He bit as hard as he could.

Damn it hurt and it was not easy. He pulled at the skin, chewing and biting.

His mouth filled with blood. The tiny implant lay on his tongue. He spat it out in his hand, a little white thing.

A wave of dizziness overwhelmed him. Damn, he was going to spew.

He leaned against the cubicle door, looking up at the ceiling. A ceiling vent blew cold air onto his skin.

There was no point. He was caught like a rabbit in a trap. Hansen knew that he had the implant; there was nowhere to hide it. If he swallowed it, they would wait until it came out either end. If he flushed it down the toilet, they would find it in the tanks. They would see, and record, everything that happened to him. He should have taken it out when he first noticed it. He should have . . .

There was no point in doing any of this.

He pulled a tissue out of the dispenser and wiped his face.

That ceiling vent was really quite big. He wondered if he could fit—

Voices in the corridor. Hansen was talking to a man in the corridor and their voices were clearly audible through the thin walls of the cubicle.

"I'm not sure, but one reason could be that he has defensive nanometrics. I know that's no longer done, because of health problems, but we're dealing with a less-than-normal person. He's a chameleon, and a very successful one at that. For one, how has he managed to enter this top-level security facility while his identity doesn't check out? Yes, it does, as far back as two years ago. He only joined us two years ago, and there is no record of Fabio Velazquez before that."

Fabio climbed onto the toilet bowl, but he couldn't reach the ceiling. He stepped onto the paper holder—

—Crack!

The whole thing broke off the wall, spreading tissue paper

everywhere. Fabio just managed to stop himself falling into the toilet bowl.

He listened, heart thudding.

The men in the corridor continued to talk. "Anyway, here is a list of known identities that he's used. It's far from complete. I'd be extremely careful of him, because one of his nicknames is 'Escape Artist'."

"I guess we know about that already. Do you think the amnesia is genuine?"

"Yes, I do. If the special branch got hold of him—and they have—they would have pretty much tried to destroy him without killing him—oh, for fuck's sake, what's the idiot doing?"

The door to the bathrooms flung open.

"Velazquez, come out!"

Shit.

Fabio grabbed a handful of tissue paper from the floor and wiped his bleeding arm. He succeeded in smearing blood over his skin. He licked the palm of his hand and tried to wash the blood off that way.

"Hurry up!"

The cubicle door rattled.

What was he going to do with the implant? In his pocket? No, Hansen would find it.

Nothing for it. He put it in his mouth and swallowed.

Then he pulled on his shirt—damn, there was blood on it—and opened the door.

One look, and Hansen's face turned to thunder. "Fuck it, what have you done, idiot?"

He yanked Fabio by his arm. Saw the raw and bleeding wound.

"You fucking schlemiel! Where is it?"

Fabio nodded at the toilet door.

Hansen walked in—

And Fabio yanked himself loose, slammed the door of the cubicle shut and ran out of the bathroom, into the corridor. He turned right, because that gave him the longest clear run and he ran faster than he had imagined he could. Hansen yelled behind him, "Stop him! Stop him!"

Fabio turned a corner into a stairwell. He went up, taking the steps two at a time. He came out into another corridor, with a lower ceiling.

Someone came up into the stairwell behind him. He ran to the left. As suspected, there was another toilet block. This one was much bigger, with toilets and showers. He went in and shut himself into a cubicle. As with the one downstairs, there were vents in the ceiling, and because the ceiling was much lower, he could reach it when he stood on the toilet's flush box. He pulled the grate out. The vent went up for a very short distance and then turned horizontal. He put the grate sideways against the wall, and then inserted his hands into the opening to heave himself up. Wow, there was a lot of space up there.

No, wait. He unlocked the door to the cubicle.

He pulled himself up into the hole, wormed around so his head faced the opening, leaned back out, grabbed the grate and pulled it in position again.

He waited, calming his breath.

The door to the bathroom opened. Someone came in.

"No, not in here either," he said.

Fabio didn't recognise the voice. Shit. He'd left a drop of blood on the floor and a smear on the wall.

The man went around the entire room, banging open all the cubicles, but he didn't notice the drop or the smear and left again. Phew.

He waited, listening to the sounds from elsewhere in the base. Yelling. Footsteps. People going up and down the stairs. The light in the bathroom flicked off.

Fabio lay quietly, waiting for the noise to die down. It was so dark that he couldn't see anything except purple blotches dancing in his vision.

He still needed to pee.

KATARINA

KATARINA HAD TO GET OUT of Calico.

Following months of frustration in her work, when repeated requests for assistance were ignored, problems were coming to a head.

After that ridiculous episode suggesting that she had nanometrics, they had taken her back to Research. In her position, with her rank, they couldn't reprimand her more severely than that without a proper process, and they knew it. People were watching her, from both sides. They knew she was loyal to the Sarajevo ideal: that ISF's function was to facilitate human exploration and settlement, not dictate it. Definitely not kill off anyone they didn't like. The Outer System Division knew it was on notice. *Improve your record of treating your staff or feel the consequences.* Space was big, but other people had survived Mars and knew something fishy was going on, and together they could piece all the events into a coherent picture that wouldn't look good for ISF at all.

That they planned to slam an asteroid into the north pole of Mars. That happened quite regularly, but in this case, none of the civilian people were warned, and what was worse, they even suggested a nearby dome as venue for a peace meeting. Why had ISF sent no real heavyweights to the meeting?

Because they intended to kill off everyone who came to it under the guise of an accident. Because some small-minded people high in command of the Outer System Division couldn't stand to be dependent on a commercial company that they didn't control and didn't understand.

And now they tried to silence everyone who took small steps to unmask their true nature.

Katarina felt torn inside. She loved the force. But it had to eradicate this cancer. Many people here didn't agree with Preston's actions either, or they refused to see his nature, because acknowledging it would upset the entire world that they loved.

Katarina fiercely wanted to believe that ISF was a *good* organisation, but her belief had been shaken badly by this crowd here.

Velazquez was a sad case, his mind broken and utterly destroyed by his superiors. Thalia and Paul were another case that she was powerless to influence. They were still locked up as far as Katarina knew. Probably for a similar transgression.

Nanometrics, ha.

It was just an excuse to lock out people they didn't like.

But how could she get out of the base, preferably with Thalia and the delegation, and with the poor sod Velazquez—before he revealed irretrievably bad secrets to people who shouldn't know those secrets.

And with Paul.

Silly, grumpy, utterly loyal, loveable Paul.

Wasn't that just like him, to wriggle his way into this delegation so that he could rescue her. The sheer pig-mindedness of him. He refused to believe that she was gone, refused to think that she might have abandoned him, refused to give up.

Her eyes misted over. They had spent far too little of the time they'd been married together.

She got up from her desk and paced around her room.

And yes, it was a much bigger room than other people had, a

fact which had lulled her into feeling positive about base command.

But Banparra was just toying with people. He'd invited the delegation with the aim of neutering that line of investigation. Throw up a lot of bureaucratic obstacles as excuse for delays, and stretch the delays as long as possible while diverting attention from something else—like this exercise that was filling up the base. The exercise that was the reason for her position here, the reason that extra ice had to be imported. But he afforded her no assistants so that she had become stressed out and only focused on her job to the point of excluding everything else, including her ability to think critically.

Nanometrics. Ridiculous.

She paced and paced around.

How to get out of this place without triggering suspicion?

How to contact Sanchez about this upcoming "exercise" that, evidently, Sarajevo knew little about.

How to let the COF assembly know that ISF was using the Io bases as a honey pot to trap critics—and maybe to repeat Mars?

That thought chilled her.

She had not actually given any orders for asteroids to be diverted, and maybe she should—oh no, she should definitely make sure that the work she did identifying potential candidates was not passed onto command.

She stopped pacing and pulled out her pad.

Banparra had already disabled her access to the research computers, but she had been distrustful enough not to keep her work there.

She pressed delete, delete.

Huge chunks of data vanished into nothingness. The little icon that told her how much space was available clicked up and up.

Then a message flicked over the screen.

You have a private message from G336584.

What the hell?

The fact that there was no name for the contact meant that she hadn't communicated with this person since obtaining this particular login. The letter G at the beginning stood for Ganymede.

She opened the message and immediately scrolled to see who it was from.

Jaykadia Law.

Damn it. She hadn't heard from Jaykadia for years.

They used to be such good friends, long ago, but a number of things had changed that. First there had been that accident with the truck that had changed their friendship.

Katarina didn't remember that much about it, but the three of them had gone for a drive and the truck had toppled into a ditch. All three of them were seriously injured and it was only because of pure luck that any of them had survived.

But somehow, after a long period of recovery, the friendship had never been the same.

Katarina had gotten married, and the other two had a succession of lame boyfriends. Katarina had joined the military and had been posted to Europa where her husband worked at the time.

They'd lost contact beyond a few visits.

Then she was posted out in the asteroid belt, and Mars happened. And when she emerged from the long dark tunnel that had her question the motives of ISF, there were still the punitive measures taken against her—life on Io, locked away from what could be termed civilisation.

Now there was this message from Jaykadia Law.

Pretty, successful Jaykadia, the youngest executive of a major company in the system, ever. Rich, pampered Jaykadia with her position cut out for her. Lonely Jaykadia, who could never find any man willing to serve second rank to her.

This message to you will probably come as a surprise, but frankly, I should have contacted you much earlier. I am sorry. I know you've been through a rough time and I kept making excuses that you didn't want to hear from me.

Fact is, I miss our friendship.

Yes, Katarina missed it, too. She missed the stupid clowning and the laughter. She also knew that time was gone and would never come back. They were adults now, with responsibilities.

I have become increasingly worried about the activities of certain sections of ISF, the most important of which affects the fate of our delegation to Io. My aunt keeps telling me to be patient, but something doesn't sit well with me. ISF have claimed the use of all my company's maintenance sheds, ostensibly for an exercise, but when I went to check out the sheds, I spotted a woman looking at some approaching celestial object on the screen. When she saw I was looking at it, she quickly moved to something else. As astronomer, are you aware of anything we should know? I'm thinking in terms of protecting or potentially evacuating certain settlements. Has ISF sent any ships to sort out the Outer System Division? Is Preston preparing a reception committee? Are we seeing a repeat of events in the past?

She was thinking *Mars,* but she was smart enough not to say it. She also knew that Katarina would think *Mars* because, likely, the mention of *you've been through a rough time* also insinuated that Jaykadia suspected why Katarina had been sent to Io.

But this letter reflected her own feelings perfectly. It was almost eerie in similarities. Despite the different career paths, she and Jaykadia were still very much alike.

Yes, elements in ISF were probably planning something under the guise of a military exercise, just like they had planned the complete destruction of Allion under the guise of a conference.

She needed to get out of here. She needed to warn Sanchez. She needed to warn Jaykadia, and everyone else she cared about.

She picked up the handwritten letter off the desk. How to get it to the delegation?

CHAPTER TWELVE

AT SOME POINT IN THE PAST, in one of his many previous identities, Fabio had earned the nickname *Escape Artist*. Because he got out of places and into places where no one thought he would go.

The ceiling duct in the toilet at the second floor residential corridor in the main base was definitely such a place.

Over the next few hours, several groups of people came in, but because Fabio managed to let himself down, clean up the drop of blood and the smear on the wall, no one paid any attention to the ceiling vent.

A few people came to use the showers and once a guy used the toilet cubicle underneath him, reading something on his pad while sitting with his pants around his ankles.

Sadly, also, the space up there—while being big enough to hide —didn't lead anywhere else. There was a square access panel that might open to let in a maintenance person, but it had to be locked from the outside, because no matter how Fabio tried, he couldn't get the panel to open.

He was hungry and thirsty, and his arm hurt. Having swallowed the implant also forced him to comb through his poop up there, and that was trickier than he thought. He could pee through the grate and have it sort of hit the right spot, but he needed to do the other business in a corner of the maintenance recess. Being dehydrated turned his poop into little hard black pellets that took ages to come out. They were slippery and needed to be held with one hand while crushing them with the other. Urgh, the smell. All for nothing. He was paranoid about accidentally shoving the implant into the toilet below so he went through all of it twice. Nothing. How long did this take?

He really had to find somewhere else to hide. Somewhere he had access to water—because he couldn't use his water allocation since it would tell them where he was—and where he could do this disgusting thing in more comfort.

Preferably somewhere off-base.

Problem was, on Io, he needed a truck. Or environment gear, but even those things were pretty useless unless he had a place to go to, and he didn't, because Prometheus was a thousand kilometres away and was also a military base. And this was over a crapload of dangerous terrain, with jagged spikes, huge heaps of soft sand that were deep enough for a truck to fall in and never be seen again. And lava lakes, lava crusts—which did the same thing as the sand bogs, but then with molten lava.

And all that while that huge fucking red and white beach ball in the sky was pumping out enough radiation to kill a person before he even died of asphyxiation.

Bugger the truck, he needed access to a shuttle. Or he needed to hide or bribe or force himself on board a shuttle.

And this required planning. Careful, meticulous planning. It required people with the right connections. And he had none of this. More than that, he had limited time.

He needed to steal stuff and would need a weapon.

And because he had no time and no means of doing anything, he'd have to do something so bold that no one expected it. Like walk into the mess and grab a tray and a can of water and walk out again—in a disguise—like a surgical gown and mask. That would make it so he had to walk into the officer's mess. Crap, talk about bold. But no one would expect him anywhere near the hospital, the place where they would detain and scan him.

First things first. Food and water. Without them, he couldn't do anything, not even, it seemed, poop.

So when the corridors grew quiet, he let himself down.

There would be security cameras all over the base, so he needed a way to turn them off, but since that was not feasible, to disguise himself.

In a corner of the bathroom, he found a cupboard that contained a humidi-vac floor cleaning machine and a number of brooms. He set the brooms upside down in the basket on the machine, so that he could hide his face between the broom heads. He would have liked a cleaner uniform, but there was none, so this would have to do.

He left the bathroom pushing the machine, bending over while pretending to read something on the pad he didn't have, so that the cameras wouldn't see his face.

The hospital was on the ground floor, so he went into the lift, said hello to the men who joined him and pretended not to be nervous.

He had one advantage: almost no one on this base knew him so they'd think he was just a new arrival having drawn the short end to do chores.

While the corridors were quiet, the hospital was busy.

It looked like there had been an accident, because the chairs in the waiting room were full. One man held a towel to his bleeding forehead, another clutched an awkwardly bent arm, pale-faced and sweating, while somewhere in the emergency room, a man screamed and swore while a forest of medical workers stood around him.

Fabio pretended not to notice or listen to the screams—that guy was really in a lot of pain—as he pushed his cleaning machine past rooms with glass walls, where patients lay in beds surrounded by machines.

At the end of the hallway, he found what he was looking for: the uniform room. He wheeled his machine inside, quickly grabbed a gown, a cap and facemask and stashed them into the recess at the back of the cleaning machine. He also grabbed a bottle of cleaning gel off the shelf.

On his way out the door, he grabbed a couple of garbage bin liners. While he made his way back to the waiting room, he lifted the full bags out of the bins and replaced them with fresh liners, stacking the full bags into the basket on top of his machine.

Fortunately, the patient in the emergency room had either been given pain relief or had passed out, and Fabio now had to side-step nurses who were assessing the other waiting patients.

From the shards of conversation he picked up, some sort of heavy container had tipped over in the loading dock.

As soon as he left the hospital, he went in search of a quiet place and found an area used for storage. He pushed the machine inside a large, low-ceilinged room, where it was pitch dark and no lights came on when he entered.

Here, he pulled on the surgical gown and cap and put the mask over his face.

If he remembered correctly, the officer's mess was just around the corridor. He also knew that if the ceiling was low, it meant there was a mezzanine level in between this and the second floor. He found the emergency box next to the door, switched on the little light it contained.

This was indeed a storage area, where boxed goods stood on pallets. He found the stairs to the next level in the far corner. They led to a loft where more boxes were stored.

This would do as a hiding place. No cameras that he could see, and there was enough air to dissipate any smell resulting from his stool-searching activities, which he might need to resume fairly soon. At least he had bags to hide the evidence and gel to clean his hands afterwards.

Food.

He pushed the machine to the bottom of the stairs, and went

back into the corridor.

The officer's mess was indeed around the corner. It was midnight, so the chairs stood on top of the tables for cleaning, and the light in the serving area was off.

However, these rooms always contained a small kitchenette with hot water and some snacks.

Fabio filled two containers with tea, grabbed a water can and put it in his pocket, and took several packets of biscuits, all while wearing the surgical gown and mask.

That was easy.

He didn't realise how thirsty he'd been until he got back to the loft and gulped both containers of tea and wolfed down all the biscuits.

Then he probed his stomach for the signs of needing to poop, but decided in the negative, so it was time for the next stage of his ridiculous plan. He needed to go to the entrance hall to the base to figure out how to get out of here.

Since a medical gown would not be suitable attire to go into that part of the base, he needed something else. He scoured the storage room and found a pallet that contained a stack of sheets of foam-core board—whatever they were used for. He used his nails to pry them loose from the plastic wrapping and carried one sheet into the hall, again hiding his face from the cameras, while pretending to be on his way to a construction site with that sheet.

The pressurised trucks would ultimately be his aim, but he needed someone with the authority to open the airlock. He also needed someone who could get him into Prometheus. Yeah, like that was ever going to happen.

This whole ridiculous plan just got a bunch more ridiculous.

But it really brought home to him that he couldn't do this himself.

Who was going to help him?

The people in the human rights delegation. Doric, perhaps.

Unfortunately, they were both in the Research base—and fortunately, there was a goods train.

Well, crap, he was in the wrong place, although he should probably check out a pressure suit because the train might not be pressurised.

The suiting room was on the other side of the hall, so Fabio walked between the trucks, carrying his sheet of board.

A group of three men in the suiting room said a quick hello, but otherwise paid him no heed.

Fabio grabbed a suit off the hooks, pulled it on, making sure to put the hood over his head, and left the room again, carrying his board.

But when he returned to the hall, an officer with a pad came up to him. He said, "I haven't seen you before. Have you submitted your departure and travel plan yet?"

"Um, I'm getting to that."

Fabio choose a random truck, leaned his board against the side, and then, because the officer was watching him, went up to the control room to supposedly submit his plans. He had no idea what to do, but he figured once he got nearer to the control room, he could find another way out of the hall that didn't catch the officer's attention.

Watched by the man, he went upstairs, and found the control room, where a number of officers sat in a circle around a table as if they were in a meeting. It was not very busy in the hall at all, so this was probably the time that they held their staff meetings.

None of them had noticed Fabio at the door.

They were all looking at a display pad in the middle of the table, which projected a hologram of a curved line crossing through a field of objects. Fabio recognised the signs astronomers used for Jupiter and each of its moons.

"It will be at least six months before it's here," one of the officers said, pointing at an entry point into the Jupiter system. "That is the last estimate. It's the earliest we can deploy surface-based weapons."

"I wish they would stop changing their mind about this," another officer said. "The troops are understandably nervous.

We've told them that this is an exercise, but no one likes to be told that we don't know how long it's going to last."

"I agree that is becoming a problem," another man said. "I've heard that some of the people in the settlements have started to question this, too. If it's really an exercise, then why don't we know when it ends?"

The first man said again, "The truth will come out sooner or later. That is inevitable. You can't just hide an alien object coming at us. We can make excuses for the amount of military activity in the system, but eventually people are going to be able to see the bright moving star in the sky for themselves. They'll wonder what it is, and they'll blame us for not doing anything to stop this alien entity that can, by the amount of light it puts out, only be using antimatter for propulsion. They'll start questioning that soon enough."

"Let's hope by that time Preston has figured out how to deal with the inevitable panic. Let's hope that Sanchez appreciates what we're doing here for humanity and that we have no time for human-rights pansies. The human right is the right to live. We're fighting for that right."

Fabio's heart was thudding. Alien object? Intruder? Anti-matter engines? Enemy activity? Where was all this coming from? Nobody had said anything about this before.

One of the men noticed Fabio. He nodded at the door and the men turned around to look. They were a mixture of Flight and Force personnel. A Flight Lieutenant-Commander, a Force Lieutenant whom Fabio suspected was in control of operations in the hall today.

"Yes, can we help you?" he said.

Fabio said, "Um, I was going to submit my travel plan, but I've just realised I forgot my pad. I'll be back in a minute."

He ran down the corridor, and down the stairs and into the hall. From there, he ran back into the corridor, still wearing his suit liner.

Holy crap, holy crap, holy crap.

THALIA

"SURELY THEY WILL enquire after us," Sol said, from his position lying on his back on the top bunk. "Governor Law will be highly concerned about our safety and will demand to know where we are."

"I'm not sure about anything any more," Paul said. "They seem to have abandoned us."

"I don't even know what is supposed to be wrong," Jun said. "I said they can check my medicine. I have the documentation now."

Thalia was pacing around the room. She hadn't quite told all the other members of the delegation about the events in the examination room, about the nanometrics. They believed she was called back because she failed her medical test because of a misunderstanding.

"Just stop it," Paul said. "Your pacing is driving me nuts."

Thalia leaned against the wall, arms crossed over her chest. But standing still wasn't easy. When she was angry or upset, she needed to walk around.

She still couldn't get over the humiliation they had caused her, back in that room at the main base. Having to hand in her ID and having every detail of her personal life read. Then being frogmarched back to the truck and taken back to the research station in the company of armed guards, as if she were going to run anywhere on her own. Fortunately, the others hadn't seen that.

She jammed her hands in her pockets.

She said, "We are in a very isolated situation. I am not sure that it will be so easy for the Council Of Four to check out where we are."

"They know where we are."

"Yes, they do, but what are they going to do about us being detained, when the only way they can come to Calico is through the military and if they attempt anything else, the action will be considered hostile?"

"I still don't understand what they said to you Thalia," Sol said. "They have no reason to retain us in this room and I haven't heard one good excuse for them to do so."

"I don't think it's about us. Something is going on outside," Jun said. "I could see it before they cut off access. There was so much activity on the other side of the base with long tubes, like they're building a rocket launch installation. Maybe they don't want the new people to find out we're here. Or maybe they don't want us to see whatever they're doing over there."

"Then why did they plan our visit during the time of a major military exercise?" Thalia said.

"Why do you keep changing the subject, when we ask you about what happened in that room?" Soul said.

"Yes, that's what I would like to know," Paul said. "What happened? Because something did. You were all defensive and your story doesn't add up."

They were both looking at her, and Thalia felt the heat rising in her cheeks. Clearly there was no way to get out of this.

"They took me aside, because they say I have nanometrics," she said in a low voice.

"What?" Jun said. "Do they have any proof?"

"They say they do. They showed me a scan where all my blood veins light up in white. That's proof, apparently. I really don't know anything about it, nor how easy it would be to fake an image like that."

Jun said, "And that is a reason to refuse us entry? Don't they know that loads of people have enhancements these days?" As the youngest in the group, he had some enhancements, like muscle stimulants, which required him to take his medicines. Paul's living tattoos, too, were a form of enhancement.

Thalia shrugged, feeling ever more confused and disturbed. "They think because I have this, I'm a spy sent by goodness knows who."

"That's rubbish," Sol said.

"That's what I said, too," Thalia said. "I haven't been sent by anyone."

He snorted. "What utter rubbish. Nanometrics is advanced, expensive technology. Who would use that on some random person who is not your target and has not been told that they have it? I really don't get it."

But Thalia remembered seeing the image on the screen, where all her veins were outlined in bright white. She had seen this before, in articles about spying and human augmentation, complete with pictures that showed what all these various conditions looked like from a medical perspective. She had been reading about things ISF did to its workers. Unless that image was faked—which was always a possibility—she really did have nanometrics.

And most disturbingly, Paul wasn't saying anything. Paul, who had more intimate knowledge of her medical details than she liked, simply because he had always come to the hospital for Kat.

He gave a barely perceptible nod, and finally started speaking.

"Everyone was singing her praises, but I never trusted that Dr Crawford."

"She saved our lives!"

"Yes, but the rumours that she worked for Allion were very strong."

"People saying those things were just jealous of her success and reputation."

"This suggests otherwise."

"Oh, you can't seriously suggest that just for some lame reason yet to be determined, she spiked me with nanometrics just so that she can spy on me years later, in case I might do something she's interested in?"

"Not just you. Here was an excellent opportunity. Three women from highly ranked families willing to spend a lot of money to nurse you three back to health. If you recovered, you would go on to influential careers. Who wouldn't like a secret window into the life of a political activist, a company executive and a highly ranked military officer?"

Thalia opened her mouth, but she shut it again.

What he said made more sense than anything else she had heard. "But why?"

The whole thing chilled her to the bone. She clamped her arms around herself at the idea that she might have been *violated* with intelligent chemicals while she lay half dead and broken in hospital.

"Why did Allion do anything? They're big in human augmentation. At the time of the accident, the company's settlements were being eradicated. A cornered cat makes strange jumps."

Thalia snorted. "I don't know if I believe this. If Dr Crawford did any such thing, she would have done it for my health. Nanometrics have lots of other uses."

"Yes, but the main reason why the technique isn't widely used is that there are ways in which nanometrics can be used to spy remotely. And this is also the reason that ISF doesn't want people with nanometrics on their bases."

"Well, it's not used in that way in my case, *if* what they say is true. I don't know any spies and Allion is dead. I just fight for human rights. I want people to be treated fairly everywhere. And I'm going to demand to speak to base command and tell them that if they don't want us on the base, they should send us home."

CHAPTER THIRTEEN

BY GIVING IN TO HIS CURIOSITY, Fabio had probably blown his chance to escape through the loading dock, as much of a long shot as that might have been in the first place.

On the way back to his hideout, he noticed an increased number of people just standing around doing nothing. In all probability, someone had raised the alarm and they were on the lookout for him.

Any time now he was going to be pulled up and asked for ID and that would be the end of his adventure.

He needed a plan.

Back in his hideout, he peeled off the hot and sweaty suit liner. It was good that he managed to get it, but if he wanted to go outside, he'd still need a suit and a helmet and a filled tank.

He was considering using the goods train for the next stage in his plan, but he still didn't know if the tunnel was pressurised. On second thoughts, it probably was, because most things that would be transported—equipment, supplies like food—would respond poorly to being exposed to a vacuum. But the air quality would be very poor, so just the suit liner minus pressure suit might do, but he would need air.

He drank the remaining water and ate the remaining biscuits. There was still no sign of the reappearance of the implant.

So. The plan.

They were looking for him all around this part of the base, expecting him to turn up in the entry hall, since they knew he had stolen a suit liner and probably planned to steal a truck.

But the entry hall was not the only place where trucks were parked. At least one was always parked at the top of the research facility. That part of the base was not as busy and he knew it better. Also, if by some miraculous chance he managed to get out and inevitably got caught, everyone involved would be an ISF officer, they would think he was an idiot and he would simply be handed back to Banparra and no one outside the base would ever know.

He needed to create a publicity fuss outside the base, outside ISF preferably. He needed people who could testify that he was right about his treatment and the treatment of other dissenters in the force. He needed to free the Council Of Four delegation as well, even if only for the reason that those people had to have some form of diplomatic immunity. And publicity, if anything happened to them. He was a nobody and no one would care if he disappeared. If they disappeared, there would be hell to pay.

Yes, that was a plan.

So it was back into the sweaty suit, and yes he had to pull the hood over his head, even if he'd attract some strange looks. Hopefully the security cameras wouldn't recognise him when wearing the hood. He did consider wearing the surgical mask, but he'd attract even more attention when wearing that, so sadly he had to take the risk. That, and walk very quickly.

And hope that he could figure out how to get into the cargo containers, shut the door for the inside and operate the train at the same time. He hoped he was right about the location of the train stop.

He tucked the water container in a pocket on his suit liner, because he could probably fill it somewhere. Some extra biscuits would be nice, but a secondary consideration.

He went into the corridor and turned left to walk past the workshops, where someone in a suit liner would not attract so much attention. But he was nervous, actively avoiding people by ducking into doorways when someone was walking the other way, waiting until they passed before continuing.

He arrived at the place where the train stop was meant to be, and crap, it was hidden behind a sliding door. He could open that door with his pad, but he didn't have his pad, because someone had removed it from his duffel.

Well, crap, what now?

The access was in a corridor where quite a number of people walked past, so he couldn't even fiddle with the panel.

And dammit, people noticed him, because he drew some raised eyebrows. This required crude measures.

He turned around and went back through the maintenance corridor. He remembered having ducked into a workshop where a variety of tools were stored.

He found the workshop, and a laser cutter.

It was a heavy thing with a big battery on a trolley, which he wheeled to the door. A storage rack held folded safety screens, and he grabbed one of those as well.

Like all rooms, this workshop had an emergency cabinet next to the door, which included two pressure suits and an air tank. He stacked those onto the trolley, and then went up to the cargo bay door dragging all his gear. Holy crap, he was sweating so much in that ridiculous suit.

He waited until not many people were around, and then set up the safety screen as he had seen maintenance crew do on other occasions.

Inside the space sheltered by the screen, he started up the laser.

"Hey, excuse me, what do you think you're doing?" someone asked.

The voice belonged to a man in overalls with the tag Lt. Fawcett.

"The door is jammed, sir," Fabio said. "They asked me to open it. Lots of stuff needs to be taken up to research."

The officer nodded and continue walking.

Sweat rolled down Fabio's back. It wouldn't be long before someone discovered that he was pulling all this bullshit and unmask him.

But the laser cut through the lock in no time, and Fabio was able to push the door open. He left the screen and the laser cutter in the corridor, picked up the suit and the tank, went inside and pushed the door shut as far as it would go. The light came on automatically.

He found himself on a small platform similar to the one he had seen at research, where a carriage waited with the cargo door open.

He went to the panel on the side and set the destination for Research, and the departure time within two minutes.

Then he pulled on the suit, put on the helmet, connected the tank—phew, cool air flowed into his lungs—climbed into the carriage, and pushed the door shut.

Oh boy, it got dark inside that thing, and he just remembered that he didn't like small, dark and stuffy places.

Why wasn't this train moving yet?

There were footsteps in the corridor, and a man's voice shouted muffled words.

Come on, come on.

He could hear someone pushing open the door to the platform. "He's not here."

And then the carriage jerked into motion. Thank the heavens. Although the people back there wouldn't take long to figure out that he was on the carriage.

It went with incredible speed. Very soon it grew quite hot inside the little cubicle.

Fabio lay flat in complete darkness, while every bump in the track made a tube under his back bite into his skin. He really didn't like this. How long was this going to take?

When he went up the mountainside with Doric in the truck, they had been driving for almost an hour, he guessed.

The carriage rumbled and rumbled. Fabio tried to calm himself by imagining getting to freedom. However he would achieve that, wherever he would go.

But while he lay there all the memories came back to him.

Red plains of sand on Mars. His hands on the wheel of a truck, his attention half on a screen that displayed the expected fallout from the explosion caused by the asteroid hit. The flashing danger zone was getting too close for comfort.

The landscape was so desolate, he could barely believe that people lived out here. Maybe someone had been telling him lies and there was really no one out here and this was all a big joke.

But he had to make sure.

He had been driving for a while on the plain when white dots in the red sand heralded the first settlement. This one was a jumble of pressurised tents sitting in a little dip. The tents were made from transparent material and Fabio could see people moving within. Some were agricultural tents on the back of a flatbed truck. Most of the tents were connected to each other through inflatable tubes.

Personnel carriers and cargo trucks sat at the edge of the settlement. A couple of people in suits came out when he pulled up next to them.

He couldn't hear what they said, because their receivers were set to a different frequency from the one on his truck.

He put on his helmet and let himself sink onto the red sand.

He held up his hands. "I'm Fabio Velazquez. I have important information for you."

He had no idea if anyone could hear him. The people seemed friendly, beckoning him to come inside their interconnected settlement. The tent even had a proper airlock with stands for suits and tanks. The floor inside was covered in rugs where people sat around low tables.

They all looked up when he came in. By far the majority of

them were women. The few men in the room were very black-skinned, all of them with bald heads.

Aggregates. Half-men, half-machine.

He didn't think he'd ever seen one. ISF considered the creation of aggregates illegal and refused to afford them status as human beings. But here they were mingling with people.

One of the women got up and came to him. She was slender, dark skinned as most of the women were, and had long sleek black hair.

"You must be Fabio," she said.

"I wonder how you guessed."

She smiled, and the glimmer in her eyes, the intelligence, the wit and humour of it, went straight into his heart.

"These are my community. These are the free rangers of Mars. My name is Priya Anyanda."

The carriage was slowing down.

Inside the cramped space of the cargo hold, Fabio managed to worm his legs under him, so he sat in a crouching position, ready to jump out when the lid opened. He disconnected the air tank from the harness and held it by the valve handle. Once he was inside the research base, he wouldn't need the tank, but it was the only thing he had that he could use as a weapon, in case someone was waiting for him.

But when the train stopped and the lock clicked and he could push open the door, it was to an empty loading dock where the light came on as soon as he clambered from the carriage.

He took off the helmet and listened—all was quiet.

Then he took off the rest of his gear, because the suit was cumbersome and heavy and he couldn't possibly run while wearing it.

The big room with the workstations next to the lift foyer was filled with light and a few people were busy at work, most with their backs to the door. A clock on the far wall proclaimed it to be the late shift, so Doric would be in her room.

Fabio ran across to the lift and went down to the floor where his room was. He found his duffel and his clothes pretty much untouched. That was something at least. He also took the harness and full air tank from the emergency cupboard inside the door, because he was likely to need them. Then he went onto the corridor—

—Straight into someone who looped an arm around his neck and a hand over his mouth.

"Mmmmm!" Fabio said, trying to worm the harness and air tank free so that he could swing them around.

The tank connected with the person's knees. He—because it was a man—toppled sideways, hanging onto Fabio's suit liner.

Fabio swung the tank again. It glanced off the side of the man's head.

He crumpled onto the floor. The man wore a tag that said Private First Class J. Dickson. Fabio seemed to remember having seen him before, although he couldn't remember when.

Shit. Now he was in real trouble.

Fabio grabbed the man under his shoulders and dragged him into the room. Fortunately, the floor was smooth, but he was heavy and Fabio was neither big nor well-muscled.

He did a quick check of the man's pockets and found an access card. That was going to be useful. He also removed the man's pad, since it would tell the superiors where he was.

Then he left the room, pulled the door shut and ran through the corridor while carrying all his stuff.

The access card let him through the barrier at the end of the hallway. So far, so good. But when he knocked on the door to the apartment where the delegation had been staying when he first found them, there was no reply.

Fabio didn't want to shout, in case he had an audience. But the private's card didn't open the door.

Shit.

He'd used his PCD before, and it would have remembered the sequence, but they'd taken it off him when they took him to the main base.

Maybe he could do something with the Private's pad. To his horror, the charge had almost run out.

He rummaged in his duffel for the illegal data patch that had opened the door previously. It had remembered the sequence, and when he attached it to the Private's pad, it sent a command to the door before starting to flash with the need to be charged.

Phew.

The door sprang open. It was pitch dark on the other side so he flicked on the light on his suit liner.

The apartment seemed abandoned, the beds neatly made, the bags gone. But as soon as Fabio stepped into one of the bedrooms, he sensed the presence of people. Also, there was no way that an ISF recruit, no matter what rank, would do such a sloppy job at making a bed.

"It's me, Fabio," he said in a low voice. "I need to get out of this place. I figure you'd be interested in getting out, too."

A soft sound came from deep within the darkness of the room. Fabio grabbed his air tank, ready to lash out if necessary.

But it was Thalia, coming out from under the bed. Her face was pale.

The light in the room flicked on and someone shut the door behind him. Jun Hasegawa. Paul Armitage let himself down from the top of the bunk bed.

"How in the hell did you get here?" Sol Whitaker asked.

The whole delegation was here.

"They don't call me the escape artist for nothing. I've come to get you out of here." Now *that* concept felt familiar and fit him like a glove. That was what he did, help people escape.

"Where are you going to take us? There is nothing out there except empty space, and lots of military installations."

"You'll be in the company of the biggest bullshit merchant in the universe. I can talk my way into anything." Sanchez's office, the Allion inner sanctum, anything.

"Who are you working for? Are you a spy?"

"They call me a spy, but I work for no one, except for the

oppressed and neglected. They don't know what to do with me, but I am their conscience. I tell them you can't treat people this way. When I was placed with Doric—"

Paul's eyes widened. "Wait. You said Doric? Katarina Doric?"

"Yes, anything wrong with her?"

"She's my wife."

KATARINA

AN ESCAPE FROM THE BASE needed to be planned.

The idea of running away filled her with despair.

It would ruin her career—

If she ever had any career to speak of, after she discovered what ISF had done at the asteroid belt.

Sanchez pretended he cared, but did he really care about what went on in the Outer System, what injustices were perpetrated in an area he couldn't control and where he was little respected?

Or did he just care about the public image of the force, only fixing up problems when they became widely known to the masses on Earth?

Was any of this worth ruining her life?

She should have dropped out of the force and found a civilian job so that she could be with Paul. But somehow, she'd had the illusion that a military career was important to her, and that she couldn't serve humanity in any other way. She remembered seeing Paul's face when she told him that she was going back.

"But why?" he'd asked.

She had told him some blather about honour and wasting the years they'd spent on her training. Not that ISF cared about that.

No, it was really because she felt that she was not proper military unless she followed in her father's footsteps, and she could feel her father's disapproval if she was going to retire and speak of doubts, or be dishonourably discharged while having exposed the things that she couldn't hide.

Of course it didn't mean that the entire force was bad. There were many good people, but what had happened on Mars was despicable, and the fact that people in the Jupiter system, like Banparra, were covering it up was even more despicable.

Preston should face a court for what he had done. But back then, she'd not had the weight of evidence or the authority needed to start that process. Not just that, she didn't have the resilience, nor the desire to spend the rest of her working life in court.

Now, accused of being a spy, framed for something she knew nothing of, she was at the end of the line.

Maybe sometime in her past she would have chosen to toe the line and look away from how an organisation was going to justify the deaths of thousands of innocent civilians for the sake of killing a competitor, but now that she was older and no longer trying to prove something, she wanted to stay true to what she had seen.

Heck, even Paul was true to his ideals. He must have spent years doggedly chasing after her, ferreting out possible places where she could be. For once, she should turn around and stop running, stop pretending that all was well with the force. The cancer could not be cut from within.

Alone in her cabin, in the depths of despair, she made the decision to run, and once that decision was made, it flowed into making a plan to carry it out.

She needed a truck, and once she got a truck, she could probably make it to Prometheus, where they were unaware of the situation, and if they were aware of it, if she brought the COF delegation as her shield, then no one would blatantly fire at them.

But first she needed to open her door.

That part was easy, because the locks inside the base were

shockingly bad, even if living in an isolated community in itself was a type of security. If someone stole something, you knew it was on base, and you could gradually search out everyone until you found out who did it.

This was not going to be one of those situations, where everybody was mobilised in order to scour the base for the missing object or person. Because she was going to escape from the base using the truck up at the entry tube.

So she used her pad to open the door.

While her pad was turned on, a general message scrolled over the screen: *Prisoner on the loose in main base. Fabio Velazquez, slight build, dark hair, last seen wearing unmarked Sarajevo fatigues, also seen wearing scrubs entering the hospital, also seen wearing overalls in the entry hall carrying a sheet of board, also seen performing fake maintenance on a wall panel.*

Katarina grinned. He was certainly resourceful.

Do not engage in fight. Capture and return to command unharmed.

That was quite odd, because Banparra was not known for being lenient with deserters. Either this man carried protection from another authority or he had some information they wanted—which fit with the way they had tried to wipe him.

Damn, she should have seen that earlier. But now it was too late, and they couldn't help each other.

She had maps. She had communication equipment, she had supplies from past field trips. When locking her in her room, Banparra had disabled her authorisation to carry a weapon, and to be honest most people in the base weren't armed. Weapons did funny things to pressure domes.

The truck would have a weapon, although nothing too drastic.

Katarina packed a bag with all the things that would be useful and that she could carry. Her warm clothes, outside boots, her suit liner, her pad and PCD, even if neither had full connectivity right now. A full water bottle. Her personal breathing mask. First aid kit including radiation pills and protective cream.

Then she opened the door to her room, checked if any of the senior officers from the new troops were in the hallway—which they weren't—and left the room.

She shut the door behind her, and ran towards the stairs.

CHAPTER FOURTEEN

WELL, IT WAS KIND OF ANNOYING that Doric was Paul's wife, and that he wouldn't leave without her—which was understandable. Even if Fabio had considered clueing Doric in to his plan, he doubted they had the time to find and rescue her, and, if they did, her presence might set off all kinds of alarm bells, because of her rank, and would she even want to come?

"I've come here especially to get her out, and I'm not leaving without her, now that I know for certain that she's on the base, and now that I know she's in trouble." Because Fabio had also told them of the scan and that she appeared to have nanometrics. But none of the delegation seemed to be surprised about this.

Sol said, "Mate, we may just have to leave without her, because things would be even worse if we're caught."

"You can go without me."

But then Jun Hasegawa said, "I know where her room is."

He held up his pad with the map. As it turned out, the accommodation quarters of the research base weren't very big, and the officer rooms were just on the other side of another barrier across the corridor.

No time to argue. "All right, let's go then."

They ran along the corridor. Fabio checked over his shoulder, but no one had yet discovered Private Dickson locked in Fabio's room.

The sliding barrier to the next section, though, was locked and remained so, even with Dickson's card or Fabio's pad.

Sol inspected the door.

"What sort of lock is it?" Paul asked.

Fabio said, "Never mind. I don't think we have time for subtlety. Stand back."

He hefted his air tank above his shoulder, and swung it into the door. The metal just bounced off, nearly knocking Fabio over.

"Let me do that," Sol said, with the implied word *midget*.

But no matter how hard he swung the tank, Sol couldn't open the door either.

Fabio's mind raced. The man he had locked into the room hadn't been carrying a weapon, had he? He was certain he would have noticed it. If he'd noticed it, he would not have left it.

But wait.

Something else bubbled up from his memory of obsessively reading the safety instructions. During a pressure or air quality emergency, all the doors would shut, but if there was a military attack warning, the big connecting doors would open. How did one simulate a military attack warning? It probably needed to be given centrally through command. Could he find the code? Damn, there was no time for this.

He put his fingers against the door lock.

Sol, Paul and Thalia were checking out the door seals and whether they could trick the door into opening by sliding something underneath.

He could sense data streaming through the lock, but, lacking technology, he had nothing to feed it.

"Here." Jun passed him a pad.

Fabio stared at lines of code on the screen.

"Passcodes," Jun said. "Try them."

Holy crap. Wherever had he gotten those?

Fabio went to the side panel. He punched the first code—it didn't work. The second didn't work either, nor did the third. But when he punched in the fourth one—

All the lights went off.

"Fuck," someone said in the darkness.

And then a small hiss and a rumbling sound.

Thalia said, "It's opening. How did you do that?"

"Just random luck," Jun said.

Fabio suspected there was more to it. He was beginning to like the quiet youngster.

When the door had moved up far enough, he ducked underneath into another dark corridor. An alarm was going off and a light flashed at the end.

He hoped someone figured out that a malfunction had triggered the external military attack alarm, because otherwise things would get nasty.

Everyone followed him. Doric's room should be just inside this door.

But when they got there, no one answered.

"Try opening the door," Thalia said.

Fabio did. It slid aside.

It was dark inside the room. The light filtering in from the corridor hit a bed with a messy covering and a cupboard with the door open, the shelves almost empty. Katarina Doric was not in her room.

"I think our bird has flown," Sol said.

"She's not dumb," Paul said, pride lacing his voice.

"That's all very well, but now we really can't wait any longer," Fabio said.

"I'm not leaving Katarina." Paul's expression was haunted.

"She's looked after herself for a long time," Sol said. "I agree, we need to go, or there won't be any escape attempt and nobody will ever find us again. Including Katarina."

Paul was very unhappy, but he was smart enough to realise that Sol was right.

Sol held a light and led the group to the end of the corridor, up a flight of stairs. Into a corridor with rows of black-painted doors on either side. Up another flight of stairs. Another corridor, this one with poorly maintained walls and floors, where trails of rust ran from the ceiling and condensation had burnt rust-coloured patches into the linoleum. Fabio knew that inside these bases, rust was always the worst in places close to the airlocks. Which meant that they were close to the top floor.

The alarm was still ringing and it wouldn't be long before people turned up. Already the sound of voices echoed from down-stairs. Those would be the troops that were housed in the corridor with Fabio.

A woman's voice called out, "Quick, this way."

A narrow side passage split off to the left. A door at the end of this passage had opened, and a woman stood in the opening, backlit by blue-white light.

Thalia called out, "Kat!"

Paul ran into the passage first, followed by Thalia. Fabio followed Sol, having trouble keeping up while carrying his tank, duffel, suit and Jun's pad.

At the end of the corridor they came to a kind of control room with many blinking lights. A soft green-white glow of light illumi-nated banks of control panels around the walls. The room held a single chair, empty. In the middle of that room a narrow winding staircase went up into the ceiling.

Fabio, Thalia, Sol and Jun went in, while Paul hugged Katarina at the door.

"I thought they'd killed you," he said.

"They damn near did."

Once in the room, different sounds drifted from downstairs: the sound of an engine, the whine of maintenance equipment. Cold air wafted from upstairs. There must be another way of getting to the surface.

Sol led the way up the stairs.

He stopped a few steps from the top. Beyond his broad back,

Fabio glimpsed the side of a truck of the type Major Doric had used to pick him up.

Katarina pushed past him and under Sol's arm. In a few quick steps, she crossed to the truck, climbed up on the step and opened the door. She gestured to him.

"Come. The rest of you, pick up a pressure suit over there."

Fabio ducked under Sol's arm and looked into the hall. The hall was much bigger than he had expected. Trucks and more trucks. Crates of newly arrived supplies. Not a living soul in sight.

Fabio ran.

At the door of the truck, Doric grabbed his arm to help him climb in. Her grip was strong and reminded him of something else. Hauling children into a vehicle. Mothers passing their offspring into his hands. Priya sat at the wheel yelling at him. *Hurry up!*

A big menacing cloud of dust on the horizon.

Some of the settlers had insisted on packing their tents and were still hauling everything into their vehicles. Fabio hoped they'd make it to safety in time. At training they always said, *Space warfare is boring. Once you can see the threat, it's much too late.*

Where was safety? He had planned to take this convoy to the nearby dome of Johnson base.

He clambered into the truck next to Priya. The back seats in the cabin were full of women with children on their laps. Silent, watching him with big, frightened eyes.

He pulled the door shut.

Go, go, go.

Fabio sank into the first available seat while the others each grabbed a pressure suit and pulled on the bottom half, because that was the easiest way to carry the damn thing.

Thalia pushed Jun up the ladder into the truck cabin. They both went to the back of the cabin.

The next one in was Paul. He already had his helmet on and promptly tripped over the bar just inside the door and almost went sprawling over Fabio's knees. He sat right behind Katarina, and put his hand on her shoulder.

Sol came in last. He ran from the stairs and simply jumped into the truck as if there was no height difference, carrying a bunch of equipment. Holy crap.

He shut the door behind him. First the outer door and then the inner door of the airlock.

Kat was going through the warming-up procedure for the truck's engine.

She shouted while not looking over her shoulder, "All of you, find a seat and sit down, in case things get nasty."

Fabio looked over his shoulder. Jun's face was pale.

"Hang on, where are we going?" Thalia asked.

"There is a shack about a third of the way to Prometheus. It's a safe spot for surface crews in trouble or for pilots to land safely in case of engine trouble. It's well supplied with food and water and long-range communication equipment that I'm going to use to call for help."

"That's not going to be much use when they shoot us," Jun said, his eyes still wide.

"I'm banking on the very good chance that they won't shoot us."

"Why not? Any news we get out will look very bad for them."

"Even if they don't care about the bad publicity it would bring —and I think they do care—I also think we have something they want."

And they all looked at Fabio.

THE WATCHER

"THERE IS ACTION," VEGA SAID.

She looked at the circle of women standing around the projection table in the control centre of Juno Station. The room was shrouded in semidarkness, as the station was just about to come out of the shadow side of the planet. Outside the window, the misty horizon lit up in a pale blue haze.

"What do you mean?" asked Taura. "Can you see that the mindshards have moved?"

"They're still at the base, but I can feel their distress. We have to act now, rather than later."

"Any idea what happened?" asked Ybella, who was the operations manager of the station and as such hadn't been intimately involved with the planning as some of the others had. Although she grasped the concept of mindshards much better than Taura did, and possibly she could feel Vega's horror at waking up in the middle of her sleep cycle with all of her brain screaming at her, *I don't know anything about this. I haven't been treated. Why would I have nanometrics?*

"They've discovered the nanometrics."

"In all three women?"

"No, just the two of them on Io. Probably in the prisoner as well, but whatever strains of dendromers he's got, it's nothing to do with us."

"What are they going to do to the women?"

"Anything that comes into their dumb brains. ISF really has no comprehension of mindshard technology. They might try to wipe them or read them. They probably think they're spies and will try to read data that the women don't have."

"Can they?"

"If they know how, yes."

"Then they might discover us."

"The chance is very small, because these women don't know anything about us either. But eventually, ISF will discover us anyway. Once they really start looking. The only reason they haven't done so is that we've given them few reasons to look. But we're ready. We have a scenario for the inevitable discovery."

Which, as Vega remembered with a shudder, involved evacuating the base, which would be a huge risky operation, especially since they had few places to move fifteen thousand people to, and the two ships available to do evacuations could only carry a hundred at a time.

"I'm more concerned about the prisoner. We can't risk losing him. We must send people immediately."

"I've been saying so all along." Taura sounded almost relieved. "Can I assemble a crew now? The *Thor IV* is in dock and all charged up. We only need to load two moths and we're underway."

"Yes. Take pilots. Take marksmen. Take Olek and his crew." Those were the best and toughest aggregates.

"Explosives?"

"Yes, take them, too."

"Does this mean that you are now finished with the mindshard stuff?"

"Yes, because the three are in the position we want. We just need to wait until they leave the base and pick them up. And no, because we still have the third mindshard. She's in an interesting position, because she has a very close relationship with Governor Law. She is highly likely to create a distraction."

Vega touched the surface of the table and a three-dimensional projection of Calico Base sprang into the air. "I'm sending everyone the details about where they are and where we are likely to be able to pick them up. Remember that there will be no revealing of who we are. We have one chance to rescue the whole of Allion. This is it."

Everyone dispersed, leaving Vega alone at the table. She stared at the projection, willing with all her mind to talk to the three women she had never met. All three would be feeling her distress now, and because of the Table of Prioritised Emotions, they would be looking for something to do to help. Because that was what you did when a close friend was in trouble. You fought; you asked questions.

Yes, do you hear that, pampered rich girl with the influential aunt? Ask questions. Many of them. I know you want to, because you have heard nothing from your friends, and because you probably have seen things that make you wonder.

Yola had been one of her mentors, almost like a mother. When she was stranded on Ganymede after the purge of Allion, she had continued to work under her assumed identity while keeping in contact with Juno Station. That in itself carried a high degree of risk.

"Dr Laura Crawford" had told Vega of the three women who were all in the hospital as a result of an accident and the amazing opportunity to connect the four of them with nanometrics.

For years, Vega had felt the joy, frustration and anger of these women while they went about their normal lives. With the same nanometrics strain, she had tracked all three of them, never interfering with their lives.

Once the dendromer molecules had been prepared, the procedure of inserting nanometrics in the blood stream was simple.

Often the receiver experienced a gradual change in character afterwards. They became more idealistic, with a heightened sense of what was fair treatment. They became less likely to follow orders.

Thalia Hasegawa had never been terribly interested in human rights before. After all, why should someone from such a rich family care about the poor sods who signed up for service?

Before the accident, Jaykadia Law had been a vapid creature, caring more about material goods than her parents. Now she had developed a good relationship with her aunt and her dearest wish was to be liked by as many of her workers as possible.

And Katarina Doric, she had taken a bit of convincing. She was a very strong character indeed.

ISF had offered her honourable discharge with full retention of her salary. She had not wanted to re-enlist in the military after she recovered. She had married and had asked for a civilian job. But gradually, she had seen that the ones who could make the most difference were the ones who could stay hidden within the structures that were the cause of their grief and those who made changes from within. So she had re-enlisted because part of the ISF culture sickened her. It was about jobs for the boys and getting your fingers into as many pots as possible. That was not the force she loved and respected, and her new placing gave her the opportunity to change it from within.

CHAPTER FIFTEEN

THE ENGINE STARTED UP with a flashing of lights on the truck's control panel.

Katarina pushed her hood down and affixed an earpiece to her ear. She typed in codes that would ensure the opening of the main airlock.

Green lights flickered.

With a jolt, the truck started moving. Kat turned on the surrounding viewscreens and suddenly Fabio had the illusion of sitting in a glass cubicle.

There was no activity in the docking area, and light was low, glinting off the sides of trucks and packaging crates.

They passed several rust-streaked posts and the wall of the hall, also streaked with rust. Kat typed on the screen and listened on her earpiece.

The airlock worked painfully slowly. First, the inner door opened and Thalia drove the truck through. No one said anything while the inner door closed and the air was sucked out. Then the outer door opened a crack. Fabio expected the wan sunlight or red-hued Jupiter-shine to come in, but the widening crack between the doors remained dark.

Crap. It was the time of the midday eclipse when for two hours, Io moved in the huge shadow of Jupiter.

The door continued opening to pitch darkness. Fabio couldn't even see stars. In the glow of the truck's headlights, small sparkles of light twinkled like falling snow in reverse. Sulphur dioxide sublimating back into the air in the relative warmth of the head-lights. The ground was covered in fine white dust from the snowed-out atmosphere.

"We're out," Kat said, her voice soft.

No one said anything for fear of being heard.

The rear viewscreen showed the view of the lit airlock narrowing as the doors closed. The only light came from the head-lights outside and a tiny green light above the truck's airlock door.

Katarina gunned the engine and, within a minute, they were bouncing over the rubber road, much rougher at this speed. She studied a map, and after a while turned into a side road, which was unpaved and much rougher. The going was slow, with the only light provided by the truck's headlights. It was so dark it was scary.

Fabio wondered how long it would be before it got light again.

"Now, tell us why you are so valuable to ISF," Katarina said.

"I don't know," Fabio said. It was getting cold in this damned truck.

"That's what politicians always say," Katarina said. "We are not politicians and we won't fall for that."

"I really don't know."

"Then why is there a special order against your name not to kill you?"

"I said I don't know. You can read my files, I can't. I don't remember. Why did you come in to interfere with my medical anyway?"

"Because there is a special order against my name, too. Because I applied to have you on my team and they granted me my wish. Because if anyone has a special note against their name, it usually means that someone will try to make their life difficult and you might not actually get to Research. Because I thought you were going to be a messenger or an ally. But you're not. You did something on Mars."

"All I remember is that I learned that ISF was sending an asteroid to strike Mars, and I learned that the area of impact was going to be fairly close to Johnson base. I asked about the civilians in that area and I was told not to interfere."

"Yes, that applied to me, too," Katarina said.

"I applied for my leave and went to warn those people. I saved a lot of them when the asteroid hit, and after the hit, because of the snow . . ."

She nodded.

Fabio couldn't see her face.

"Then I tried to take the people to Johnson, but we found the base in disarray. One of the domes was broken. First I thought that this was from the weight of snow, but—"

Another memory flooded back.

He remembered coming back to the dome after the full effect of the impact had rolled over the area. Johnson had been covered in a thick layer of snow, but the resulting wind and shockwave had kept the tops of the domes clear. So he'd been surprised when he came in leading all those women and children, finding the pressure lost, people dead and dying on the ground.

Were the domes breached through the shockwaves?

Surely one of the domes was still intact?

He led the group through empty corridors, cumbersome as it was to walk for long distances in suits designed to do in situ maintenance work.

Then they entered a small dome that had housed a public open space. Snow covered the ground, benches and planter boxes, and the palms and plants had all frozen.

A group of people came in from the other side, and by the patches on their suits, Fabio knew that they were ISF troops. The patrol leader carried a considerable weapon, a VF-class handheld cannon—model C3 or something similar—and Fabio remembered wondering why he'd be carrying a weapon like that into what was essentially a rescue situation. The rest of the patrol fanned out over the dome.

And then they noticed Fabio and his group.

Even though Fabio's suit had no connection to the soldiers', he sensed that "oh, fuck" moment as the troops stood and stared at them.

Two of the men raised weapons at the group of women and children. Fabio could barely believe his eyes.

He said to Katarina, in a low voice, "I saw troops firing at the survivors."

"Wait—you saw ISF personnel firing at civilians?"

"Yes."

"Did anyone try to stop them?"

"Who could stop them? I should have, but I'm skinny and I've never held a position where I would be allowed to take a weapon off the base. I was a coward, but I didn't want to be shot. So I ran. Sorry, I'm not sure what happened then or where the people I rescued went, or whether any of them got away. At some point I must have run into someone I knew or we couldn't go any further or . . ." He searched his memory but came up with nothing. That part had been a big hole where, clearly, some interaction with ISF was supposed to go.

But the soldiers had shot women and children. He remembered that.

Katarina nodded. "These were Allion people and they were witnesses. They had no vested interest in ISF and were not supposed to live to tell the tale. Some people in command call you the cause of the greatest fuck-up in military history. I struggled to see why, but now I understand. No one was supposed to live to tell the tale. Because of you, a fair number of people did. Some, within ISF, they could control, but others they could not. Some, even within ISF, they can't control anymore. We're sick to death of what this organisation has done in our name without our knowledge. Whoever decided to use the talks between ISF and Allion at

Johnson as an excuse to wipe out Allion is a criminal, and I would like to demonstrate that ISF is nothing like that."

"I am proud of you," Paul said. He placed his hands on his wife's shoulders from behind.

"Which is not a position that's going to make us very popular at Io," Fabio said.

"No, because that's the position of Sanchez, and he is the real enemy to many of these people."

"Wait—I discovered something when I was in the other part of the base."

He told them about the conversation he had overheard about the alien object coming towards the system.

Katarina Doric was silent through all of it and still didn't say anything when he had finished.

"I had heard rumours of this," she said finally. "I heard this from someone who judged it a crackpot theory."

"Wouldn't you know this, working in astronomy?" Thalia asked.

"Astronomy is a very big field, especially in the military. We are in what they call applied astronomy, that data would come in from defensive astronomy—which is only a small department—or exploration astronomy, depending on where this object was first discovered."

"Is it true, though, or just another smokescreen to justify the activities of certain people?"

"I don't know. We can only get the answers once we're out of here safely."

Then she spent some time fiddling with the communication equipment. Thalia and Sol composed a message to the Council Of Four assembly that Katarina sent, using the truck's long-range capability.

"Mind you, none of this is secret, so they will know where we are and will come after us as soon as they get a fix on the origin of the communication."

Fabio wondered whether they would make it to the shelter.

JAYKADIA

"YOU HAVE HEARD THIS—WHERE?"

Jaykadia's aunt had initially been annoyed to have been called out of a meeting, but that expression changed the moment Jaykadia had told her of the object she had seen on the screen.

Encouraged by her aunt's interest, she continued, "I thought it was part of the exercise, but I went to dig around a bit, and there has been talk of this object amongst amateur astronomers for a while, with a lot of speculation about what it could be."

"So it's real."

"It would appear so. I read one discussion where they spoke extensively about the possibilities. It's a point of light. It's coming in our direction. It's in interstellar space and currently just outside the solar system. It's moving very fast but has slowed down considerably, from a considerable fraction of light speed when they first discovered it to barely ten percent now. It's not moving in a direction that objects are known to move, and there is nothing out there that would cause an object to lose speed in the direction it's moving. Most importantly, because the light shows up in the visible spectrum, the prevailing opinion is that it's the output of an engine braking, and the only type of engine that produces that much visible light is one that uses antimatter. No known human technology has antimatter engines, or can propel a ship at those speeds, so this is why the *alien ship* possibility is the most commonly suggested."

"Hmmm." Her aunt raised her hand to her mouth. "Are they suggesting that people knew about this for a long time, yet no one has gone public with it?"

"I don't know about that, but I definitely think that the *occupation* of my maintenance sheds has something to do with this. I've kept a close eye on what they're doing, as you suggested, and it seems they're setting up a nerve centre for a major operation. I've also looked into satellite data and it seems they're building a launch installation on Io, and I wouldn't be at all surprised if that's why we haven't been allowed to speak to the delegation."

"Because they have unilaterally decided that an alien ship—or whatever it is—is hostile and therefore requires no consultation with us for them to shoot it out of the sky? Because clearly, if this is a ship, they plan no negotiation with it, and not only that, they plan to blow it up in or near our system, where we may be harmed by any fallout."

"I've never heard them say any of those things."

"No, but I can read between the lines. I think I shall cut my meeting short today and will request to speak with Preston as soon as possible. Thank you for letting me know about this."

"What do you want me to do about the people in my maintenance sheds?"

"What would you want to do?"

"Kick them out, obviously, because many of my engineers are very unhappy. *I* am unhappy. They treat me like I'm a child, circumventing questions, and every time I see those people I get this *Shouldn't you be with your mother?* look. We are spending a lot more time and money on maintenance, and some of our crawlers can't go out at all, because we can't maintain them properly, or we don't have anywhere for them to unload their harvest. Meanwhile, Preston has broken our trust—"

"That's it—trust. He has betrayed our trust. We are resilient and we're not crazy. We run commercial companies and commerce is a game of give and take. Sometimes you give more than you take, sometimes it's the other way around. But we are only prepared to play that game under the understanding of mutual trust."

Her aunt signed off, because she had a meeting to get back to, and Jaykadia stared unseeing at her screen.

Some would suggest that mutual trust had been broken after Mars.

There were many rumours about what happened, and few looked good for ISF, but for the practical people of the Outer System, having principles and objections was not a smart way to survive.

When you lived out here, you did what was necessary and got the supplies you needed, even if some of those supplies came from less reputable sources, because you had no other options.

That time was coming to an end.

What would you like to do? her aunt had asked.

She wanted them out of her sheds, and, failing that, she wanted to have an end date for this exercise, and if they couldn't give her one because it wasn't an exercise, she wanted formal declarations about what happened and what events led to the necessity of building weapons and why the population was told nothing about this.

But, oh, she knew Preston was a master in diversion and he would find something that justified his actions, hoping to bog down discussions in irrelevant minutiae while he continued doing exactly as he wanted.

He'd say, *I'll meet you next week*, not because he wanted to be formal and pretend to be well-prepared, but to buy himself another week of inaction in which he didn't have to move his troops.

It was infuriating.

And she was frankly pissed off that the military was playing games. Not only had they played games with her, but now they were playing games with everyone. Hell, if this really was an alien intruder, then everyone should know about it. Everyone in ISF *would* know about it.

So, back to that question, what was she going to do?

Her aunt had asked a taunting question in return, and that question, *What would you like to do?* almost sounded like an invitation.

Do whatever I've told you not to do, I'll pretend I didn't see it.

Do something rash, and we'll fix it up later.

You're young and prone to make hasty decisions. Go for it.

She could march off to the maintenance sheds and tell the ISF troops to get out, but they'd just laugh in her face. What was she to them? Just a young pretty face who happened to have inherited this company. Who didn't—at the heart of it—know what she was doing. Who wasn't part of the established elite, even if she came from the right family. People merely tolerated her as owner of Ganymede Mining. But listen to her, no, not even her own senior management would do that.

With exception of the workers. Maybe they just liked her because of the amusement factor, because they could see her trying so hard to fit the mould of the grey-faced men, trying to do things their way.

Maybe they just liked her because none of the other executives ever came to the suiting hall and never attempted to hear their concerns in person.

Whatever was the case, *those* people would do as she asked. And *they* were the ones with their fingers on the switches. They were the ones who opened doors—and shut them, because they knew how to do it—which the executives didn't—and because someone told them to do it. They operated huge lumbering mining crawlers. They controlled the fuel distribution and the power plant.

She had tried to be a good little girl and not upset anyone.

She was through with that.

If ISF could have an "exercise", she could have a "technical malfunction". Let's see how serious Preston was about this exercise, especially the timeliness of it. If it was really about this approaching ship or object, they would be on a strict time schedule, and any hitch would send him into her office immediately.

CHAPTER SIXTEEN

THE TRUCK BOUNCED OVER the uneven terrain.

It was so rough and noisy inside the cabin that no one spoke except a few occasional words, and even those needed to be shouted.

Fabio was tired. He couldn't remember when he last slept well. He kept drifting off, but the road was so bumpy that every time he dozed off, his head would connect painfully with a metal support strut next to his seat.

And when he closed his eyes, shards of memories crowded his mind.

Arriving at Johnson on Mars, and receiving an angry message from his superior officer. *I have informed the local authorities that you will not be allowed to travel outside the settlement, both for the sake of your safety and that of others.*

Well, they had attempted to keep him at the base, but obviously didn't know about his nickname. The "escape artist" had done his work. Yes, he was of slight build, and yes, windows really did need to be locked, even ones that only opened a crack. He'd boldly demanded a loan truck and had received one. He'd left the base before anyone had discovered that he was gone.

Then he remembered sitting down in the tent-village on colourful rugs with brown people who sat cross-legged on the floor. A couple of children—all girls of course—brought bowls made from a resin mixed with red Mars soil.

Priya sat next to him.

She was lively and bubbly and kept talking as the night progressed. He'd shown her the trajectory of the asteroid, and she had ordered everyone in the settlement to pack up. He asked her if she didn't need to pack and she said, "I travel light. Everything I have I can carry in a single bag."

"Me, too."

That was because he'd never been able to build up enough possessions.

"You travel a lot?" she asked.

He told her that he worked on an assignment in the asteroid belt and would probably work somewhere else afterwards.

If he was still welcome to come back after having left his position without permission.

And if he wouldn't end up in some military jail.

It got later and later. He ended up spending the night in her van, which was . . . interesting. He remembered the strange smell of the fabrics and oils and spices that she used.

In the morning, while they lazed together and he traced his finger over the curve of her dark-skinned shoulder, she said,

"If you travel to the Jupiter system, I have something that needs to be taken out there."

He remembered being puzzled why she asked. Didn't she have her own people? But he said he would take her thing, and then became alarmed as she returned with a container of dark fluid attached to a tube.

"Don't worry, it won't hurt," she said as she stuck plaster over his skin and told him not to touch it—because the patch itched.

The dark fluid dripped into his arm through the tube.

"It's a charged fluid that will interact with your nanometrics and will stay suspended in your blood for anywhere up to a year. Then it will flock together and form a biological capsule that will be invisible to scanners and will work its way up until it sits under your skin. It's quite easy to extract it from there."

"What's in it?"

"You will find out."

And, as Fabio remembered, as his head banged against the metal strut once more, he hadn't yet found out anything. He assumed that this had been more than a year ago and that the thing he'd extracted from under his skin—that still showed no signs of reappearing—was it.

He'd been able to piece together that Mars was much longer ago, and that he had somehow managed to sail through all the medical procedures without the capsule once triggering a question. Because it was undetectable. And might have been lodged deeper inside his body at the time.

But what did it contain?

Something that was important, and something that Priya was willing to defend unto death.

"Crap," Katarina said in a way that made no bones about the fact that real trouble lay ahead.

"What?" Paul had also been dozing in his seat behind her.

She nodded at a screen in front of her and Paul looked over her shoulder.

"Oh fuck," he said.

Sol got up from his seat to look at the screen, while bracing himself on the metal struts.

"The chase has begun," he said.

Fabio leaned over. The screen displayed a grey landscape with the road clearly visible. The truck was a red dot in the middle. But another red dot moved just inside the edge of the screen.

"We're about fifteen minutes from the storage bunker," Katarina said. "And the reason I wanted to go there is that the depot contains some serious weaponry. We may need it."

"Has the Council Of Four responded yet?" Thalia asked.

"Just an acknowledgement, but I'm sure the wheels are spinning and the engine is running."

JAYKADIA

THE MOMENT THE POWER went off in the maintenance sheds at the Ganymede Mining Company, Jaykadia's screen lit up with messages.

First there were the red flashing warnings.

There was no power to the life support systems and air quality would start to deteriorate significantly within two hours. There was also no water, since there was no power to the pumps. *Immediate action needed.*

Yup.

She swiped the warnings aside and then counted down before she received a message from whoever was in command of the ISF troops in the sheds.

But first another, unrelated message arrived: from her aunt. The COF assembly had received a message from the delegation to Io. They asked for assistance to leave Io. Apparently, ISF accused them of being spies.

Her aunt said, *We've issued a general alarm, and a vessel has responded.*

Jaykadia asked if there was any response from Base Commander Banparra, and her aunt told her there wasn't, but that

Preston had sent a message that he was "disappointed" in the low
level of trust displayed by the civilian population.

Had Preston done anything recently to inspire that trust?

And now a message came from the man himself: to come to the
maintenance sheds immediately because *our operations are severely
hampered by a power outage that is caused on your end of the supply.*

Right, let's play this game.

Jaykadia dressed in her overalls and went out, through the residential and commercial areas of the settlement, who were unaware
of any power games being played out over their heads.

She stopped at the entrance to the workers' suiting and change
room.

She'd heard that people still came here, despite the fact that
there was no work to be done, but she hadn't expected the cheer
from all those people, mostly men, mostly much older and bigger
than her, who had been sitting in the room talking.

When she came in, they all cheered and clapped.

It almost choked her up. She had to be doing something right
to justify their loyalty.

"I'm here to ask two of you a favour," she said. "It may not be
entirely without danger, but I hope to at least get a reply on when
we can have our maintenance rooms back."

At least fifty hands went up.

She picked the two tallest and most well-muscled men.

She told them to put on a set of the newest, clean company
overalls with the company logo.

"I need to speak to Vice Admiral Preston, but if I go alone, I'm
likely to be dismissed as a 'cute little girl'. You're going to pretend
you're my bodyguards."

The men took that task with solemn faces, although one of
them—his name was Wyatt—joked about whether they'd get guns.

Guns would be good, but all domes had a strict no firearm
policy, so just the men's sheer size would have to do.

Flanked by the two men, Jaykadia made her way through the
company's offices, where it was busier than normal. Bodyguards

were not very common in the settlement, except maybe for visiting dignitaries, and she got a lot of strange looks.

They walked through the tube to the entrance to the maintenance sheds.

Since she had last come here, ISF personnel had placed a kind of tunnel inside the tube that visitors were meant to walk through one by one, presumably a safety scanner for weapons. Wyatt went in first. Lights blinked on the inside of the tunnel. Jaykadia went in after him. A voice told her to stand still for a few seconds and a blue light tracked over her skin. Then an array of lights flashed and went off again. That was it? She joined Wyatt on the other side of the machine.

Two men in white uniforms were just coming out of the door, probably warned by the machine that people were coming, but Jaykadia didn't like the look on their faces.

"I'd like to speak to the officer in charge," Jaykadia said.

"You can't come in, I'm sorry," one of them said. "We are not allowed to let civilians into the facility."

"This happens to be my facility," Jaykadia said. "I'm Jaykadia Law, the owner of Ganymede Mining. I'm here to speak to Vice Admiral Preston."

He gave her the usual dubious look, but nodded. "I'll check." Oh, no, he was not happy. She wondered what his orders were. Turn civilians away at the door? Pretend nothing is wrong?

The man disappeared into the door, leaving Jaykadia and her two miners to stand uncomfortably at the entrance with the remaining guard, who stared doggedly at the end of the passage.

From inside the door came sounds of talk and the whining of electronic equipment. It sounded like a drill. She was wondering what they were doing inside.

After a while, the man came back. "Come with me please, ma'am."

Jaykadia followed the man into the hall, where, as she had half-expected, work went on as normal.

Well, almost normal.

They had clearly brought in generators for the lights, but many of the computer screens—while remaining on—displayed nothing except error messages.

Even though only a couple of days had passed since she was last there, so much had changed. They had set up an entire communication centre with workbenches and screens. They'd even put down rugs over the concrete floor.

Seriously, how long did they plan on staying? All without telling her? Did they mean to ruin the company?

The office where the man took her was closer to the door than the one she had visited before. A man waited inside, with Major stripes on his uniform. Jaykadia knew this because Kat was a Major last time Jaykadia had seen her.

"How can I help you, madam?"

"I was told to come here to see Vice Admiral Preston."

"I'm sorry madam, but he is currently busy."

"Then I will wait here."

"I'm sorry madam, but you can't. You will have to go outside."

"Wait a moment," Jaykadia said. "You are here because I own this facility. I was told to come here to speak with him, and so I will see him."

"I can ask." He didn't sound happy.

"Please, do."

He left. Office was a very big word for a bare room with just a desk, two chairs and a notebook, the real life variety, although the paper would be reusable plasti-paper. There was not a single piece of equipment inside. Jaykadia wondered if this room was built for the purpose of talking to people from outside ISF.

Eventually a man's voice sounded outside. "I will deal with it, Watson."

Jaykadia recognised the man who came in. Vice Admiral Preston.

He made a formal greeting, but while he sounded friendly enough, his face showed extreme annoyance.

Well this young upstart woman is finally getting under their skin.

About time, too.

She said, "You insisted on seeing me? Do be quick please, because I don't have much time."

"We appear to have lost power, and any inquiries to your staff result only in 'we'll see what we can do' replies."

"Yes, we'll see what we can do. One of the main power generators went down, and when this happens, the residential areas receive priority, as you will understand. I also see that you have your own power generators. We really will address this problem as soon as possible."

"We have sensitive computer systems that need a steady supply of power to operate."

"I'm sorry, I truly am, but we're working on it."

"I want you to give this utmost priority."

"My settlement and the company are my priorities."

He gave her a hard stare.

"It's an exercise, right? Unexpected situations arise during operations, and everyone needs to be prepared."

He opened his mouth, and shut it again. His face went dark.

"Don't tell me how to do my job."

"Then don't tell me how to do mine. I am questioning why I gave permission for you to use this hall when you do so under false premises and you detain our delegation."

His eyebrows went up. "I think there must be some sort of misunderstanding, because we are not detaining anyone."

"I might ask the delegation on Io if they agree."

Comprehension dawned on his face. "That has nothing to do with us, and is a matter for the local base commander."

"Who is under your command."

"Yes he is, but it is his judgement to protect his base."

"And clearly, a delegation of four unarmed people is a threat to his base."

"I'm not at liberty to go into the details of this case."

"But I am at liberty to withdraw my permission for you to use this hall."

Now the comprehension *really* dawned on his face. "You would not do that."

"Wouldn't I?"

He stared at her for a moment, nostrils flaring.

"It's an exercise. Maybe I'd enjoy seeing how you improvise as much as our company has been forced to."

"You would *not* do that." He made it sound like a threat.

"Or what? Would you raise arms against me?"

He closed his eyes. "Heaven help me."

"I have no interest in upsetting you for the sake of being a pain, but I do request that our delegation be allowed to leave, or report in, or even do the agreed inspections."

"They are safe and will be allowed to contact you."

"Oh, and why am I getting strange messages about them? Why has there been no word about what's going on?"

"That's not my respon—"

"It is, though. I'm beginning to suspect that we're not hearing the whole truth. Not about the delegation, about ISF's plans, or indeed the reason for this unannounced military exercise, if it is indeed an exercise."

She met his eyes squarely. His lips pressed into a thin line.

"Or is there some reason that I will need to warn the community of impending danger?"

"No, no. I will make sure that the delegation is put on a return shuttle as soon as possible."

"Thank you." She turned around and then changed her mind. She wasn't going to let him off so easily.

"What's this then about an approaching object?"

His eyes widened. "Where did you hear about that?"

"A few places. Amateur astronomers talk about it."

"Amateurs."

"Is it all nonsense, then? Is there no object?"

"Oh, there is, but it's unlikely to be what they think it is."

"Then what is it? People who know about this seem to think

that it can only be an artificially propelled object travelling at speeds that our ships can't achieve."

"An you know everything about our technology?"

That caught her on the back foot. Was he saying that ISF did have this technology and that the object was merely a test ship or something like that? Was that what this whole "military exercise" circus was all about?

He nodded once and went to the door of the meeting room. "Now if you don't mind, I am very busy, no thanks to you."

CHAPTER SEVENTEEN

FABIO HAD THOUGHT the truck couldn't go any faster. He was clearly wrong.

Katarina flatfooted the vehicle, and it accelerated to a speed he had thought impossible for something this size.

The road wasn't any less bumpy, and he had to hang on with both hands to avoid being thrown from his seat. Paul hung onto the back of Katarina's seat with white-knuckled hands. Jun's face looked pale.

Thalia didn't appear to have an issue with the speed or movements of the vehicle and neither did Sol.

Fabio wished Katarina would keep her eyes on the road and she'd stop looking at the screen.

It was unmistakable: the red dot was coming closer. What would they do when it got close enough to fire at the truck? He was sure that the people in the other truck would know about the weapons in the depot and would do everything possible to stop them reaching it.

The first rays of light crept over the jagged landscape as Io moved out of Jupiter's dark shadow. A faint wisp of mist rose into the air as the thin atmosphere sublimated back into the air.

"There," Thalia said, pointing at the screen.

Fabio couldn't see anything worth noticing from his position, but they had to be getting closer to the depot.

But they turned a corner and he could see it, too: a strangely blocky shape in an utterly hostile landscape of jagged rocky spikes poking out of loose sickly yellow sand.

They truck had almost reached the small concreted area next to the blocky building when something exploded next to the vehicle. Katarina swore. The truck swerved and hit a patch of deep dust with the wheels on one side. It almost came to a standstill. The caterpillar wheels churned up a cloud of dust that created a cloud of dust even in this thin atmosphere. The dust particles glittered in the stark, lifeless light.

"Come on, come on!" Katarina revved the engine, but it would not go any further.

"Damn it, damn it."

She jumped up from her seat, ran across to the door, pulled on her pressure suit, jammed on her helmet and stepped into the airlock, all within moments. As soon as the lock cycled, she opened the outer door, jumped onto the sand and ran for the depot. She disappeared into the shadow of the building.

Meanwhile, Thalia had climbed into the driver's seat, but she couldn't get the vehicle to move any more than Katarina had. It was well and truly stuck in the sand.

Meanwhile, Sol went to the back and pulled on his suit. Fabio followed and helped Jun pull the helmet over his head.

Only one person fitted in the airlock at a time. Sol went first, and then Jun.

They ran along the road, following Katarina's footsteps.

Next it was Fabio's turn.

He checked all his gear. A small suit malfunction out there and you were dead.

At the depot, Katarina had come out of the blocky building carrying a huge gun on a stand, which she proceeded to set up within the shelter of the building.

The airlock opened. Fabio jumped into the dust.

He remembered jumping out of the truck at Johnson, and landing in a thick layer of fluffy snow. He'd sunk in to over his knees.

The dust on Io was a bit more solid. Now that he was down here, there was less light to see the footsteps of the others ahead of him.

More disturbingly, there was no sound, so no way of knowing if he was being used for target practice. It was nice of the group to suggest that ISF wanted him alive, but he wasn't so convinced.

He ran, bent over so that he didn't present too much of a target.

Something hit the rock close to him. The blast sent shockwaves through the ground and threw up dust. Fabio ducked behind a rock spike, although he had no idea where the fire was coming from. There were jagged rock spikes all around him, blocking his view.

He remembered hiding in the ruined dome at Johnson, with dust-coloured snow falling down around him. There were dead bodies on the ground, now being covered in snow. He had no idea who was shooting or why or who they were aiming for.

Priya leaned into him. He knew she had been injured, but hadn't realised how badly until it was too late. He was still on a high, because he'd enabled so many people to get to safety, and during the boring ride Priya had spoken of some of the fabled Allion technology that ISF could only dream of.

"The antimatter engine," she said. "ISF has offered us any amount of money for one of the two prototypes. Think of it, they could get from here to Earth in two weeks if they had this engine."

"But you're not selling?" Fabio guessed.

"We will sell, but not yet. It's not commercially viable."

Those mundane, yet optimistic words kept repeating in Fabio's mind after she had slipped from his grip in the corridors of Johnson. When removing her suit, he found it was soaked with blood. A projectile had hit her in the side.

Staring in shock at her lifeless eyes, Fabio had lost all semblance of self-control.

He'd grabbed a nearby dead soldier's gun and gone on a rampage. Who had he killed? He didn't even want to think of it. All he could feel was the discharge of the heavy-duty gun, all he could see were sprays of blood dripping down the walls. The conference at Johnson had hosted a number of semi-important ISF officers, who had come here to fake interest in a peaceful agreement. It was all a ruse. They were only at the base to watch Allion get wiped out. Fabio had killed many before he was captured.

A traitor? No, because Sanchez had been livid when hearing this story.

"I will do anything I can to cut this cancer from our force. Preston will hear from me, and hell, he won't like it."

Mars was why ISF had split into Inner and Outer System divisions. Mars was why he had spent years in detention being shuttled from facility to facility. And all of a sudden, Fabio knew what he was doing here: he had to expose Preston, and ISF didn't want to kill him, because he had something they wanted. Priya's capsule. And in a roundabout way, she had already told him what was in it: information that led to the technology to produce an antimatter engine.

But now he was stuck here in between a couple of jagged rocks on Io, with no weapon and no way of getting out safely. He crawled through the dust, which was loose in parts and caked into a crust in others. Sometimes, his foot or knee would sink through.

He couldn't hear any shooting. His helmet feed appeared to be out of order. The display was on, but all he could hear was weird static, and his calls for the others were met with silence.

The wall of the depot shelter was now in view, but in order to get to it, he would have to cross the bare concreted space. The truck still stood on the road behind him. He couldn't see Katarina, but he presumed she had gone inside the building or stood in the shadow, waiting to fire.

He could try to risk it and run. But no. A glimmer of movement behind him revealed Thalia and Paul. Sol and Jun were hiding behind the truck. What were they doing back there?

Trucks were closing in all around the bunker. He could see at least three. The whole escape attempt was futile.

A woman said in his helmet comm, "Get back into the truck."

Fabio didn't recognise the voice, but something about the accent jigged his memory. He wondered if Thalia and Paul had heard it, too. He wondered if this was why Jun and Sol were back at the truck.

"Get into the truck," the voice said again. "Hurry up, because I don't know how long I can keep this channel open."

Fabio gestured to Thalia and Paul, and he ran. The dust was quite deep in places, and several times, he tripped and fell. He had no idea if anyone was aiming at him, and no idea where the others were, though he thought the others might have passed him.

The truck came into view just as Katarina was climbing into the airlock. She carried the big gun on her shoulder as if it was a mailing cylinder.

She gestured at him, *go, go, go!* and closed the airlock.

Fabio reached the truck as the airlock opened again, with no idea where they were going in the hopelessly bogged vehicle. There was no time to ask.

He was the last in. Paul was just removing his helmet, and let loose a string of swear words.

Katarina jumped into the driver's seat.

Outside, at least five trucks had stopped around the depot. Men in suits were now coming out. The low sunlight glinted on the barrels of their guns.

It was too late. Fabio had not regained enough of his memory to be of any help. He'd be captured, put in prison and he would die there, probably as early as today.

"Sorry, sorry," he said.

"Why?" Thalia said.

"Because it's me they want, and I think I know why, but there is a piece missing that connects it all together so that it makes sense. I have information that they want. It belonged to Allion and is about how to produce antimatter engines. They must be detailed plans or something."

But Kat clapped her hand over her mouth.

"What is it?" Paul asked, and he asked it again, because she didn't reply.

"Antimatter engines," she said. "The approaching object."

"Yes, I've seen that. What is it?"

"It puts out light in the visible spectrum, and many very knowledgeable people pored over it and concluded that it could only be an artificial construction. It's going too fast and in the wrong direction to be anything else. It's a ship."

"No," Fabio said. "It's not just a ship. It belongs to Allion. Priya said they had two prototypes. Well, ISF has combed the system extensively. Where are they?"

"Destroyed?" Thalia said.

"No. They've done what antimatter ships are designed to do: they left the solar system."

"Interstellar travel," Jun said. "The stuff of theories."

"No," Kat said. "Allion was always the stuff of theory, daring to do things that most companies and institutions from Earth never dared try. Sometimes their work blew up in their faces—spectacularly so—but when they succeeded, they took themselves another twenty, fifty, a hundred years ahead on the technology curve. It's a ship, and they're coming back."

Before anyone could suggest that if this was true, those people wouldn't like what they saw, Paul called out, "Look!"

They looked where he pointed.

Two of the trucks were moving away from the bunker at great speed. One of them appeared to be firing into the sky.

"What's going on?" Sol asked.

Katarina said, "It seems we are getting help from above—crap!"

A flash tore over the landscape throwing up a cloud of dust.

One of the trucks had fallen onto its side, the other had been blown into bits.

The remaining three trucks now also started moving.

Katarina pointed the camera up, but the sky was dark and revealed none of its secrets.

Then something came from above, thud, onto the roof of the truck and then onto the ground.

It looked like—

Somebody walked across the roof of the truck, jumped onto the engine panel and into the dust. He carried a large gun across his back. Fabio didn't recognise the make or model.

He casually picked up the gun stand that Katarina had left outside the door of the truck.

"He's not wearing a suit!" Jun said.

"Damn, that's an aggregate," Thalia said. Half-human, half-machine.

The man set up the stand, leaned his own weapon on the stand and fired.

The rocket hit the closest of the trucks, shattering the front left corner of the cabin. The pressure blew out in a puff of air and flying debris. At least some of the troops inside had been wearing suits because they ran out and around the vehicle.

The drivers of the other trucks reversed away, but this fighter did not miss.

"Holy shit," Paul said. "He's doing that all by himself."

But the man decided it was enough and jumped back on the truck.

A couple of the other trucks exploded.

Then a big clunk made the truck shudder, and the next moment they were lifted right off the ground. The last thing Fabio saw of the surface was the aggregate man jumping onto the outside of the vehicle and riding on the roof like a trapeze artist.

Holy crap.

The ship that had to be up there and that reeled them in moved at a steady pace. It was hard to see in the top viewscreen, because most of it was dark as space itself. Fabio guessed that it was of similar size as an ISF cargo vessel, but the bits he could see didn't look like a clunky transport ship. *Streamlined*. It moved with grace. The cargo bay had doors in the bottom, which was a strange place for doors to be in a space-faring vessel, where side-couplings were a lot more common.

They were being winched up into the hold.

THE WATCHER

THE IMAGE FROM THE TINY camera was grainy.

It was bad luck that the rescue was happening just as Io moved through Jupiter's shadow and the light was too low to get a decent picture.

The butterfly satellite that the ship had released before going further down to the surface should have had a good view of the area, but the picture quality was rubbish.

The two moth fighters released from the wellship *Thor IV* were clearly visible, because their beacons showed up as dots of light in the projection. They flew over the landscape below, in which Vega could make out a blocky building and a number of ground vehicles approaching the blocky building.

"I'm going down at the next pass," Olek said.

Vega couldn't see him, but likely he'd be hanging onto the outside of one of the moths, wearing a harness with a magnetic clip and a retractable tether.

He was their secret weapon, not to be noticed until he was already too close.

Vega sometimes joked that they should produce female aggregates, but the male ones were good to look at, and they impressed and intimidated even the ISF soldiers.

How great would it be to be able to go out in space without having to wear so much cumbersome gear?

The moths turned around and came back in the direction of the blocky building. One of the ground vehicles had become stuck in the sand, and a person had run to a flat area next to the building.

"Someone's going inside," Taura said, standing next to Vega.

"It's one of the mindshards. I can feel it. She's scared, she has defected. The ISF soldiers are after her, and when they catch her, they are likely to kill her."

"Where is the prisoner?"

"In the vehicle."

Yes, she should absolutely concentrate on him, even if it was easy to get distracted with all the directions her mindshards were pulling her. Because another mindshard was also in the vehicle, and the one who still remained on Ganymede had just challenged the very person responsible for the deaths on Mars.

Vega couldn't know what Jaykadia had done or said, but she had sure spied on some snippy conversation between ISF officers about *that pretty young thing* who led Ganymede Mining and who now, apparently, refused to cooperate.

A couple of other vehicles had pulled up at the blocky building. All occupants had now left the stranded vehicle, and were making their way in the direction of the building. This was good. They were all wearing suits.

One of the pursuing vehicles fired at the abandoned truck. The impact made the vehicle shudder, which was visible even in the poor image. There was no visible damage to the truck, but it might not work anymore.

The moths were on their way back and had almost reached the building again.

But, no, one of the pursuing vehicles had noticed the craft flying over. It reversed and fired into the sky.

The other vehicles were too close and too heavily armed for the moths to land, unless—

She asked the pilot of one of the moths, "Have you got a channel to their suit cams?"

"I can try," the voice came back, crackling with static. And then, "Yes, I do. Go ahead."

"Get back into the truck," Vega said, and she repeated that until the figures turned around and went back to the stricken vehicle.

"Go, quickly," she said to the team. "Take the whole vehicle."

Olek jumped from the moth's side. He had switched on his camera, and Vega could see the tether unrolling as he fell. And then a shudder when he landed—on the roof of the vehicle.

The other vehicles were coming closer, and Olek jumped off the vehicle, grabbed something out of the dust—which turned out to be a stand—and used it to balance his weapon. In short order, he despatched the first of the oncoming trucks. The others backed away, but now they needed to be quick.

"Request backup," he said.

But the two moths had moved on and needed to turn around before they could come back again. Olek jumped back onto the truck. A rim ran along the side of the roof of the truck. He tested its strength, pulling hard on the metal edge. It didn't budge.

He wormed a pad from his belt and attached it to the vehicle, under the rim, and did the same on the other side. Then he jumped off into the sand.

But Vega couldn't see what he did next, because a flash went off nearby. One of the attacking vehicles exploded.

Olek remained down in the sand. He was all right, wasn't he? She couldn't see him anymore.

Another flash. A second vehicle exploded.

Olek clambered onto the roof from the other side of the vehicle. He had crawled underneath and was pulling up one end of a transport harness.

He looped the rope on the harness around the pads on both sides.

Both moths had passed the area and needed to turn around again. There was another aggregate—possibly Kimley—on top of one of the moths, firing at the trucks.

Olek aimed his harpoon and fired.

His tether unreeled as the hook flew up and up—and grappled onto one of the moths. The tether drew taut.

The truck left the ground, seemingly floating over the jagged landscape, although Olek's cam showed that he was working hard to stabilise the vehicle so it didn't rotate or sway.

"We've got them," Olek said through the comm. "It was dicey and we had to destroy five vehicles, but we got him."

Vega blew out the breath she didn't realise she was holding. She turned to Taura. "Prepare part two of the plan."

Taura nodded and left the room to do all the technical things that now needed to be done, all those things that were Taura's expertise.

Vega was so relieved, because frankly, she'd started to doubt that the mindshard technology would deliver. Empathy was all very well, but it was not as clear as *directions*. A person could take several routes to act on their empathy. To guess that four people would all be motivated to choose the side of the oppressed was a huge gamble, but it was not detectable through spy monitoring, even if the nanometrics required were. That was the weak spot that had almost been her undoing. ISF had discovered the nanometrics, even if they had no idea what their function was. To them, nanometrics meant *spies* and *data*, but the four people had only been *agents* without their knowledge. ISF had almost destroyed the man who carried the most important data.

But now it was over.

"Put me onto the prisoner as soon as you can," she said to the pilot of the moth.

While she waited, she told the projector to find a soothing image of some starfield or of the swirling clouds of Jupiter. She sat on the floor with her legs crossed and her eyes closed.

Fifteen thousand people on Juno Station would be safe now. They would have somewhere to go.

Not long after, Olek's voice came over the comm. "I'm here with him now."

An image sprang into the air of a thin, pale-skinned man with dishevelled dark hair.

That was the man they'd all been looking for, the one Priya had chosen? He really did not look like much.

She said, "You don't know me, but I have heard about you. My name is Vega Antares and Priya Anyanda was my soul sister."

CHAPTER EIGHTEEN

THE TRUCK WENT HIGHER and higher into space.

Fabio couldn't even see the surface anymore, because the giant crescent of Jupiter dominated the view.

"Where are we going?" Paul asked. "Where the fuck are we going? There is a man on the roof, not wearing a suit. That is fucking Jupiter out there, he should have been dead ages ago. Why is he alive? What sort of robot is it?"

"He's an aggregate," Fabio said.

"What the fuck are you? Some kind of spy?"

"I'm Fabio Velazquez. I am the last survivor of the chameleon program, which was ISF's answer to the aggregate program. I am still a Lieutenant in ISF, although I don't know how long that will last. I worked in mining astronomy, Research Division. At Mars, I rescued a community of people from certain death when I found out that an asteroid was on course to collide with the area where they lived. I went against the orders of my superior and went to warn the communities down there. As it turned out, they were Allion communities. As it also turned out, the asteroid strike was meant to look like an accident and no one was meant to survive. As a result of my actions, the perpetrators of the planning—who are in ISF but do not speak for the whole organisation—had to go into Johnson and damage the dome to make sure there were as few witnesses as possible. Because people were coming in from outside knowing what had happened and that it was not an accident. Some of these people were killed, but some made it out."

"So you were that one man, never mentioned by name in any of the stories about Mars," Thalia said. "You said nothing about this when we first met you."

"That was because I remembered nothing. And I'm not sure I did do anything to justify praise."

"Yes, you did. You saved lots of lives."

Fabio shuddered, remembering the feel of a weapon discharging, remembering the sprays of blood, remembering the long boring periods of lying on his stomach in a medical treatment room, remembering the fear of waking up and not being able to move.

"I don't know. Memories are coming back, but I'm not sure of their correct order. Whatever I did, I've spent the past few years paying for it."

Something clanged hard against the outside of the truck.

Thalia took in a sharp breath.

Sol said, "It's all right, the weapons can't reach us up here. I think we're being taken into a hold."

"It's not that. It's . . . what sort of ship is this? It creeps me out. Like my memories aren't my own. I'm feeling things. . . ."

Katarina turned around. "Yes." Her voice was full of agreement.

Paul stared from one to the other, then turned to Fabio. "Yes, since you know so much, tell us. What sort of ship is this?"

"Nothing to do with me, I assure you. I guess we'll soon find out."

The fact that there was a lot of sound outside had to mean that they were inside the ship and pressure had returned.

Voices. One male, one female.

The airlock alarm started blaring.

Katarina turned it off. A moment later, the outer door opened and then the inner door.

A woman came in. She was slender, rather flat-chested, dark-skinned with long glossy black hair. Her eyes were Asian but her nose and full lips were African. Her skin was perfect and unblemished.

Both Thalia and Katarina gasped.

"I've seen you before," Thalia said.

The woman smiled, reached out and touched Thalia's forehead, and then Katarina's.

"I doubt it," she said. "Because the price on my head is higher than any reward ever offered."

She came to Fabio, reaching out to him. Her touch made him shiver. "Do you have it?"

He nodded, too embarrassed to say that the capsule was somewhere in his digestive tract and had so far refused to come out.

She smiled. "Give it to the crew on the main ship."

And then she simply vanished into thin air.

"What the hell. . . ?" Paul said.

"Who was that gorgeous creature?" Sol said.

"What was she talking about to you?" Paul met Fabio's eyes. "Do you have what?"

"The Allion people I rescued gave me something to carry to their comrades in the Outer System."

"So, you're an Allion spy?" Sol said.

"No, but I come up for people who are treated unfairly."

"As I remember, that was the main failure of the chameleon program," Katarina said. "They were honest, painfully so. They said things that people didn't appreciate hearing at times that they didn't appreciate hearing them. They could not be cajoled into the obedient mould of the military."

A man now came in. His skin was ink-black, with a greenish sheen. He looked human enough, but Fabio knew this was an aggregate.

He clamped a hand around Fabio's upper arm and pulled him

up from his seat. Except "up" was a strange concept, because gravity had begun to decline. They went outside the truck and into a narrow docking bay, where the truck looked strange next to two slender single-pilot craft.

Were they for fighting?

Clearly, they were now in a much bigger ship.

The man took him to a tiny room where he ran a scanner over Fabio's body. An image came onto the screen with a spot in his belly clearly marked.

He gave Fabio a cup of water with a strange metallic taste. He was only satisfied after Fabio had drunk all of it, and afterwards he told Fabio to undress and strapped him in a soft padded couch.

"The ship needs to move. This will be uncomfortable, but it's safe."

He tied the straps, tied an oxygen mask over Fabio's face and tied him to other equipment.

Fabio wasn't sure which was more uncomfortable: the fact that the ship pulled serious Gs or that everything in his bowels streamed out. He guessed that was the point of drinking the fluid, but his skin was getting sore from sitting in his own waste while he drifted in and out of consciousness.

It was not for nothing. When the ship finally slowed and the man came back to help Fabio out, the thin-as-water shit had mostly been absorbed by the liner of the chair, except for the little capsule.

The man used a steam nozzle to wash him. He was given clean clothing: a loose pair of trousers and a red shirt with a shape more suitable for women than men.

The man took him back to the others, who were staring at a projection screen of a giant space station floating above the clouds. It was a circular structure, with a "wheel" made up of transparent bubbles and interconnecting tubes. Long flexible ropes dangled off the side of the revolving structure, disappearing into the distance.

The ship matched speed with the outside of the station, and connected to a mooring tube

A voice said, "Welcome to Juno Station. You are the first outside visitors in the history of the station. Please remember that the station and the ship is the property of Allion Aerospace. You are welcome to speak to any of our workers."

"Holy crap," Paul said.

Katarina nodded. "Does anyone know that this amazing thing is here?"

Holy crap indeed.

When the doors opened, an arrival committee waited at the entrance to the ship and this included the gorgeous woman that he had seen in the earlier projection.

She hugged Thalia and Katarina, both looking bewildered. She used the word *mindshards,* the meaning of which, he guessed, would be explained soon.

"Come," she said to Fabio. "My name is Vega Antares and I am the current executive director of Allion Aerospace."

She took him to a room filled with natural light filtered from the clouds below. The room was empty and the floor oddly soft and bouncy. Light nozzles in the ceiling projected a holographic image of the legendary Allion logo in the middle of the room.

Fabio still could barely believe that all of this existed. This was supposed to be a dead community.

"This is what you brought," Vega said.

A picture sprang into the air showing a—what was that giant thing that almost didn't fit into the room?

"This is the starship *Forthright.* A number of years before the Mars debacle, it left the solar system because we developed a way to surf space-waves created by travelling at near lightspeed. When a ship surfs a wave, it travels faster than light. It also moves out of our communication range, for obvious reasons. That alien ship coming in our direction? That's the *Forthright* coming back. These are the ship's plans with details about the electronics and navigation that we can use to communicate with them while letting them know that we have the right code for them to start talking to us. Problem is: they're set to go to Mars and we need them to slow down before they get to that stage. Mars is no longer our main base and if they insert into orbit there, it will certainly lead to trouble."

"You have a contingent of ISF waiting for you here," Fabio said.

"I've got another mindshard who has just dealt with that."

JAYKADIA

"**THIS IS ASTONISHING,**" Governor of the Council Of Four, Anise-Leontine Law, said, looking at the screen.

Jaykadia was still a bit flustered from having travelled all the way from the mining settlement to Galileo City. She had received the anonymous letter this morning. She thought she knew where it came from and understood quite well that this had the potential to do a lot of damage, so she had elected to see her aunt in person.

Her aunt read on.

"It says that Preston is directly responsible for killing thousands of people on Mars. The asteroid was diverted under his orders while he knew, or would soon be aware, where it was going. He knew that there were talks scheduled in that area. He never did anything about the threat to civilians. And after the impact, did his best to cover up his actions when it became clear that people had survived, people who could not be gagged and silenced about what they had seen."

"It is quite something, isn't it?" Jaykadia said. "I just didn't know what to do with this and I value your opinion."

"Oh, this absolutely should come before the assembly. Preston has deceived us even more than we thought. This is no longer a political game. It should become a court case. I will send a copy of this to Admiral Sanchez."

"So, do you still want me to bend over backwards to the military 'exercise' in my maintenance sheds?"

"Absolutely not. Tell them that they can pack up. Tell whoever sent this message that any Allion refugees can freely visit the civilian settlements without fear for their lives. This is ridiculous."

Jaykadia nodded. She had no problem working with or for the military, but the way in which Preston had sought to control everybody in the system for the sake of eradicating competition was ridiculous.

There would be a lot of fallout from this, including what Allion doctors were doing in public hospitals applying secret technology, but she felt smug about this little corner of victory. The workers in the suiting room would be happy when they could go back to work.

Her aunt said, "I will mention the details of this incoming ship to the assembly."

"No," Jaykadia said. "I think that should stay between us. We don't know who else is trying to get their hands on it. We want them to arrive safely, without risk to them or us. If some idiot tries to blow a ship with antimatter engines, there's no telling what sort of debris or flares could result. I don't think I want to find out the danger an explosion like that would pose to us here."

"True. Safety comes first."

"Safety, and then trade. If the technology is for sale, then I'm interested."

"I'm sure you are, like a good child of your father's."

Both Thalia and Kat returned to Galileo City a few weeks later. It was strange to see Kat out of her uniform, but she declared that she had turned her back on the military forever.

Jaykadia didn't believe her, because Kat never left the military.

Jokes went that she had been born with a gun in her hand. She did, however, give a long and detailed account of the ISF's activities in the asteroid belt before the COF assembly.

Apparently, a few weeks after that, Sanchez contacted her with the offer of a significant promotion and pay raise, so that was the end of her not being in the military. She was going to work at Sarajevo, so Paul could go home and continue to be cranky and be in love with her.

Thalia had a much different story. She spoke of an amazing modern space station in the clouds of Jupiter called Juno Station. She spoke of having travelled on the legendary wellship *Thor IV,* one of the few ships able to escape Jupiter's enormous gravity well, and of the spacey, light-filled rooms, all populated by women from poor countries on Earth and men with greenish-black skin who did not need space suits to step into a hard vacuum.

There had been a man with the group called Fabio Velazquez, and he had elected to stay with Allion. They had promised to record and then destroy all his anguished, jumbled-up memories, and replace them with pleasant ones. They were hugely interested in his genetic material, being a chameleon.

Why was the ship coming back? No one knew until they could communicate.

What would the small Allion community do? No one said anything about it.

It would be interesting, but for now, it was much less likely that they'd end up being blown to bits or taken prisoner.

That suited the Council Of Four fine.

Because it was always better to go into trade with another party than to declare war on them.

ABOUT THE AUTHOR

Patty Jansen lives in Sydney, Australia, where she spends most of her time writing Science Fiction and Fantasy.

Her story *This Peaceful State of War* placed first in the second quarter of the Writers of the Future contest and was published in their 27th anthology. She has also sold fiction to genre magazines such as Analog Science Fiction and Fact, Redstone SF and Aurealis.

Patty has written over twenty novels in both Science Fiction and Fantasy, including the *Icefire Trilogy* and the *Ambassador* series.

pattyjansen.com

facebook.com / patty.jansen

twitter.com / pattyjansen

instagram.com / jansen_patty

MORE BY THIS AUTHOR

In the Earth-Gamra space-opera universe

RETURN OF THE AGHYRIANS

Watcher's Web
Trader's Honour
Soldier's Duty
Heir's Revenge
The Return of the Aghyrians Omnibus

The Far Horizon (For younger readers)

AMBASSADOR
Seeing Red
The Sahara Conspiracy
Raising Hell
Changing Fate
Coming Home
Blue Diamond Sky
The Enemy Within

The Last Frontier
The Alabaster Army

Hard Science Fiction

In the ISF-Allion universe
Shifting Reality
Shifting Infinity
Charlotte's Army
Juno Rising

SPACE AGENT JONATHAN BARTELL
Contamination
Observation

Epic Fantasy

GHOSTSPEAKER CHRONICLES
(formerly For Queen And Country)
Innocence Lost
Willow Witch
The Idiot King
Fire Wizard
The Dragon Prince
The Necromancer's Daughter
Ghostspeaker Chronicles Books 1-3

Epic, Post-apocalyptic Fantasy

ICEFIRE TRILOGY
Fire & Ice
Dust & Rain
Blood & Tears
The Icefire Trilogy Omnibus

MOONFIRE TRILOGY
Sand & Storm
Sea & Sky
Moon & Earth

Short story collections
Out Of Here
New Horizons

Self-publishing (Non-fiction)
Self-publishing Unboxed
Mailing Lists Unboxed
Going Wide Unboxed

Visit the author's website at http://pattyjansen.com and register for a newsletter to keep up-to-date with new releases.